# DEFENSIVE STANCE

## LAS VEGAS RAMBLERS

### BOOK ONE

# DEFENSIVE STANCE

## LAS VEGAS RAMBLERS

### BOOK ONE

## Kasha Thompson

WEBSTER AVENUE PUBLISHING
LINCOLN, CA

DEFENSIVE STANCE

Paperback ISBN: 979-8-9862679-3-7

Copyright 2023 Kasha Thompson



This edition published and arranged by Webster Avenue Publishing.

Printed in the United States of America. First Edition July 2023.

Character Illustration: Mary Rudkovskaya

Cover Design by: Webster Avenue Publishing

Interior Layout by: Webster Avenue Publishing

Editing: Courtney Driver of Whoproofedit.com

# BLACK LOVE NOV·EL

/blak/ /ləv/ /nävəˈ

noun

1. a novel, with black main characters that examines the complexity of falling and staying in love.

2. a story centered around black love with just the right amount of sweet, savory, and spice.

# CONTENT NOTES

Please note Defensive Stance discusses topics which could potentially trigger certain audiences. Some readers may consider the following as spoilers.

Moderate coarse language
Several sexually explicit scenes
Death of a parent
Anger management
Drinking, drug use, and gambling

*To my reading ass bitches.*

# DEION

IT WAS THE FOURTH QUARTER AND THE TEAM WAS DOWN BY five. The Ramblers were in Portland at the Moda Center, one of the top five loudest arenas in the NBA. Chants and boos from the crowd seemed to reverberate in my chest. As I advanced the ball up the court, I silently regretted staying up until three in the morning the night before. I'd been to Portland over a hundred times, and while you might not associate it with a banging nightlife, it did live up to its motto "Keep Portland weird."

Last night proved to be bizarre with an underground speakeasy and a tattooed fire-eater who also wasn't afraid of sticking my dick down her throat. I passed the ball to point guard, Colin Pratt, and maneuvered my way to the side of the rim so I'd be in the perfect position to drain a three pointer. Threes were my specialty, all though I'll admit my hot hand was more frequently cold as I entered my fifteenth year in the NBA.

Pratt did what we'd rehearsed a million times in practice, he fed the ball to me. The three wasn't open so

I dribbled to the hole using my back to drive the defensive player with me, easily sinking the basket.

The Portland rookie mumbled under his breath, "Fucking bitch." That was his second mistake. His first mistake was thinking he could guard me.

The disrespect forced me to halt my advance to the other end of the court. "What did you call me?" I cocked my head to the side in disbelief.

The rookie screwed his face trying to play dumb. "Do you have a problem?"

"Nah I ain't got problems but I damn sure got some solutions." Primary of which was busting him upside his head.

"Man fuck you." He waved my words off like I wasn't froggy and ready to jump.

Heat flushed through my body. The screams from the zealous crowd were drowned out by my pulse throbbing in my ear. "Fuck me? Bruh that's exactly what your mom was saying to me last night when I was ramming her from behind." I thrusted my hips for maximum impact.

I did not know this man's mother, but it seemed like the appropriate response in the moment. Now as you can imagine, player twelve of the Portland Trailblazers received my words with all the disrespect I intended. He lunged forward scratching at my shoulder in an attempt to grab my jersey.

One thing about me, I talk a good game and always come prepared to back up every last syllable. I clocked homeboy in the side of his head before lowering my stance into a fighting position. The rookie swung but missed, and I took that opportunity to make contact with his ribs. I would have dusted the college dropout if the referees hadn't swarmed, pulling us apart.

Pratt wrapped his arm around my neck, dragging me away. "Chill Deck. Let it go."

My eyes bulged and my breathing was erratic. "Let what go? I'm good," I told Pratt before screaming across the court at the rookie. "Welcome to the big leagues bitch."

There was nothing I hated more than a rookie who thought he was hot shit because he was the star player in high school or college. Don't nobody care how many points you scored in the NCAA championship game. These new cats walk in here with chips on their shoulders, and I'm just the motherfucker to knock it off.

The refs called a technical foul on both me and the rookie. Shaking free of Pratt's hold, I stalked over to the nearest ref, my lips curled in disgust. "What the fuck do you mean technical foul. He attacked me. I was just defending myself," I shouted inches from the ref's face. My ass was pushing it and I knew it, but I was too wound up to extinguish the anger that was boiling into a rage.

"Go to your bench McCabe," Referee Sims ordered.

Off the court, Sims and I were actually cool. But we weren't in the lounge of some nondescript hotel. This was work, basketball was my profession and I took this shit seriously. And right now, Sims could catch all this smoke. I did not deserve a technical foul when I was provoked. So what, a dude just got a free pass to swing at me and I was supposed to be the bigger, more enlightened person? Fuck that.

"You didn't see him lunge at me, but you saw everything *I* did?" I pleaded my case bending to make eye contact.

"I'm not gonna tell you again, Deck."

"Fuck you, Sims." I hoisted my two middle fingers into the air.

"You're out, McCabe." Sims blew his whistle as it was announced I'd been ejected from the game. Meaning with nine and a half minutes left on the clock I was being banished to the locker room. The crowd rejoiced at my exit. Ray Charles's "Hit the Road Jack" began to play as the Portland fans waved their arms with jeers directing me off the court while singing at the top of their lungs.

I hated away games because in most cities the fans were hella disrespectful. Just straight assholes. While sitting on the bench before the second half, some Portland fans seated behind me were obnoxiously shouting, saying my game was trash and I needed to retire because at this point I was embarrassing myself. Who pays close to three hundred dollars for a seat and then spends the entire game harassing the opposing team?

My teammates pulled me away, probably afraid I'd do something worse, while I continued to rant. "Straight bullshit."

With hurried strides, I passed Coach Justus Chappel whose eyebrows were low and pulled close, creating a crease in his forehead. He was pissed and I was gonna get a verbal tongue lashing when this game was over. I didn't fear no man, but Coach Chappel had a way of making you second guess all of your life decisions.

Walking through the crowd heading out of the arena, a Portland fan threw a half-filled drink at me. The cup ricocheted off my chest before tumbling to the floor. I'm from Houston, Texas but it didn't really matter where you grew up because there ain't nan nowhere on this planet where throwing a cup at a man isn't considered disrespectful.

This next part is a little fuzzy. All I know is I charged into the stands and physically assaulted a man in attendance. It took several security guards and a few members from my team to prevent my fist from making contact with the fan's face. These men dragged me away as I tried to claw my way back to the individual who asked for an ass whipping the minute he cocked his arm back and flung his cup in my direction.

In the locker room I punched the air. I was angry, but not stupid enough to hit a solid surface. A player last season had gotten so upset after a loss, he punched a concrete wall, shattering most of the bones in his hand and breaking his wrist. So until I could find a gym's punching bag, this air was going to get these fist combos from the residual rage still coursing through my veins. Jab, cross, left hook.

Fans were not supposed to antagonize the players. If a fan assaulted a player, and make no mistake that cup was the definition of assault, they could end up with a lifetime ban, never allowed to attend an arena game ever again. On the flip side players were definitely not supposed to physically attack the fans. The consequences for that were automatic suspension and for some unlucky bastards, termination.

After silently fuming alone for several minutes, the locker room door opened and Pratt entered, followed by my other teammates. My stomach tensed into tight coils. I'd let my team down which was never my intention. Should I have kept walking, yes. But backing down wasn't in my DNA. The dejected expressions on the team's face told me all I needed to know. We'd lost and my antics most likely contributed to that.

Yes, it was the preseason but every game, every win still counted. If the preseason was filled with losses, it didn't bode well for the regular season. These early games set the tone for the rest of the year. You wanted to float into the regular season on a high note, not dragging your feet because you were broken and beaten. The Ramblers only had one win after playing three games in the preseason. I could forecast sprints and grueling practice drills in our future.

Clearing my throat, I offered a flimsy apology. "Hey guys, sorry about losing my cool."

"What the fuck were you thinking?" Number four, Dennis Lowrey asked.

"It was unfortunate and, in my defense, not my fault." I wagged my finger.

"Deion you ran up on a fan in the stands." Pratt's eyes were like saucers.

"He threw a cup at me. What did you want me to do?" I shouted. I was sorry but any one of these players would have done the same thing. Except for maybe Monroe, he was raised in the church and had only been in the league for a little over two years. He hadn't yet acquired the bad habits some of us seasoned players exhibited.

"Walk away Deck. Sticks and stones," Monroe suggested. See didn't I tell you he was a choir boy.

"I live by the philosophy of don't start nothing won't be nothing."

"Well, you fittin' to be living on ramen and hot dogs when they shit can your ass," Dennis said.

Firing me would be a financial loss. My ten-million-dollar contract was guaranteed whether I played or not. I learned early in my basketball career to always secure the bag. A forty-million-dollar contract is great, but not if it isn't guaranteed. If you got injured or were a hot head like me, you weren't walking away with anything but thoughts and prayers.

Plus, in my case a trade would be difficult because no one else would take me. I came with a reputation and most organizations viewed me as a liability not an asset So it didn't make sense for the organization to waste all that effort and have teams laugh in their ear or slam the door in their face when they mentioned my name and a potential trade.

Pratt let out a harsh breath. "Damnit Deck. You'll be lucky if you get slapped with a fine and suspended for several games."

"And I'll accept whatever punishment the Ramblers' organization deems fit."

When I acted badly, I was always willing to take the punishment. And by confronting a fan I'd acted very badly. But I couldn't lose this job. Basketball was all I had; it was my refuge. When my wife left me after years of neglect on my part, the game was there to help me reset. It didn't matter what team I was on, if you passed me the ball I was gonna make it do what it do. But in the past few months not even the game could block out the shit tumbling around in my head.

After enduring the disappointed faces of my teammates, I was summoned for the obligatory sit down with Coach Chappel. "What the hell is going on with you?" Coach yelled before I even had a chance to comfortably take a seat.

"Nothing, I'm fine." I hitched an indifferent shoulder.

Justus pushed out a long breath. He was leaning on the desk in the office space reserved for visiting coaches. When he spoke again his tone was softer. "Does this have anything to do with your father—"

"No," I objected. I did not want to talk about my pops.

"I'm just saying you've always had a short fuse but this … this feels different."

"I don't know many people who would have reacted differently if in the same situation." I pinned my arms over my chest.

"Bullshit, most players aren't risking their careers over a medium sized Coke cup."

"It was a large cup. The straw could have scratched my retina."

Justus rolled his eyes. "I received a call from Thornton. And you know I hate talking to that man."

Grover Thornton was the majority owner of the

Ramblers and his opinion mattered. You never wanted to talk to Grover. Quite honestly it was best to just fly under his radar like a stealth aircraft. He was a shrewd businessman and he wasn't what I would consider a people person. Thornton didn't give a fuck about your past actions. All that mattered was what you'd done for him lately.

"I know you do." I ducked my chin in contrition.

"He wants you to go to anger management."

I laughed for a long time, wiping tears from my eyes. "Nah, I'm good."

"That wasn't a suggestion. It's a requirement for continued employment with the Ramblers."

"I don't need therapy. I'm good. I don't have shit I need to figure out."

"We all have shit that needs figuring out."

"You attack one entitled fan and now everyone thinks you have mommy issues," I joked with a scoff.

Coach rubbed his beard. "How is your mother, by the way?"

"She's good, looking to downsize. She doesn't want to tool around that house all alone."

"Well tell her I said hello and I'm jonesing for her peach cobbler."

"For the last time I am not gonna help you shoot your shot with my momma," I teased.

"Deion, I do not know how to break this to you but your momma is fine."

My mother had me right outta college and she was often mistaken as my contemporary and not my elder. I'd posted a video with her on my social media account last week and the comments section was filled with remarks on how we were a stunning couple. I didn't find that shit funny, but my mom ate it up.

"Coach, I'm already feeling like crap, could we not?"

"When we get back to Vegas I want you to reach out to Doc Walton and get a reference to an in person local anger management group."

"This is bullshit and you know it."

"How long are you going to continue to play the victim?"

"Until somebody believes me." I tossed my hands in the air.

"Deion McCabe the man who cried wolf." Coach opened the office door indicating it was time for me to leave. "By the way you will also be fined and suspended so get your checkbook ready."

# SLOANE

"Welcome to Sunset Counseling Center and our weekly anger management group. Take your seats. Looks like we have some new faces so please let's get started so everyone gets the opportunity to share," Shelly, the anger management counselor called out.

I found a chair in the circle and examined the faces of the people who were meant to be my "family" for the next few months. If you couldn't tell, that was me being sarcastic. The pamphlet for this center called group sessions a safe place where strangers become family as they bond over shared trauma and learn useful coping tools to deal with intense emotions.

I had a family and they were plenty. The last thing I was looking for was new kinfolk. I was here because I had to be, not because I was hoping to soften my sharp edges. My edges were sharp and prickly for a reason; they kept me safe while keeping others at bay. When you allowed people to get too close, they could inflict irreparable damage.

"Let's go around the room and introduce ourselves. Name, why you're here and what you hope to get out of this group," Shelly said, scanning the sign-in sheet. "Deion, do you want to share what brought you to anger management?"

"Nope."

Deion McCabe was a shooting guard for the Las Vegas Ramblers. Even in a plain T-shirt and navy sweatpants, he stood out. He was six foot five so you couldn't miss him. I'm sure some women would find his rich-brown skin, broad chest, and big feet attractive. He looked how I felt, like he didn't want to be here slouching in his folding chair, sunglasses covering his eyes, tattooed arms planted firmly across his chest.

I chimed in, feeling charitable I thought I'd help him out. "I think we all know why he's here. He went ballistic on national television."

"I didn't go ballistic," he objected leaning forward.

I arched a skeptical brow. "You attacked a dude while his teenage son watched."

"I was defending myself." His tone was laced with annoyance like he was tired of explaining his actions.

"From what? The short balding man who threw a paper cup at you."

"So if someone did that to you you'd just walk away?"

"No, I'd beat their ass. But maybe I'm not the best person to ask seeing how we're both attendees of the same group."

Shelly jumped in. "This is good. Conversation is cathartic. Sloane do you wanna go next?

"Do I have too?"

"You don't have to do anything, but the point of the group is to share and learn."

I huffed out a long breath. "OK. I'm Sloane Kaplan. I'm a cancer, literally and figuratively." I paused for laughs that never came. The therapy group was a tough crowd.

"Why are you here?" Shelly clearly wanted to keep me on task.

"I drove into my probation officer's car while he was still in it."

"Whoa," one of the attendees said.

"Bullshit," the guy next to me shouted. "How are you not in jail?"

"Because he was also my boyfriend so he got fired. They agreed not to suspend my license and I agreed not to sue for abuse of power."

Deion McCabe removed his sunglasses, his eyes narrowing in on me. Never one to back down from a staring competition, I returned his gaze.

"Do you know why you did that?" Shelly asked.

"Yes, because I was angry."

"But *why* were you so angry?"

"Because he was a lying sack of shit, Shelly." A woman can only be lied to so many times before something in her snaps.

He'd lie and I'd choose to believe him even though my internal lie detector could detect the falsehood from a mile away. Marco wasn't even a good liar. It was actually insulting he thought I was that stupid. *You were supposed to meet me for dinner but you fell asleep and when you woke up your phone was dead and after trying to charge it to no avail you realized you needed to get a new phone. But because you were so busy you couldn't get to T-Mobile for close to a week and once your new phone was set up I was the first person you called.* Incriminating photos on your friend's social media page, which clearly showed you turning up at numerous clubs on the strip, be damned.

"Up next … Harold."

"Uhh … yeah my name is Harold Rice and I'm here because I shot at my twin brother."

I released a guffaw. "And you guys were judging me. Is there some type of award for least managed anger? Because I think Harold is the front runner."

"You both tried to kill people. I don't see a distinction," Deion said.

"I did not try to kill anybody. It was a slow speed crash. Fifteen miles per hour. He had his seat belt on for fuck sake. Harold on the other hand loaded a gun, aimed it, and pulled the trigger." I turned to Harold. "You could have killed your brother … do better."

When I'd been ordered to attend anger management, I never expected such a ragtag bunch. We had a police officer. That made sense. A soccer mom who'd lost her shit while driving on the freeway. I almost felt sorry for her because who hadn't experienced road rage. The I-15 during rush hour traffic was the worst and found me gripping my steering wheel and screaming obscenities on more than one occasion. Then there was Harold "Bang Bang" Rice, the maladjusted banker and a smattering of other sullen characters. Last was the basketball player, who was by far the most unexpected addition.

I'd seen clips from the game in which he went all

Wreck-It Ralph. If you were paying me millions of dollars, I would suck it up and keep it moving. A fan could call me a bald headed, cootie-licking, snot rag and I would walk on by like my name was Dionne Warwick. It didn't surprise me he was forced to attend therapy, but I thought guys like him were provided private sessions with cucumber water and sounds of nature softly playing in the background.

I guess his team wanted him to learn a lesson. And one way to do that was to make him drive to the sketchy part of town to pay his penance. As each group member retold their story, I could distinctly notice a tilt of superiority in Deion's demeanor. This asshole thought he was better than us. His indignant smirk made me want to jump up and punch him square in the nose. But I was reminded of what Shelly always said, "Anger is just one letter short from danger." I did my best to suppress a laugh.

"Sloane is there something you wanted to share with the group?" Shelly asked with eager eyes. This woman loved it when we were engaged in the conversation.

"Umm … I was just thinking about what you said a few sessions ago."

"About?"

"About dealing with our anger and getting to the root of it. You know doing the work, journaling, drinking ice lattes …" I trailed off. I didn't have a point but Shelly was always a positive thinker waiting to spin our bullshit into golden words of wisdom.

"That's so true Sloane and ice caramel lattes are the best." She released a robust chuckle.

I smiled bright at my new position as teacher's pet. Scanning the room, my gaze landed on the lanky basketball player who wasn't buying my bullshit. I flashed him a discreet finger before pretending to listen intently for the remainder of the hour-long session.

When the session ended, I high tailed it out of there. Normally I would hang around and pocket some of the refreshments, but I'd promised my brother Chet I would meet him to check out some car. Yes, my brother's God given name was Chet. What my Black ass parents were smoking when they named him, I would never know. I was just glad they stopped smoking it when it was time to name me.

Pulling up to an auction lot, I parked and located Chet out front. He offered a wave as I walked toward him.

"Hey Sissy, thanks for coming."

"This car better be worth it."

"You know I wouldn't call you out here if it wasn't." His step had a lot of pep in it. Which was typical Chet when he had some hare brained scheme he hoped to insert me into.

The car was a 1994 Mustang Cobra in faded cherry red. In my opinion the car was hideous. Years of neglect caused the paint to chip, the interior was tattered, and the wheels were bald. But this specific model had amazing resell value. With some cars going for as much as forty-thousand dollars. At this particular auction lot, the starting bid was one dollar so you could drive away with a steal of a deal. The vehicle had one-hundred-and-eighteen-thousand miles which was really good for a car that old.

Chet could turn this hooptie into a beauty and make a nice profit. It was imperative to feign disinterest. We split up and worked the crowd of potential buyers, peppering in some misinformation about accident history and vehicle damage. The goal was to make people think this car was a risk and the return on the investment was low. I stood next to the vehicle and loudly claimed my nonexistent husband had just sold his 1994 Mustang and was practically robbed.

"All the offers were super low. He finally sold it for nine grand just to get it out of our driveway. Don't believe what you see online because the resell value is not there."

A few moments later Chet pointed out the loose tail pipe and cracked windshield. "Maybe someone can scrap it for parts. But if you're looking for a reliable ride that won't have you stranded on the side of the road … this ain't it." He shook his head walking away. When our duplicitous deed was done, we hung out on the rickety bleachers waiting for the auction to begin.

"Have you spoken to your father?" Chet asked.

"No. I'm just working under the theory he's still alive until I hear otherwise."

"He's still alive. I had to bail him out of the county jail the other day. I almost called you."

"I'm glad you didn't, I bailed him out last time."

"That man has nine lives. Any other person they would have already been thrown under the jail."

My father didn't have much in way of a job, savings,

or reliability but lucky for him he had connections. He was friends with most of the people who ran the hole-in-the-wall casinos and bars he frequented. And most of them had his kids' numbers saved as their favorites for whenever he stepped out of line or got too drunk. He'd also went to school with the Sheriff in his county and had been calling in favors since their freshman year.

"What did he do this time?"

"Stole some money from a stripper."

"He's a winner."

My father had been in prison more times than I could count for petty larceny, public intoxication, public indecency, and small amounts of drugs on his person. Each time he got released he promised he was a changed man. Once, he came out claiming he'd found religion. The Lord had shown him the light. He started going to church and met this nice God-fearing lady who gave him a warm bed and some walking around money.

Six months later we found out he conned her out of close to ten-thousand dollars. Changed man my ass. Shit the entire Kaplan family had seen the inside of a jail cell at one point or another so I wasn't exactly judging. But I was working really hard to stay on the straight and narrow. And when I tell you that path was ridiculously straight and painfully narrow, I meant it. I've made mistakes in the past … and the not so distant past, but I was a better person now. Going to anger management and staying out of trouble. The fact that my words were reminiscent of my fathers were not lost on me.

"He asked about you."

"I'm sure he did."

"He misses you and Ace. Genuinely."

"Don't let him play you, Chet. You're smarter than that." I wagged a warning finger in his direction.

When I was younger, I wholeheartedly believed my father's apologies. But I was thirty-four, a grown ass woman with a child of my own, and flowery words and hand-wringing no longer fooled me.

Chet tossed his arm around my shoulder. "So are you ready to help me intimidate these fools so I can drive away in that sweet ride?"

"Let's go get 'em."

# DEION

AFTER MY SECOND ANGER MANAGEMENT CLASS, I STOPPED at the snack table to get some coffee for the road and found Ms. Reckless Driver stuffing the leftover donuts into a zip lock bag.

"Really?" I asked.

"This is a no judgment zone ... remember," she scolded me.

"You're right, do you playa." I raised my palms in surrender.

"They're just going to throw them out in an act of unnecessary food waste. If you knew the amount of food we just throw away as Americans it would make your head spin." She moved on from the donuts to the fruit, stuffing bruised bananas and snack-sized oranges into her oversized purse. A purse which I was almost certain she used to steal things from convenience stores and Walmarts. "And Vegas is the worst offender." She started counting out items on the hand that wasn't clutching a bunch of mini, white chocolate Kit Kats. "Food, clothes, toiletries, you name it we toss it. Grocery stores chuck boxes of misshapen fruit just because it's not aesthetically pleasing."

"So you're just balancing the scales." I cast a cynical eye in her direction.

"I'm doing my part to help Mother Nature heal."

"How's that all working out?"

"It's thankless. And honestly, I can only fit so much shit into this purse." She tapped her quilted tote bag.

"Are you one of those dumpster divers?" I asked added milk to my coffee cup.

She put her hand on her generously well-curved hip. "Do I look like a dumpster diver?"

That was a loaded question. I'd never met one in person, but if I had to dream up what a dumpster diver looked like it would not be this woman. She had impeccable skin with a smattering of freckles and moles that danced across her face. Her golden-brown natural curls were piled atop her head in a messy bun. During group I noticed her fingernails. They were long, pointed, and decked out in a funky painted pattern adorned with jewels. For a moment I imagined how pretty they would look clawing at the skin on my wide back.

Sloane was short and her frame was solid. Maybe she was average height for a woman, shit when you were as tall as I was everybody was short in comparison. The casual ribbed dress she was wearing … and she was wearing the hell outta that hunter green dress … clung to her abundant curves. I could make out a piercing in her belly button pressing against the fabric along with a small pooch. She reminded me of the sculptures of Greek women whose bodies offered a soft place to rest your head. I doubt she worked out, she didn't look like the type of woman who spent hours spinning her wheels on a stationary bike. Most likely she was staying in shape from trying to evade the cops.

"You don't smell like wet garbage so probably not," I said.

"I shower, that tends to help." She pushed an unruly strand of hair from her face. "So the Ramblers sent you to anger management?"

"The executives didn't take too kindly to a player choking out a white dude on live television."

"I thought it was hilarious." Her eyes held a wild quality that captured my attention.

"That shit almost got me fired."

"I've been fired before and it sucks. But if you let shit slide eventually motherfuckers start lacing up the skates."

"Yeah, well I ain't Bow Wow and I'm not letting nobody roll bounce on me."

The corner of her full lips shifted into a slight smirk. "You know the saying, 'What doesn't kill you makes you stronger'?"

"Yeah."

"I believe that life is constantly trying to kill us. Physically, emotionally, mentally. And when you accept that fact it becomes easier to navigate through it. You lower your expectations, you expect the worst in people, you never look for the silver lining. You just accept that this is it." She threw up her hands with a sense of defeat. Like the years had not been easy on her.

"That seems extreme."

"I just think it's realistic. And I believe in being honest with myself. You should try it sometime. It might actually help you improve your ball handling."

The thing about being an athlete is that everyone feels compelled to offer you unsolicited advice. They wanna act like what you do isn't hard work. And that if they wanted to, they could lace up their shoes, dust the potato chip crumbs from their soiled T-shirt, jog from their well-worn couch and make the winning basket from three-point range. "I don't remember asking for your two cents."

"Fair, but let's not act like you're giving it one hundred and ten percent out there. Shit, I think most Ramblers' fans would take eighty five percent of your effort. You're not having fun and it shows."

My brow furrowed as I considered her words. There was a time when I lived for this game. All I wanted to do was shoot the ball, practice my free throws and run drills. I fell asleep at night thinking up ways I could hone my craft. The last thing anyone could claim was that they out hustled me on the court. But that all changed when my dad passed. Everything seemed different. Yes, I was a grown ass man but at thirty-six I still needed my father. He was our rock, he was the blueprint.

Some of what Sloane said resonated, life was constantly trying to drain us and oftentimes it was slow, wearing you down over time until the things that brought you joy no longer made your heart sing. Other times it was instantaneous, in the blink of an eye nothing made sense and everything tasted bitter. It was always too hot or too cold. Too much or not enough. It was never just right. This past year without my pops left me searching for balance, for something I could put my trust in. No matter where I searched, on the court, chilling with family and friends, or in between some random woman's legs, I couldn't find it.

"Do you have heart and hustle at your nine to five?" I threw her words back at her.

"It's an eight to four in the morning. And no I don't. But I also don't get paid a gazillion dollars to do it." She hoisted her bag, which was loaded with contraband, over her shoulder.

"Are you a stripper?"

Sloane's head reared back in disbelief. "Is that judgment?"

"Just curious."

"Vegas is a twenty-four-hour city. We're not all strippers."

"You're right. No offense." Once again, I found myself trying to atone for my assumptions.

"Hmph." She was eyeing the exit but there was something about her that made me want her to stay.

"So what happened with you and that probation officer?"

"He was fired."

"Yeah, but are you two still together?" Don't know why I asked other than curiosity.

"No, I tried to kill him. That would be toxic." Her tone implied she thought I was slow.

"Admitting you were wrong is the first step."

She brandished her hand like a stop sign. "When did

I admit I was wrong? He had it coming and I'd do it again."

"OK Sam Jackson," I croaked.

"What?"

"Samuel L. Jackson from the movie *A Time To Kill.*"

"Never heard of it."

I placed my hand over my heart. "Oh my God, you'd love it. It would tap into your deep-seated need for revenge."

"Who said I had a need for revenge?"

"You drove your vehicle into another vehicle causing damage. Your actions speak volumes. Plus, I can see the desire for revenge swimming in your eyes."

Sloane ripped her sunglasses from atop her head and shielded her field of vision.

I chuckled. "Try not to side swipe anyone before group next week," I said heading toward the door.

"I make no promises," she shouted, as the door swung shut behind me.

***

AFTER THE GROUP SESSION, ALL I WANTED TO DO WAS HEAD home take a hot shower and crawl into bed. The night prior I was unable to sleep and finally accepted the sleep train missed my stop. So I got out of bed and started my day at five in the morning. Per usual I hit the gym and put in two hours of strength and conditioning. I then reported to the Ramblers' practice center to sign my discipline paperwork which included a suspension for several games along with turning over a check for one hundred thousand dollars, the cost of my fines.

Not even going to lie, that stung. I was too old and my NBA future entirely to precarious to be blowing a hundred grand on avoidable fines. My focus should be on stacking my money to ensure a stable future, not giving cash away. Since entering the league fifteen years ago, I'd amassed a respectable wealth.

The first few seasons I was stupid, buying cars and jewelry I didn't need and spending money on outrageous parties and lavish trips. With my father's guidance I wised up quickly. I remember him asking me if I wanted to bust my ass and sacrifice my health on the court every night just to have nothing to show for it in the end. "Son, you need to think about your future. Don't blow your money on cheap thrills. Invest and multiply."

So that's what I did. Sure, I still partied and spoiled myself every now and then, but nowhere near the level I was on my first three years in the NBA. I knew my pops would be pissed to see me handing over a check that could go to open up a franchise restaurant or a car wash. It was too late now, that money was gone and I'd learned my lesson.

When I entered my house the smell of fried meat assaulted my senses. I stalked to the kitchen to find my little brother in front of the stove grooving to the Isley Brothers in a ruffled apron and swim trunks.

"Hey, what the hell are you doing?" I yelled. But my brother didn't acknowledge me, he just kept performing a two-step before sliding in his socks across the floor.

"Alexa, turn off the music," I shouted. The sounds of Ron Isley's velvety smooth voice ceased.

"Yo, what the fuck?" Raphael protested.

"How come every time I'm in the kitchen … you're in the kitchen?" I asked, quoting a line from one of my favorite movies.

"Cause that's where all the food is."

I gestured in the direction of the backyard. "Your guest house has a fully stocked and functional kitchen."

"I know but I can't fry chicken in there. The smell gets on everything."

"So you decided to walk across the garden and fuck my shit up?"

"I opened the windows." He pointed to the windows and patio door that were wide open all while the heat was on full blast.

"Alexa, turn off the heat," I ordered.

"Chill, I made enough for you." Raphael snapped his fingers. "Hey taste this potato salad I followed Dad's recipe to a T but something is missing." He handed me a spoon with a generous portion.

I tasted it smacking the potatoes against my tongue. "Add more pickle relish," I said tossing my spoon in the sink.

"Good looking out. How was anger management?"

"It was a waste of fucking time. The counselor keeps trying to get me to express my feelings. I'm not sharing my deepest and darkest with a group of strangers."

"Sometimes it's easier to share things with people you don't know because there's no fear that you're letting someone down."

Raphael moved into my guest house shortly after our father passed away. Before that, he was a vagabond. He wouldn't admit it but I think my mother talked him into it. She was afraid I wasn't coping and I may have said some fatalist shit. So my baby brother was here to keep an eye out, steal my clothes, and have sex in my hot tub.

"Maybe but if I needed to talk, you're a stone's throw away."

"And I'm always here if you need me but I'm not a trained professional."

I scratched at my tapered fade. "Weren't you enrolled in those therapy classes a while back? You got a certificate and everything."

"That was *massage* therapy. If you need help relieving muscle tension, I got you." He pulled several golden pieces of chicken from the hot grease.

"Hey, Pratt invited me out tonight. Do you wanna roll?"

"Are you paying … cuz you know my funds are funny."

I smirked. "Of course, I'm paying." I'd been paying for him most of our lives. He wanted to start a taco truck, I gave him the startup money no questions asked. Didn't even mention that people were not going to buy tacos from a Black guy in Vegas. He wanted to enroll in botany classes, I paid his tuition. I don't even know what that shit is. His latest endeavor was The Kush Consultant, a weed dispensary. That business was actually doing really well. We were partners and were looking to open our second location.

"You have to promise this won't be like last time when we went out and then you dipped after an hour. You didn't even cut out with a shorty. You just got bored and left."

"Are you ever going to let that go?"

"No. You used to be the life of the party and now you are in bed by ten."

"Well not tonight. Because tonight we're turning up. Alexa play, 'Yeah' by Usher.

The AI genie complied and my brother resumed his dancing while fixing us both plates.

# SLOANE

"Ace, I'm home," I said, tossing my keys on the kitchen counter and heeling off my shoes.

"Hey Mom. How was anger management?" this ten-year-old boy who literally stole my entire face asked.

"I'm still angry. But now I'm angry and hungry."

"So you're hangry?" He laughed.

"Yes." I pulled items out of a grocery bag. "How does breakfast for dinner sound? Your mother is awfully tired."

"So that makes you trihangry?" He placed a box of his favorite sugary cereal in the small pantry.

I chuckled. "I guess it would."

"I'm down for breakfast. Can we make pancakes?"

"You know it." I shook a bag of the just-add-water pancake mix.

"I know something that will cheer you up." He scrambled to the living room.

"Oh yeah, what?"

"I got an A on my science project." He held up the report that accompanied his project on processed foods. My son took a burger and fries from a fast-food joint and then we prepared the same meal using fresh ingredients to compare the decomposition time and demonstrate how processed food took considerably longer to decompose than unprocessed food.

"Of course you did because your momma didn't raise what ..."

"No fool."

"That's right, baby. Now come over here and help me scramble these eggs," I said washing my hands in the sink.

Ace pulled his stool up to the counter after washing his hands and started breaking eggs. I was praying for a growth spurt. His father was tall and my brothers were both tallish, so Ace's chances were good. But at ten he was always in the lower percentile for both weight and height when we visited the doctor.

"Oh ... check this out." My face brightened. Guess who's in anger management with me."

"The Hulk?"

"No. Doesn't The Hulk need his anger so he can smash things?" I handed him the salt and pepper to add to the eggs.

"Yeah, but he should learn to control it so he doesn't smash the wrong things."

"Good point. It's not The Hulk. It's Deion McCabe."

Ace's clear brown eyes overtook his perfect face. "No way? Did you talk to him?"

"Briefly, he seemed normal."

"You should ask for his autograph."

"Why would I do that?"

"Because it could be worth something." Ace wriggled his eye brows.

"Maybe five years ago, but today … I doubt it."

Ace was afflicted with the same get-rich-quick spirit every Kaplan was born with. My family was used to making money by one of three ways: luck, getting over on somebody, or through the five-finger discount. People in the area knew to lock up their belongings when the Kaplan crew was in attendance. I didn't want that for my son. We were breaking generational curses over here.

My childhood was fucked, which led to a fucked up entrance into adulthood. Ace was impressionable and mimicked everything I did. His life was not going to be a dead-end disappointment like mine turned out to be. He was special and I'd been entrusted as his guide. So no boosting cars or selling dime bags for this kid. Not on my watch.

After dinner I prepared for work. I was a cocktail waitress at Enclave nightclub in the Venetian Hotel on the Strip. Not my dream job but it paid most of the bills and allowed me to spend time with Ace in the day. This weekend Ace was staying with his dad. As parents we'd agreed to trade off weeks. One week Ace was with me, the next he was with his daddy. I'd made a lot of mistakes in my life, but having a child with Ace, Sr. wasn't one of them. We couldn't figure out the love part but the co-parenting piece we had on lock.

Senior was an amazing father and that's all I wanted for my kid, to have a father he could depend on which was something I never had. My father was around but he was far from dependable, and even as a preteen I often felt like the adult and my father the unruly petulant child. Now that we were both grown not much had changed, he was still getting into trouble and I was still expected to bail him out. It was exhausting.

After dropping Ace at his father's, I headed to Enclave to start my shift. I was a bit of a tomboy having been raised by a single father with two tough-as-nails brothers but you wouldn't be able to tell from the way I was dressed. Removing my oversized shirt and tossing it in the locker, I revealed the red leather booty shorts that laced up on the sides and the black bustier which enhanced my modest B cups, making it appear I'd benefited from surgical enhancements.

My hair, which was usually in an absent-minded bun, was free with my tight coils brushing my shoulder as the circumference of my hair took up most of the attention. I wasn't bad to look at when I made a bit of effort. As I worked the floor my moist and juicy curls danced to the pulse-pounding music with each step. And my hips ... these hips had a mind of their own and demanded your full attention when I entered a room.

Who would have thought the thing I attempted to hide in overalls and baggy clothes when I was a teenager, would be the same thing that made men covet me. I'd been getting catcalled since I was seven. I developed early and grown ass men took notice. All the attention was terrifying with random men saying things to me I didn't fully comprehend. One time my father beat a man bloody for staring at me too long. I was in shorts in the safety of my home, but the man's gaze followed me around the room and Stanley Kaplan took exception to it.

My father did not play about his baby girl. He was lacking on so many levels but he was not going to allow his preteen or teenage daughter to be preyed on by a grown ass man. The funny thing is, when I turned eighteen my father would use my curves to his advantage to distract random groups of men while he picked their pockets. He called it using the talents God gifted me with. So here I was with my ass cheeks hanging out using my *talents* to turn a buck.

By 1:00 a.m. the club was at full capacity with drunk party goers getting their lives to a XYZ Baby song. I swayed my hips at the bar as the rapper talked about oral sex in graphic and inappropriate detail. My boss, Fabio, wrapped his arm around my waist.

"Honey, we have some VIP guests." He pointed to the second floor. "Looks like athletes or rappers. And they appear to be into Black women. So tonight's your lucky night, sweetheart." Fabio patted my ass before walking away.

Getting groped was kind of part of the job description when you worked in the hospitality industry. If it wasn't the manager, it was the guests, or the bouncer. I'd lost count of the men and some women I'd cursed out for getting too handsy.

Looking up to the VIP section, my stomach trilled with excitement. This was rare, because of my brown skin I was hardly ever selected to service VIP. I wasn't considered exotic or interesting to look at. Usually I was relegated to serving the group of college friends who were all married and settled down and decided to reconnect in Vegas to prove they were still cool and not just pathetic adults pushing forty. They tipped well enough but not like the VIP crowd. A few weeks ago a leggy blonde server received a ten-thousand-dollar tip. The most I'd ever gotten from a single customer was five bones. Don't get me wrong, five hundred dollars is good money, but it isn't shit when others are clearing thousands from the table.

I adjusted my boobs so they were perky and bouncy in my skin-tight bustier and added a whole lot of jiggle to my walk so my natural ass turned heads as I made my way up the stairs. Standing in front of the exclusive section of seating, I flashed a seductive smile. "Welcome to Enclave. What are we celebrating tonight?"

"Being young, Black, and rich," a man with a mouth full of diamonds said.

"I can dig that. What can I provide to make the celebration a memorable one?"

"Shit what are you offering?" Another man's eyes tripped down my frame.

"Liquor, lots of liquor and weed if you're into it."

"What do you think, Deck? Should we get a few bottles?"

I turned to the man he was addressing and found Deion McCabe sitting between two women who appeared to both be vying for his attention. Deion stood towering over me because he was a genetically fortunate basketball star and I was a mere mortal. "This is your eight to four?"

"Yep, told you I wasn't a stripper."

"Could you just hook us up with a variety of libations and some hookah."

"That I can do."

Deion retrieved his money clip from his pocket and peeled off ten one-hundred-dollar bills from the stack of money in his fold, handing them to me.

"I haven't done anything yet."

"Don't worry I'ma make you work for it." His eyes were intense and seemed to be attempting to penetrate my hard outer shell.

"You keep tipping like this and I'm liable to do just about anything."

He chuckled, leaning in so only I could hear him. "I sure the fuck hope so."

I practically floated back down the stairs, this night just got very interesting. Tucking the crisp bills into my bra, I headed to the stock room to pull bottles. Shit if this rich lonely ball player needed me to switch my hips and coo seductively while serving him and his friends drinks, then he'd come to the right place. I was aiming to have his thick money clip empty by the end of the night.

Back in VIP I laid out the bottles and carafes of orange, pineapple, and cranberry juices for mixing. Then running back downstairs I returned once more, and with the help of another waitress to set up the hookah pipes and flavored tobacco. At Enclave it was all about offering a superior experience. In Vegas the night life options were endless so we needed incentives to draw the crowd in. We had a bevy of beautiful men and women on staff. Your choice of premium weed and top shelf liquor and the Enclave offered awesome music, not that top forty bullshit. Our DJ's played the type of songs that keep you stuck on the dance floor. We guaranteed you'd leave wet and sweaty at the end of the night.

After setting up the hookah, I leaned over giving Deion a perfect view of my tits. "Do you wanna take the first hit?" I asked Deion, ignoring the racially ambiguous woman whispering in his ear.

"Ahh nah. I don't smoke. Smoking will kill you." He winked at me, licking his full lips.

*Was this man flirting with me while also flirting with the woman next to him?* I guess he decided to cast a wide net in hopes one of his lures would end up with something dangling off it. To be fair a man like Deion McCabe didn't have to do much to pull a woman. He was handsome, but not a pretty boy. He exuded confidence with a distinguishable air of someone who would grab you by the throat and make you beg for it. Clearly he could fight, which I know the average person wouldn't consider a turn on, but it happened to be high on my list as a panty soaker. And most importantly, he was rich and famous.

"When I come back you guys better be ready to do some shots." I addressed the crowd of predominantly men. Most of whom stared back in lecherous silence.

Making my way back down the stairs, I walked past number twelve, Colin Pratt. Deion McCabe was his right-hand man on the court. On the ground level, I headed to the dance floor looking for women I could recruit. That VIP section was like a sausage fest and the two women who were in the space were firmly dialed in on the superstar. But you know what they say … it ain't no fun if the homies can't have none.

Being a cocktail waitress at a popular Vegas night-club frequented by the rich and notable, you were expected to go the extra mile. Celebrities were used to white-glove service and it was our job to make their experience an unforgettable one, or more like the nights where you wake up and you can't remember a gotdamn thing because you had so much fun. Those were the best nights.

Plus, pretty women made men want to spend cash. It was a win-win for all involved. The men got to flex and showboat and act like hot shit. The women got free everything, awesome pictures for social media, and if they were lucky maybe they got flown out to a tropical destination. And I … I got paid. Because when people were happy and drunk they tended to reward me with cold hard cash.

"I hope you don't mind a little company?" I flashed a bright smile while holding bottles of tequila in each hand. A procession of hot babes followed me into the section. One of the original women flashed me the evil eye, clearly unhappy with the growing competition. Standing in the center of the crowd I yelled, "Let's get you good and drunk."

The group cheered.

Turning to Deion, I shouted so he could hear me over the music, "Get on your knees."

To my surprise he complied without hesitation. Kneeling before me, he placed his hands on my hips. I gave his scruffy beard a not so playful tug, which forced him to wince, before I tilted his head backward. With my hand cupping his chin, I shoved my thumb into his mouth pulling on his jaw so it remained open. "Don't you move handsome." Raising a bottle over his head I poured tequila into his open mouth as his groupies and entourage cheered him on.

Deion's gaze was trained on my face. His hands were respectably situated on my hips but his eyes, which resembled the golden hue of the Don Julio he was consuming, held nothing but carnal intent. He tapped the side of my hip when he couldn't drink anymore. When he stood it forced my head to arch upward to meet his face. There was a mischievous smile pulling at the corners of his mouth. Retrieving his money clip from his pocket, he once again handed me a thousand dollars. Money talked and Mr. McCabe was speaking my language.

# DEION

WHEN COLIN SUGGESTED WE HIT UP THE CLUB, MY normally introverted self surprisingly agreed. Raphael was right, I'd grown into a bit of a homebody only venturing out for work and the occasional sneaky link. What should have been Colin, my brother, and a few pretty women morphed into the entire crew linking up. Apparently, Colin spread the word and our VIP section was now overrun with faux alpha male energy.

After attending the anger management meeting, I was looking to shift my mood. Staying in for the night all alone harping on what a fuck up I was wasn't a healthy option. But now that we were at the club, I was regretting my choice. It was loud, smoke kept wafting into my face, and the women were trying too hard.

Despite all that, I plastered on a smile and bobbed my head to the bass heavy hip-hop music. Inside however, I was counting down the minutes until I could make my escape. I was distracted with thoughts of my father, the Ramblers, and how I was going to turn my season around. That stunt I pulled on the court had placed a target on my back. With words like unreliable, temperamental, and menace being bandied around in association with my name. Even now in the plush luxury of VIP with my brother, friends, and an assortment of beautiful women I couldn't get my brain to switch over to energy saver mode.

The only bright spot was Sloane. Every time she entered our section I snapped to attention and my eyes followed her around the room like a lost puppy dog. I could tell she was pretty when we talked at the group meeting earlier with not a stitch of makeup and her hair in a messy bun. But tonight, she was serving more than just drinks. How she squeezed all that ass into those tiny pom pom shorts was beyond me. I was looking for a distraction and the anticipation of her passing this way again was doing the trick.

"Shit, I don't remember the last time we did this," Pratt said.

"That's because you ran off and got married and now Charmise got you on a short ass leash."

"She doesn't trust me," Colin said, almost with a hint of pride.

"She shouldn't because your ass is trifling." Pratt married Charmise a few months ago after dating her for over ten years. And by dating I meant demanding she be monogamous while he racked up conquest in every zip code. But in the end, I guess they both got what they wanted. Charmise got her stunning five carat ring and Pratt got his ride or die who was willing to turn a blind eye as long as he came home to her.

Pratt eyed a pancake-assed brunette twerking poorly

to an E40 classic. "So we don't get our wires crossed which ones you got?"

He was referring to the women in our section. When you and your homeboys went out it was always best to strategize so you both weren't wasting your efforts on the same woman. Pratt's tastes in women were vastly different than mine so we didn't need to compare notes. He liked snow bunnies and I liked thick Black women. Don't get me wrong I would fuck anybody. OK, that wasn't true I would fuck any woman with curves, natural or BBL. But when it came to love I preferred to keep that Black.

"I'm good, it's all you."

Pratt offered a smug purse of his lips. "I saw the way you were eyeing our waitress. She's not gonna sleep with you though."

"Oh yeah, why not?" Not that I was interested. Maybe it was the fact that she liked hitting people with her car that was holding me back.

"Because she looks like the type who can detect bull-shit," he joked.

The bumper car driver from anger management was back. *Why wasn't I nicer to her this afternoon?* She was buzzing around our section making sure everyone had what they needed, clearing empty bottles and taking orders for specialty drinks. Sloane wasn't even writing this shit down. Either we were gonna get our drink orders fucked up or she had one hell of a memory.

My buddy Chipmunk was doing the most per usual, trying his best to capture her attention. We called him Chipmunk because his voice sounded like Alvin from

The Chipmunks all high pitched and at top speed. Kids could be cruel in junior high and the moniker kind of stuck even all these years later. It didn't help that his voice never developed beyond the eighth grade. I also got my nickname, Deck, when I was young. At ten I was lanky with a significant height advantage over most of the other kids so they started calling me Deck because they claimed I was taller than a double decker bus.

Chipmunk was my friend but he was being obnoxious as hell. Annoying the women in our section because he had zero game and hitting on Sloane any time she made an appearance. For a vertically challenged, out of shape man who still lived with his mom when he wasn't mooching off of some woman, he was hella confident.

When Sloane disappeared down the stairs, I tapped Pratt's knee. "Why is it that when we're at home we wanna be outside, ripping and running. And then when we go out we can't wait to carry our asses back home?"

"What, bro can I get a hit off what you're smoking?" he joked.

I didn't smoke. Smoking fucked up my endurance. Players with lackadaisical fitness regimes didn't make millions. That meant no smoking, limiting processed foods, lots of veggies. I drank in moderation. I fucked in excess. My body was my temple and what I put into it fueled me. Standing, I gave my limbs a stretch. I was getting too old for this shit because it was too loud and I couldn't understand what the whack ass mumble mouth rapper was saying. All I could hear was the bass washing everything else out.

In search of a restroom, I headed to the main level. I had to pee but I also wanted to hide for a bit. The restrooms were unisex individual water closets which was great if you wanted to be alone or get some sloppy toppy from a willing participant. When the door opened to one of the six restrooms Sloane was on the other side. She practically bumped into me, her eyes focused on fidgeting with the cups of her bustier. Delight settled all warm and gushy in my stomach; it was an unfamiliar feeling so it caused me to take notice.

I gently pushed her back into the restroom, closing the door behind us.

Sloane immediately protested taking a defensive stance. "Listen guy, it's not that type of party."

"Can you relax?" I said, locking the door.

"No, because you currently have me held hostage in a bathroom closet."

"What, hostage?" I raised my hand to signify I had no ill intent.

"It's kidnapping. You just kidnapped me."

I advanced toward her but her next words stopped me in my tracks.

"I will kick you in your ball sack so hard your grandsons will be walking with a limp."

"I just wanted to talk."

She held up a finger of warning. "If you touch me—"

"I'm not gonna touch you … unless you ask me to." At the sink I splashed my face with cold water and grabbed several paper towels to pat my skin dry.

Her body relaxed and she leaned against the wall. "What do you want, Wackadoodle?"

"How long have you been working here?"

"You pulled me into the bathroom for a rundown of my resume?"

"I pulled you in here because I wanted to talk."

"About?" She placed a hand on her curved waist.

"Anything."

"Therapists are typically paid." She eyed me, her expression was impassive but I knew she was hoping I'd take the bait.

I respected the hustle. Time was money. Pulling out my money clip, I counted out five hundred dollars before handing her one.

She released a slow huff of air, tucking the bill deep inside her bra. "I've worked here for over a year. Before that I was at a fancy strip club ..." She pointed her long finger in my direction. "Serving drinks. But when the opening at Enclave came along, I jumped on it."

"Do you like it?"

She looked at me expectantly. With a chuckle I handed her another hundred.

"I like the money. I don't like smelling of alcohol and tobacco. My kid hates the smell ... but that's probably a good thing. Say no to drugs and all that jazz."

My eyebrows inched up my forehead. "You have a kid?" I dangled another hundred in front of her.

"Yeah, a son. Ace ... he's ten."

I relinquished the bill watching her store it safely with the rest. "I got a kid too. She's twenty, goes to UNLV. So fucking smart. I can't believe we're related." Destiny was the best thing I'd ever made. She was bright, kind, and inquisitive. Fortunately, she was blessed with her mother's beauty and my height. And as a teenager she had more sense than I ever did. Everything positive I accomplished was for her. All my hard work and trying to create a lasting legacy was because of her.

"What's Ace into?"

"He loves science and electronics. And he's currently obsessed with learning how to pick a lock."

"Really?"

"I have two brothers who spent a good part of their youth boosting cars."

There was a knock on the bathroom door.

"Occupied," I yelled.

"Why are you hiding in the bathroom when you should be partying with your friends?"

I held my left hand out and used the right to point to my palm. Sloane handed me back one of my hundred-dollar bills. I resisted the urge to press the bill to my nose so I could inhale her essence.

"You know when someone talks about being in a room full of people and still feeling alone?"

"Yeah."

"It's a dash of that, mixed with a sprinkling of imposter syndrome and topped with a hefty amount of are these friends just using me."

"I think it's safe to say most of them are using you."

My face pulled into a surprised expression. "You think so, huh?"

"I'm a good judge of character and I can read people from a mile away."

"Oh yeah?" I crossed the small space to stand directly in front of her. "What story am I telling?"

There was another knock on the door, this time louder.

"I should go." She pushed past me but I grabbed her arm. And just like she promised, she kicked me in my nuts. It wasn't super hard but it was enough to fold me in half allowing her to make her escape.

So this is the part where I admit that shit was a turn on. Slap me, choke me, pull my hair, and make me your slut. I felt fairly confident, if given the chance, Sloane could deliver in all categories. The thought of it had me reaching for my dick tempted to stroke it. But shaking hands with the milkman wasn't what I craved. I wanted the waitress with the brass knee to tease me until I begged her to stop. When I regained my composure, I returned to the VIP lounge and the upbeat vibe had been replaced with yelling.

"I told you not to touch me," Sloane screamed, her body weight shifting from side to side like she was readying herself for a title fight.

"I didn't do shit. Why are you tripping?" Chipmunk spat out.

"You stuck your tongue down my throat, you fucking perv."

"What?" I said, turning to Chipmunk with fire behind my eyes.

There was always one or two guys in the crew who habitually crossed boundaries and Chipmunk was one of them. If I had any sense, I'd cut his ass off. But he'd been my friend for years. And even though he was a mooch, who used my name for clout, loyal friends were difficult to find. But that didn't mean I wouldn't punch him in the throat for stepping out of line.

"It's just a misunderstanding. This bitch is blowing shit out of proportion."

"No boo boo, you're the one who's out of proportion with those stubby ass legs." Sloane advanced like she was ready to set shit off.

"Whoa, hey whoa. Hakuna Matata or whatever the fuck they say in anger management." I said, firmly planting myself between them.

"Your friend was outta pocket," she said.

Chipmunk inched closer. "What happened to the customer always being right?"

"That doesn't mean you get to do whatever the fuck you want," Sloane yelled from behind me.

"I'm the one in VIP."

"You're in VIP because you're a dickrider who can't pull women on his own and who needs a grown ass man to financially provide for him because your pockets are light. So you can miss me with the rich and famous bullshit."

"Shots fired," Raphael shouted. Shit was always a game to him. When I left VIP he was two sheets to the wind but I guess the possibility of Chipmunk getting his ass handed to him had woken my brother up like some smelling salt.

"I see now why you're in anger management," I whispered to Sloane, while using my arm to block her attempt to move forward.

"Fuck you bitch," Chipmunk shouted, spit flying from his mouth.

"Munk chill, that's a lady," Raphael said.

"Fuck me bitch? Is that all you got? Cause I could do this all day. You couldn't handle the shot when I poured it for you all coughing and choking like a punk. Your chain is fake and clearly missing cubic zirconias and you haven't tipped all fucking night."

The crowd in VIP all jeered pointing and laughing in Chipmunk's face. It was clear he wasn't going to win in a verbal assault with this one.

"Suck my dick." The laughter at his expense was making him more combative.

Without missing a beat Sloane said, "I'd have to find it first."

"You're messing with the wrong one."

"Mofo I am two seconds away from busting this bottle across your big ass head with the receding hairline," she countered.

Chipmunk advanced like he thought he was gonna do something but I shut that shit down with a stiff arm to his neck. "Where the fuck do you think you're going? Back your dumb ass up before I embarrass you," I yelled, my deep voice, almost a rumble. Chipmunk was always starting some shit and it was pissing me off. Him physically threatening Sloane was where I drew the line and I was ready to lay his ass flat on the ground. The stunned faces of my crew told me they knew it.

"I don't need to be protected. I could stomp the piss out of him."

"I have no doubt you could. But I'm fully prepared

to choke out anyone who tries to put their hands on you." For some strange reason I was unable to articulate I was protective of the cocktail waitress.

"This is some bullshit," Chipmunk said, his hands balled into tight fists.

"I suggest you take some of the bass out of your voice. If you want to get to her you're going to have to come through me and I guarantee your ass it's gonna be a short fucking trip."

"Don't get cursed out and knocked out." Raphael chuckled.

"Is everything OK up here?" The club manager, who begged for a picture with me earlier, asked. His eyes darting from Chipmunk to Sloane.

Like the bitch he was, Chipmunk started to sing like a canary. "Your waitress was rude and she threatened to physically assault me."

"Only after you groped me."

"Sloane, is this true?" the man with the bushy eyebrows and excessive chest hair asked.

"Fabio, he grabbed me and tried to shove his tongue down my throat."

"Liar, I just asked for another drink and she kneed me in the balls."

Damn, I thought I was special. Apparently, we were all getting our nuts crushed by this woman.

"That shit doesn't even make sense. Why would I hit someone asking me to do my job?"

"Sloane, I've warned you." Fabio rubbed his hands together like he was wiping them clean. "This is the last straw. You're fired."

"Whoa … hold up. Now just wait a minute," I protested.

But before I could defuse the situation a bottle sailed past Chipmunk's head narrowly missing him. I turned to Sloane and her hand, that just seconds ago was holding a bottle of Cîroc, was now empty. After that, shit got chaotic. Sloane wiggled her way past me, fist flying while people screamed and fled VIP. Security ultimately dragged her down the steps and Chipmunk was left pinching his nose to stop the bleeding.

# SLOANE

"Fuck em," Tammie said.

Tammie Yarrow was my neighbor. She lived in the apartment right across from mine. I also counted her as one of my friends. Tammie was like a seasoned auntie and a walking cautionary tale all rolled into one. If it could be done Tammie had done it. Sex at fifty thousand feet, dating a suspected serial killer and potentially being an accomplice. Most notably, she was an all-star poker player having won tournaments where the grand prize was mucho dinero.

She took a long sip of her coffee, which I had no doubt she'd topped off with something a little stronger. "If that hairy motherfucker let you go it's his loss cause you're the best bottle girl in the city."

I chuckled at Tammie's words. But she was right, Fabio was Chewbacca hairy and I was one hell of a bottle girl. But all that didn't make being fired any less stressful.

"They're hiring at the Corral if you're interested," she said only partly in jest.

The Corral was just like it sounded. It was clouded

with cheap weed smoke with a playlist on repeat in lieu of an actual DJ. The clientele was questionable. A woman had to be extra vigilant because she could easily be assaulted, drugged, or caught up in the middle of some bullshit that ended in a hail of gunfire. Was I desperate? Yes. But I wasn't looking to subject myself to that kind of working environment. I still had my job at the race and sportsbook at Caesars Palace. Hopefully I could pick up a few extra shifts until I sorted this thing out.

"I'm gonna pass on the Corral," I said.

"I guess the rumors about Deion McCabe being an asshole are true."

"A huge asshole." It was his fault I'd lost my job because he couldn't keep his little minion in check.

"What about Colin Pratt? Is he as handsome as they say he is?"

"I didn't notice." Pratt wasn't my type; he gave off cocky dickhead energy. The type of guy who'd come from the hood but once he made it out he never looked back. I liked my men a bit rough, less refined, who weren't afraid to get dirty. Men more like … Deion McCabe to be honest. If he wasn't such a douche, I'd let him hit with little to no effort.

"I know you're used to being around the rich and the famous so I have to live vicariously through you. Ain't no one worth noticing frequenting the Corral."

"Now come on Tammie you've been around for a minute. Don't act like you and the Rat Pack weren't bumping uglies," I teased.

Tammie flashed her middle finger. "I ain't that old,

bitch." She croaked and we both shared a good laugh. With a stretch she lifted herself from my couch. "Don't worry about this too much. You'll find something. One thing about you, Kitty Kat, is you always land on your feet."

Heading to the door, she let herself out. Tammie was right; I was born with steel woven into my spine. Which allowed me to balance all the bullshit I was lugging around with me. Every time I took a step forward, I was inevitably knocked two steps back. I called it the Kaplan curse. I didn't believe in ghosts or fairy tales but the Kaplan curse was very real. My father and his father before him were bound by this force that wanted to see us fail. I don't know who my daddy or granddaddy pissed off but they were working overtime to keep their foot on the necks of every Kaplan descendant.

My cell phone rang and I searched the cushions looking for it. When I finally answered the phone I slid to the ground slightly winded. That's what you get when your cardio only consists of climbing the stairs to your apartment and out running the neighbors ornery cat.

"Hello?" I huffed.

"Sloane, baby."

"Who is this?" I knew it was Fabio. He was the only person I knew with a voice that thickly accented.

"It's Fabio."

"What do you want? I returned my apron and access cards."

"Today is your lucky day," he hooted loudly.

"Can you get to the point ... quickly." I wasn't in the

mood to play Fabio's games. He shitcanned me and was now calling with bells accompanying his voice. Clearly, he wanted something so he needed to just spit the shit out.

"Do you want your job back?"

"Of course, I do," I said, through gritted teeth.

"Then maybe we should start with being a little nicer."

I faked a light airy tone. "I'm sorry. Please go on." He had to know I was being snarky. My voice was never cheery, it was deadpan and dripping with sarcasm.

"I just got off the phone with Deion McCabe. He's a nice guy. And he's clearly taken a liking to you."

"What do you mean?" I placed the phone on speaker setting it down on the coffee table.

"He asked me for a favor."

"What type of favor?" If Fabio were in my living room I would ram my arm down his throat and rip the words out of his mouth.

"He asked me to give you your job back. He said the misunderstanding was on his part and you had nothing to do with it."

"Are you serious?"

"Yeah, I reminded him you assaulted a patron and threw a bottle and that's bad for business."

I poked out my lips expelling a considerable amount of air to stop myself from spewing profanities. "I apologize for losing my temper. It will never happen again."

"Well Deion just gave you a get out of jail free card."

"And how exactly did he do that?"

"We are both business men and we came to an

arrangement that was beneficial for both of us."

I didn't need to know the dirty details. All that mattered was I was gainfully reemployed. "I'm glad it all worked out."

"You're on the schedule for tomorrow night. See you then, my beautiful flower."

I looked at my phone in disbelief long after the call disconnected. I've been fired plenty of times and on most occasions the termination stuck. Deion must be a smooth talker because while I didn't deserve to be fired, I went out in a blaze of glory. And I was certain all that remained were the charred remnants of the bridge that led to employment at Enclave or any of their affiliated nightclubs and restaurants.

So it would appear I was in Deion McCabe's debt and I didn't like that shit.

---

AFTER OUR NEXT GROUP SESSION, I MARCHED RIGHT UP TO Deion and gave him a piece of my mind. "Fabio told me you put in a good word for me." I pinned my arms over my chest.

"I did."

"Why?"

"Because my boy was outta line and even though you were talking reckless you didn't deserve to lose your job over it."

Typically, people didn't go to bat for me. At a pretty young age I learned I only had myself to rely on and even family often disappointed you. I didn't like favors or handouts. I was perfectly capable of taking care of myself. Eventually, I would've found a new job, I mean this was Vegas we were talking about. Granted my next establishment probably wouldn't have been as plush as Enclave.

"You placed me in your debt and I'm not comfortable being in that position." Deion's gaze coasted over the length of my body lingering on my backside. It was brief but I caught it and so did my stomach which zinged at the slight hint of interest.

"I don't intend to make you pay up. I know you couldn't afford it."

My eyebrows inched toward my edges. "You don't know shit about me." The zippy buzz in my tummy dissipating.

"You steal donuts from group. That's kinda all I need to know." He exited the double doors headed to the parking lot.

I followed closely behind, pulling my sunglasses from my head to shield my eyes from the morning sun. "What crawled up your ass and died?" He ignored me, never slowing his pace.

"Look, I always repay my debts," I shouted to his back. "I'm very Game of Thrones in that way." His long strides forced me to jog to keep up.

"Consider us even. Now leave me alone," he called over his shoulder.

"No." I stood between him and his car. "Now what are you gonna do?"

"Listen lady, I'm tired. My morning practice was horrible. And then I had to show up here and listen to

Harold cry about not being the favorite son. I just wanna go home."

"What made practice so horrible?"

He took a deep breath realizing he wasn't getting past me until he answered my question. "I'm finding it hard to focus." He tugged at his beard.

"When I have trouble focusing, I smoke a little weed or find a fine man with a stiff dick to eat me out."

He didn't even bat an eye at my words. "I don't smoke and neither should you and sex isn't helping."

"Well maybe you should talk to somebody."

He screwed up his face in disdain. "Like therapy?"

"Yeah, I used to go. It was good ... but then she wanted to talk about a bunch of crap from my childhood and I just kinda stopped showing up."

"Why if it was working?" His tone led me to believe he was genuinely interested.

"Because it hurt." I said the words before my brain had a chance to think about it. "But I'm fine now and it could be a better experience for you."

Therapy was a court appointed thing from a prior offense. I made fun of the process at first but I found a really cool Black female doctor who didn't take my shit and wouldn't allow me to make excuses. After a few sessions I started looking forward to it. Ace was young but I could see the patterns. I was passing my baggage down to him like that shit was a family heirloom.

When I gave birth to Ace, I vowed to create a space that nurtured his creativity, allowed him to explore his feelings, while teaching him to communicate his emotions not in flashes of anger but with his words. But when the therapist probed about my childhood and my parents I just shut down and eventually stopped going. That was over four years ago.

"I don't need therapy; I need my hot hand back."

"You *have* been playing even more crappier than normal."

He narrowed his eyes. "Thanks."

"When did you lose it?" I asked, leaning against his expensive car.

"What … my hot hand?"

"No your virginity. Of course, your hot hand."

He released a long huff. "I don't know. I can't call it. It's just MIA."

His eyes were a bit sunken and his shoulders were slack. Seemed like life was hitting him with a solid one-two combination punch. Part of me was just happy life was focusing on someone other than me at the moment because it had whooped my ass from Reno to Vegas and back again.

My face lit up, "Get in the car," I said heading for the passenger side of his Maybach SUV.

"Excuse me?"

"I'm gonna need you to forget everything you know about me and ignore your better judgment."

"None of that sounds like it's in my best interest."

"You know what, that's fair. But I think I know a way to get your mojo back."

"How?" He raised a skeptical, thick eyebrow.

"We're off to see the wizard," I said, jumping into the passenger side, making myself at home in the caramel-colored leather seat.

# DEION

I FOLLOWED SLOANE'S REALLY BAD DRIVING DIRECTIONS. She was the type of direction giver who called out a turn or need to exit right before you were about to pass it.

"So you're actually friends with old boy?" she asked, while opening my glove compartment to snoop.

"Who Chipmunk?"

"Chipmunk." She said the word like it was a foreign language. "I know his momma did not name him Chipmunk."

"No, she named him Aaron. Chipmunk is a nickname."

"Well it suits him because he's short and whiny."

I chuckled. "He's a childhood friend so it's complicated."

"The hell it is. I have tons of friends from my high school I no longer fuck with."

I gave her a skeptical eye. "*You* no longer fuck with them or *they* no longer fuck with you?"

Humor danced across her face, her eyes appearing to twinkle. "Same difference."

"Look, I'm sorry about my friend."

"He's a creeper."

I didn't object, choosing only to shrug my shoulders.

"If you know this then why are you still hanging out with him?"

"Don't you have people who are questionable morally but you're still close to?"

"Yes, but I'm related to them. Makes it a little harder to disassociate." She slammed my glove box after rummaging through the contents and finding nothing of interest.

"Chipmunk is like family."

"I can't believe you're calling a grown ass man Chipmunk and he just lets you."

We were traveling in the car pool lane, and after passing another exit I asked, "Do I need to start getting over?"

"We have a few more exits." Sloane shifted her body so it was angled toward me. "What did you promise Fabio to get my job back?"

"Who said I made any promises?"

"Because Fabio doesn't do shit out of the kindness of his heart."

I shot her a quick glance. "Which exit are we?"

"We still have a ways to go. Answer the question."

I rapped my fingers against the steering wheel. "A commercial."

"Come again."

"I have to do a promotional spot for Enclave. No big deal."

"For free?" Her head recoiled.

My shoulders lurched.

"Don't you usually get paid millions for shit like that."

"Pratt gets paid millions. I'm more in the thousands."

"Well, when you're a hundredaire like me either is big money. Why would you agree to that?"

"Because you got fired due to no fault of your own. And I don't need those kinds of bad vibes."

Her silence was deafening seeing how she hadn't stopped talking since we'd climbed into the car. The last thing I wanted to be known as was a Captain Save-em. I wasn't looking to rescue her from shit. My only goal was to right the scales. I'd done enough fucked up shit on my own I did not need to have this one-off event muddying my ledger at the pearly gates. Plus, she had a kid and I didn't want to be the reason they struggled to make ends meet.

Sloane finally took notice of the road and screamed, "Oh shit that's our exit."

I was forced to abruptly cross over three lanes of traffic so we didn't miss the approaching exit. It was obvious this woman lived her life fast and loose. Fuck rules, fuck directions just white knuckling it through life. After several more blocks of ill-timed directions I pulled into a parking spot and stopped the car.

"Do you know why we're here?" she asked.

"Because you like nature?"

No, I didn't know why we're at a park at eleven in the morning on a Tuesday. On the drive over I asked her where we were headed and all she would say was "You'll see" before releasing a fiendish laugh. I could only assume we were at this park so she could put me out of my misery and bury me under a shady tree.

"Every day top tier ball players show up to that court over there." She pointed to a basketball court buzzing with activity.

I knew some of the most amazing ballers never made it to the league. Securing an NBA contract didn't mean you were elite, it meant you were lucky. Over the course of my career I played with some phenomenal ball players on and off the court. When I was younger, I'd go to the park in Houston looking for some three-on-three action or a pickup game. I'd play a few games and then hang out and watch others play. All of it a learning opportunity.

*When did I get too good for some homegrown competition?* I couldn't tell you the last time I'd played with someone not pulling in seven figures. A scrimmage or impromptu game with professional players was always tempered because everyone was afraid of getting hurt and losing their golden ticket.

Most of us NBA players were out here playing scared. One bad move, one wrong body fake could have you riding the bench for months on the injured list. And once you were hurt, I mean really hurt, broken leg, jacked up rotator cuff, it was rare to ever get back to the same level of play.

"So what are you suggesting?" I asked.

"I'm suggesting you lace up your sneakers and have a *White Men Can't Jump* moment."

I flashed her a skeptical glare.

Sloane released a pained meowing sound. "Don't be a scaredy cat."

Her words didn't move me.

"What, are you afraid?"

My shoulders hopped. "Kinda."

She looked up at me, her taunting face morphing to one of surprise. "Why, you're a good player. I mean lately you've been playing like a fudge nugget but over-all, you're a talented player." In spite of the insult her words were gentler than I was used to from her.

"What would you know about that?"

I'd grown tired of people telling me to get over it and just play. That what I was experiencing was all in my head. I'd tried moving past this. With sleep boogers still clinging to my eyes I'd join Raphael for morning medi-tation. There were sticky notes with words of affirma-tion posted on my bathroom mirror.

At the Ramblers' training center, I practiced running back and forth over the court while draining three pointers or going in for a layup. Afterward I'd meet up with my trainer and workout again until my body was fatigued. I prayed to God, Buddha, and Wilt Cham-berlin and none of that shit worked.

"I grew up with a household of men. And I work part time at the Caesars Race and Sportsbook. I know good players when I see them."

Scrubbing my face at her basically comparing herself to a talent scout, I said, "Street ball and NBA ball are not the same."

"Yeah, cause in street ball the guys have nothing to lose. They leave it all on the court. While you NBA types are worried about endorsements and making the all-star team."

"Being in the NBA doesn't exempt you from having problems."

"And I'm offering a solution. Just play one game."

I leaned back in my seat with a stubborn bend to my jaw. She was not going to let this go. And if I declined, she would never allow me to live it down. This woman who was so sexy a few nights ago, while still stunningly beautiful with her voluminous curls framing her diamond-shaped face, was now annoying as hell.

She reached into the back seat grabbing my sneakers and tossed them on my lap. "No pain, no gain. Fear is just an illusion. It's only pressure when you're not prepared. Success is like rent and it's due every damn day."

"OK, shut up I get it." Swinging open the car door, I changed into my sneakers. "Rent is due," I mumbled to myself.

Exiting the SUV, Sloane had an excited hop in her step. "This is gonna be good."

We walked toward the court, the whole time I'm doing my best to pump myself up. *You're a beast and can't nobody do what you can when you're in your zone.* Hopefully no one recognized me and assumed I was just another tall brother from around the way. Vegas was a transient town, so me being a Las Vegas Rambler wasn't an advantage. Half the city's residents still had a hard on for their hometown team.

Stepping onto the blacktop, we came to an abrupt halt. "We got next." Sloane shouted, to the men running back and forth on the court. Turning to me she whispered, "I've always wanted to say that."

The mix of men stopped mid stride recognizing me immediately.

"I know that ain't who I think it is." One dude squinted. "Deck McCabe, what are you doing out here? Don't you have fans to beat up or some shit like that?" His words were accompanied by a chorus of laughter.

"He's out here to whoop some ass and take names," Sloane interjected puffing out her chest.

"No I'm not." I waved her words away. "Just looking for a friendly game of ball. Not trying to showboat."

"We're not gonna take it easy on you," a man with a salt and pepper beard said.

"I wouldn't expect you to. I'm hoping to play with the best ballers in Vegas …" I tilted my head in Sloane's direction. "And I was told I could find them here."

It didn't really take much convincing to get the group to play with me. Who doesn't want to brag to his old lady about the time he played with an NBA player and almost beat him. The game was fast paced and the players were aggressive. It was three on three and the shit I got away with at Quest Center Arena wasn't flying on this blacktop. I glanced over at the benches and saw Sloane taking pictures and chatting it up with the crowd of spectators that were forming.

A dude with the heart and size of Spud Webb passed me up and took it to the hole for an easy layup. He mean mugged me all the way down to the other end of the court clearly thinking he was hot shit, like he bested a legend. What he didn't know was that a twelve-year-old could probably cross me up right now. My head was barely in the game, I'd slept like crap the night before, and this morning was leg day so I was a little spent.

It took me a minute to warm up. And by a minute I meant two full games. But as we played and the guys ribbed me when I missed a basket or was slow to get the rebound it all came back. Basketball could be fun even when your game wasn't all the way together.

I found myself returning their verbal jabs with ones of my own when I drained a three pointer or stole a possession. At one point after an assist that allowed me to sink an easy bucket, me and my teammates exchanged daps and back pats while taunting the other team's lack of defense. A smile pulled at my mouth, white and broad, at the on-court camaraderie.

The final score after three games was two to one with my team winning the final match. At the end of the game, the players circled around me. We exchanged handshakes and they asked me questions like "What's it like to play in the NBA?" and "Do you think Colin Pratt is the greatest alive?"

One man retold his favorite play from my basketball career years ago when I was playing in Kansas, and I dunked the ball over the top of a rival player after a fast break. "That shit was so disrespectful. I loved it," he cackled.

"That needed to be on a poster it was so pretty," another man cosigned.

Not going to lie, the unexpected adulation made me beam. On the bench I found Sloane counting out cash.

"Did you bet on these games?" I asked, my body stiffened and the muscles in my neck were visible.

"Yes, and that last game you cost me a hundred dollars."

"You bet against me?" My voice was high pitched and nasally.

Sloane seeped in a deep breath. "I mean you weren't really giving me a reason to bet on black."

"That's fucked up," I said, dropping on to the bench next to her.

Sloane tucked her winnings away and settled in on staring at me. "That was fun … right? Admit it, you had fun." She nudged me with her shoulder.

It was fun, but I wasn't gonna give her the satisfaction of knowing that. She seemed like the type of person who loved throwing things in people's faces … words, actions, her fist.

"How much did you win?"

She smiled brightly. "Two fiddy."

"Good, then you can buy lunch."

# SLOANE

I watched as Deion squirted ketchup, mayo, and mustard on his plate. Mixing the three together, he smoothed the concoction on the bun of his veggie burger with a butter knife.

"You're a vegetarian?" I asked.

"No, I just like the taste of veggie burgers," he said, before taking a big bite.

Deion's legs were so long his knees touched my booth. I had to angle my limbs, positioning myself in between his wide stance.

"Are you from Vegas?" he mumbled around the food in his mouth.

"Is anyone from Vegas?" I joked. Vegas was a migratory city. Everyday a new crop of hopefuls would hop off a bus, touch down on a plane, or cruise into town. Each looking for a fresh start, hoping to strike it rich, or become famous. "I was born in Reno but we eventually settled in Vegas," I said, forking my omelet and taking a bite.

"Do you like it here?" he asked, his scrunched-up face revealing he did not.

"I'm not exactly a world traveler so I don't have much to compare it to."

"It's hot as hell here." He eyed me waiting for a cosign of his statement.

"Houston's hot."

"Houston is tolerable. Vegas is like dancing on the devil's tongue." He wagged a sweet potato fry at me.

His words made me smile, my dad often said the same thing. "Well, I like things hot. Keeps everyone on their toes."

"I guess." Deion stole the avocado I'd pushed to the edge of my plate adding it atop his burger. "So tell me this, how many jobs do you have? You work at Enclave and then you work at a sportsbook and let's not forget you hustle people out of their money at every opportunity."

I ignored his snide comment. "What can I say, I'm a go-getter. And I've never been afraid of honest work or a well-crafted shell game."

I likened myself to that shell game … you know the kind where you have to guess which cup was hiding the queen of hearts card. People were so busy trying to figure me out they missed what was happening right before their eyes. Like right now Deion was focused on my work ethic but what he didn't know was I was sizing him up for some work of my own. The kind that required little to no clothing and him putting his athleticism to the test. I'm talking about seated shoulder press, split squats, hip thrusts, and deadlifting all one hundred and seventy pounds of me to his mouth.

What can I say he was hot and at peak physical

perfection. I wanted to be stretched and conditioned by Mr. McCabe and when he was done, I would stumble to the showers dripping wet and sore. *God please let this man be a freak.* That was probably not an appropriate prayer request but he knows my heart and I needed to get laid. Since breaking up with my probation officer I'd been in a bit of a slump and I was hopeful the ball player could knock the cobwebs loose.

Deion was staring at me like ketchup was decorating the side of my face. This whole time he'd been talking I was daydreaming about his dick and hoping I would be unable to fit it all in my mouth.

"What?" I said.

"I asked, what other countries have you visited?

*Countries?* I think Deion could see the bewilderment on my face.

"States?" he asked, narrowing the scope.

"Like I said I haven't been to many places. Mostly spots that can be accessed via car. Cali, Arizona, Utah."

"Do you have a fear of flying?" He relaxed against the booth nibbling on fries.

"It's not a fear. It's a lack of funds. Don't get me wrong I've flown before but I'm a single mom and shit like that is a luxury."

"Sure, I get it."

"Not everyone was born with a silver spoon in their mouth and a solidified legacy." I spat out.

This man was born into money and couldn't fathom people having to stay close to home because missing work meant a short paycheck. The thought of being able to travel out of the country was unimaginable to me. I was poor and I wasn't pretty or genteel enough to get flown out to some easy breezy destination.

His eyes creased at the corners. "Have you been Googling me?"

You didn't need to Google Deion McCabe to know who his father was. Morris McCabe, was an NBA legend. My dad lost a shit ton of money betting against the senior McCabe. His father was a hall of famer and your favorite player's favorite player. Deion was born into basketball royalty. That legacy was hard to escape.

"It's just common knowledge." I attempted to remove some of the sting from my words. "I'm not trying to shame you. I'd much rather my daddy was a basketball icon instead of a Jack-of-all-trades."

"Oh yeah, what does your dad do?"

I expelled a long breath. "A little bit of this. A little bit of that. And a whole lotta nothing."

Unlike Deion my father wasn't the pillar of the community, so the last thing I wanted to do was spend time talking about him.

Glancing at his watch he asked, "Are you ready to go?"

"Uh-hm." I tossed back my coffee and dumped all the sugar packets and tiny creamer cups into my purse.

"Listen, you do not have to steal sugar packets. If you need sugar, I will get you sugar. We can pull up to Costco right now and I will buy you an industrial size box of sugar."

"It's not stealing, it's being frugal. Only one person in my household uses sugar so I don't need a buttload of sweetener."

"You sound like my brother." His phone chimed and when he checked it his face flushed. "Shit."

"What's up?"

He raked his fingers through his beard. "I have a thing I need to be at, like now." Deion slid from the booth, dropping a hundred dollar bill on the table. I thought I was supposed to pay but I didn't object. He looked around trying to figure out his next move. "Do you mind tagging along and then after I can swing by and drop you off at your car?"

"This isn't some kind of drug deal is it? Because I'm on probation."

"It's a Ramblers' event."

I could just order a RideX to take me back to my Honda. But there was something about Deion that I found intriguing. OK, I was trying to smash and if we said our goodbyes now it would delay the possibility of his balls slapping against my chin.

"Uhm, that's fine. Lead the way," I said.

Deion's eyes sized me up as if he was only now realizing sex with me was on the table. I kind of thought it was cute he didn't immediately assume he could bag me. He sunk his teeth into his juicy lower lip. "Great let's go." Claiming my hand he led me out of the diner.

The event was a youth basketball league which the Ramblers' organization sponsored. Several players from the team were in attendance. Sitting in the stands of the gymnasium, I watched Deion move through the crowd of kids and parents, all smiles. His intense, brown eyes narrowed and his nose crinkled as the corners of his mouth ticked upward to reveal an even row of white teeth with a slight gap separating his two front teeth. He didn't smile often but when he did it was as if I was a depleted battery connecting to a charger, his smile filling me up with wanton desire.

Deion was good with crowds. He didn't strike me as a people person but he seemed to enjoy engaging with the middle school kids. Maybe it was the love of the sport and being around future athletes that found him in a jovial mood. He was showing a boy with a huge afro how to hit a three pointer from the side of the court. Throw after throw Deion drained each one. He didn't seem to have a hot hand problem right now.

A woman scooted next to me on the bench. "Which ones yours?" she asked, pointing to the court.

I shook my head. "None of them. I came with the dude with the tattoo sleeve and wizard beard." I pointed to Deion who was now watching the kid do his best to replicate what he'd just been taught.

"Wife?"

My lids hardened. "No."

"Girlfriend?"

I levied a glare in her direction. "No, we're not even friends." You could never trust someone who asked too many questions, it was giving undercover cop.

"Well, he sure is handsome."

"I guess. Look I'm not interested in small talk." I crossed my arms over my chest.

The woman flashed a shocked glare and slid down the bench away from me.

I wasn't trying to be an asshole, that mode just came

preset with my model. There was nothing I hated more than small talk. Especially small talk for the sake of filling the silence and nothing else. Also, I didn't trust many people so I wasn't interested in idle chit chat. But her questions got me thinking if Deion and I weren't even friends, why had I agreed to come here. I could have offered to take a RideX and even gotten him to pay for it. Sure, I was hoping to get laid but this child-friendly event probably dashed all hopes of that happening today.

I guess I enjoyed his company. He was a bit of a grouch much like me. But there was something else, a sadness in his eyes which I recognized because I saw that same despondency when I looked in the mirror each morning. Or maybe I was bored. It was my day off and this was Ace's week with his father. All I had planned for today was a large meat lovers pizza, a true crime marathon and internet porn which would lead to solo sex.

After the basketball drills, mini exposition game, and photo ops, Deion came bounding back toward me. All eyes were on him, as attendees in the stands pointed and stared as he took a seat next to me. I wasn't certain if they were gawking because he was Deion McCabe, two-time NBA champion and winner of three MVP awards or if the rubbernecking was due to the fact he was Deion McCabe, the most controversial and polarizing player in the NBA.

"All done. Thanks for hanging out. I'm sure you didn't have sitting in a poorly ventilated gymnasium on your list of to dos for today," he said.

"It's cool. It was nice watching the kids' faces light up when you and your teammates entered the room."

Deion rested his arms on his knees tossing me a raised eyebrow. "Don't tell me you're getting all soft on me Kaplan."

"Kids are my kryptonite." I leaned in closer pointing to a child whose small frame was swimming in his uniform. "You see that little man over there."

"Yeah."

"He could not take his eyes off of you. He'd watch you shoot and then pick up the ball and give it a try missing every time."

"That ball is almost as big as him." Deion chuckled.

I joined in on his laughter. "I know. It's adorable. I don't think he stopped smiling the entire time."

Deion once again eyed me suspiciously.

"Stop it. I love kids. They're the best of us."

He checked his phone for missed messages. "Speaking of kids, do you need to pick your son up from school?"

"No, his father and I trade off, so Ace is with him this week."

His lip twitched upward as he shook his head thoughtfully.

Silence fell between us like we were both trying to devise ways to continue spending time in company with each other. I wanted to offer myself to him; it was usually a full proof strategy. I'd ask a guy if he wanted to have sex with me. Most times the answer was a resounding yes. The few times I'd received a no my ego was bruised, but I'd just shrug it off in search of the next willing participant.

Deion rubbed his hands on his knees. "So should I take you back to your car?"

"You could." I hoped my tone implied he had other options.

Deion angled his body toward me and brushed my curls from my eyes. His gaze was exploratory, locking on to my face in search of his next play. Probably deciding if I was worth printing off a non-disclosure agreement. He ran his smooth tongue over his lips causing the pulse in my crotch to flit. "Do you want to come back to my place and have ... lemonade in the backyard?"

I sure hoped lemonade was some type of euphemism for sex. "I like my lemonade tart, just a touch of bitterness with a firm kick."

"My lemonade will definitely cause you to pucker."

I honestly didn't know what we were talking about at this point but my interest was piqued. "That sounds delightful."

# DEION

THE RIDGE WAS A GATED COMMUNITY IN A NEVADA SUBURB of Summerlin. Contrary to popular belief, I didn't often bring women back to my place. And truthfully, I was probably taking a risk with Sloane who would most likely use the opportunity to case the joint. But it was hard to resist this particular woman.

She had thick thighs, which were my weakness. And those thighs connected to a supple ass that jiggled ever so slightly when she walked. On her head sat a mass of curls she was constantly brushing from her large brandy-colored eyes. Her smile was wicked, like she was two seconds away from doing shit she shouldn't.

Then there was her rebellious, stubborn nature. She said exactly what she was thinking, your feelings be damned. I was ready for her to take control and dominate me. Being submissive to her would not be a problem. I was an active listener and I followed directions. Hearing her sultry voice tell me I was indeed a good fucking boy would ruin me.

Sloane dropped her bulky smuggler's purse on the marble floor. Some of the items her sticky fingers had collected along the way spilt out. *Was that a mug from the diner we ate at earlier?*

"You live here by yourself?" she asked, her head on a swivel as she scanned the long hallway and twenty-foot ceilings before disappearing into the adjoining room.

I'm only gonna say this once, if I end up as the victim on a true crime podcast, I only have myself to blame. *Deion McCabe was a popular basketball player with a hot temper but on one fateful night in November he met a woman with a temper the size of a five-alarm fire.*

"Do you like true crime?" I asked, as she breezed back into the living room.

"I love it. Even though most killers are sloppy."

"You think so huh?"

"Yes, I've spent many hours plotting out the perfect crime. I should have gone to school for that CSI shit because I would crack the case wide open every single time."

"Note to self not to make you mad."

"I do drive my car into stationary objects so it's probably a mental note you should keep in the forefront of your brain."

"What exactly would I have to do for you to consider vehicular homicide."

"I'd have to like you enough for that."

"You don't like me?"

"It all depends on what happens in the next few minutes." Sloane tucked her shiny hair behind an ear. Her big brown eyes were taunting me to make a move.

Now that Sloane was here, I wasn't sure what I wanted. Or how to properly ask for it. If this went poorly, I'd have to interact with her every week at the anger management group. And even if it went well, one-night stands were meant to be just that. I had enough problems, fucking around with a parolee with a fiery temper was probably a path I should avoid.

My brain was working overtime to talk my dick out of this. *Take her back to her car and go home. But have you seen her ass? I mean be fucking for real. I ain't walking away from that. And honestly what man could? I'm certain them baby making hips have destroyed one or two happy homes.*

Sloane busied herself touching my things. I bet her momma stayed slapping her hands when she was a kid. Her fingers swept across a picture of me, Raphael, and our parents on the mantel.

"Your people?" she asked absentmindedly.

"Yea."

"Handsome bunch. I always thought you looked like your father but you are your mother's child. Does the fireplace work?" She bent at the waist taking a look.

"What are you a realtor?"

She ignored my question just like I'd ignored hers. "Where's my lemonade? I was lured here with the promise of a refreshing drink. Or was that all a ruse?"

"Are you serious?" I thought it was obvious, that in this instance, lemonade was a metaphor for sex. Maybe it was foolish of me to assume she was interested in the same singular thing I was.

"Were *you* serious when you offered me a tall, dripping glass of lemonade?"

With an aspirated huff I led her to the kitchen and got to prepping her fresh squeezed lemonade. I used the bowl of lemons my housekeeper displayed each week, claiming it was a calming visual aesthetic. As I stirred in the sugar I asked, "Do you know what the word euphemism means?"

"Yeah, I think we had to do that to my dog when I was ten. He had cancer." The corners of her perfect bow-shaped mouth ticked upward.

Pouring her a tall glass, I handed her the drink. "Here … I hope you choke on it."

Sloane chuckled, tipping her glass in my direction. "To choking on it."

I gripped the counter painfully aware I was losing the battle to keep my dick flaccid. As her throat worked up and down as she drank, it wasn't hard for me to imagine her devouring me in a similar way.

She tapped her glass down releasing an exaggerated ahh sound. "That was refreshing."

"Thank you, I ran a profitable lemonade stand when I was younger."

I tossed the used lemons and stored the rest of the lemonade in the fridge while Sloane walked around my home, very possibly pocketing small trinkets. I found her in the second living space tapping the keys on the piano.

"Do you play?" she asked.

"No, it came with the house."

Sloane's fingers swept the keys before walking to the next room, the swing of her hips propelling me forward in hot pursuit. I could watch her walk for hours, preferable while naked with a bend and snap mixed in for good measure. Now that sleeping with Sloane was a viable option the realization of how starved I was for physical contact was sinking in.

Even though I'd played team sports my entire life and was considered a popular kid growing up I was a bit of a loner. And it was difficult to find a woman who was willing to chill with me on the couch when there were parties to attend and fashion weeks to sit in the front row of. If I fucked with you that meant you were special or in Chipmunk's case, I'd known you since childhood so you were grandfathered in.

"Is anger management working for you?" I asked, as she stopped to admire the artwork on the wall.

She laughed. "You were at the club … what do you think?"

"I think those were extenuating circumstances."

"I don't know. I've been a fighter all my life. With my words and my fists. I don't think you can reform something that's been innate for thirty-four years. What about you?"

"I don't have an anger problem. People try me and then I have to check them. I don't ever start shit."

"If we were in group right now, they would say you have to stop seeing yourself as the victim and take accountability for your actions."

My face brightened. "So you are actually listening and not just faking it."

"I never fake it." She lifted an indifferent shoulder. "I'm at those stupid meetings for forty-five minutes and there's only so much daydreaming I can do." Sloane stopped at a piece that was essentially paint splashed on a canvas. "This is god-awful."

"It's a Bassey and it's worth over two hundred thousand dollars." I corrected her.

"Just because something is expensive doesn't mean it's good."

"If you don't understand art just say that."

"I understand you have to be one stupid motherfucker to pay that much for a canvas with a rainbow of colors splattered over top."

*Was this her attempt at foreplay?* "I like it." I said with a firm nod of my head.

"No you don't, you bought it for the price tag and now you're stuck with this ugly ass art on your wall."

"I bought it because it spoke to me."

"You have bad taste."

"That may be true seeing how I'm here with you." I smirked.

Sloane flashed a contemptuous glance in my direction. "Do you think insulting me will get your dick sucked? You just lost a point."

"A point for what?"

"For insulting me when you should be telling me how pretty I am."

"How many points do I have?"

"You *had* five, now you have four."

"Can we just agree I have eclectic taste?"

She didn't respond opening the sliding door to the atrium leading to an intimate, private, outdoor space with lush greenery and a small pond. I decided to move the conversation away from art. Which was subjective. And while I purchased that piece at the height of my reckless spending, it retained its value even if it looked like it was created by a seven-year-old. A very talented seven-year-old, but seven all the same.

"What are you on probation for?" I asked.

Sloane made a loud buzzer noise like the type you'd hear on a game show when you answered a question wrong. "Point deduction."

"Is that topic off limits?" I scratched my head. I was all for playing games but she had to at least share the rules. Maybe she was looking for me to level up the conversation into sexy talk territory. I cleared my throat and dropped my voice a full octave. "I bet you taste like peaches. Wet and juicy." I hoped to turn this violation around.

Sloane gasped clutching her invisible pearls. "Point deduction."

"Point deduction for what?" I felt like she was the referee and I was pleading my case.

"Freaky offensive play."

"Freaky?" I raised an eyebrow offering up a glassy stare. "Don't pretend you don't like it a little strange." She didn't come off as a pillow princess. Sloane was definitely active both verbally and physically in the sheets.

She pursed her lips till they were a thin line.

"Can you please review the tape."

"No."

I leaned against the wall, with an indignant fold of my arms, scheming on ways to right this ship. "I'm sorry I brought up your probation. I get it. I have stuff I don't want to talk about either."

"Like the fact that your contract expires at the end of this season and it might not get renewed?"

So she *had* Googled me. "Yes, among other things."

After a few tough years being bounced around from team to team I'd landed on my feet with the Ramblers. But when my four year contract expired I wasn't so sure the Ramblers would be interested in doubling down. Could I retire and be financially secure? Yes. But I wasn't ready to throw in the towel, and still believed some of my best playing years were ahead of me.

I was so lost in my thoughts I didn't see Sloane make her way to my side of the atrium. She pushed her hair from her face looking up at me. Her breast raising and falling inches from my body. Sloane hooked a finger in the collar of my shirt leading my lips toward hers.

*This woman is gonna be my downfall,* was my last thought before she plunged her tongue into my mouth. You know when people claim the world slows down when they kiss someone? Kissing Sloane was the opposite. Everything seemed to speed up with each moment frantic and fleeting like the world was burning down around us and all we had was right now.

Sloane's lips were warm and the corners of her mouth were sweet, most likely from the lemonade. I ran my hand along her jaw before cupping her face to pull her closer. My fingers inched further back, curling around her neck which elicited a rough moan from her mouth. Sloane pulled away, her eyes low and dreamy. I was captivated by her face and didn't notice her flat hand slapping me square across my cheek.

I pressed my hand to my skin in shock. Stepping

back, I gauged her motivation. My dick was already tenting my pants. A beautiful woman, whose kisses stole my words, and she had a heavy hand. "Sloane … are we gonna need a safe word?"

"What we're about to do absolutely requires a safe word."

I advanced, scooping her up so her legs were around my waist. Her kisses were frenzied and intense like if she could, she would bite my head off like a praying mantis who decapitates its mate after a sexual encounter. It wasn't pretty, the scene of us stumbling back into the house and down the hallway clawing at one another in an attempt to get closer.

Sloane pulled at my lower lip with her teeth before loosening her hold and landing on her feet with a giddy laugh. She placed her hand on her hip. "Do you need me to sign something?" She asked a bit out of breath.

"No … I don't do that."

Sloane's thick, perfectly arched eyebrow danced up her forehead. "No NDA, what are you living in the stone ages?"

"Are other men making you sign NDA's?"

"No, but I've never slept with a celebrity before. There was that one guy from Big Brother but he was faux famous so that didn't count."

Sure I knew plenty of players who required an NDA before being intimate, Colin Pratt among them, but it wasn't my preference. Signing paperwork wasn't an aphrodisiac. Any woman could claim she had sex with me, whether it actually happened or not. And what was

I protecting with an NDA anyway, that I had sex with women? I think that was a well-known fact.

Sloane searched for a paper and pen opting for a takeout menu on the glass coffee table and a green highlighter. She read aloud as she wrote: "I Sloane Kaplan promise not to tell anyone living or dead about my night of freak nasty sex with Deion McCabe. If I speak about this night he is authorized to give me one wet Willie."

She handed the not so legally binding document to me and I read it through. At the bottom of the note were two boxes both checked, one read STD free and the other HIV negative. "Seems official."

"I took some online paralegal courses," she bragged.

"I also get tested regularly and am free and clear of all diseases. Now that we've gotten that out the way ..." I tossed the homemade NDA onto the table. "Alexa, start my mellow grooves playlist."

Melodic music streamed through the speakers mounted throughout the house. A baritone voice crooned about all the things he wanted to do with his lady. Sloane's body swayed back and forth. We were a foot apart but I could feel the electricity coursing between us. If I just extended my hand, I could pull her closer and neutralize the tension.

Back in the courtyard I was fueled by the sting to my left cheek but now that the pain had dulled, I needed to work up my courage. I wanted to please this woman in every conceivable way and I wasn't looking to rush. Sloane stood there expectantly waiting for me to take control and I was returning her energy with a hooded glare.

"What's wrong?" she asked.

"I'm admiring the view. You were right about one thing?"

"Just one?"

"You are stunning and it shouldn't have taken me this long to tell you."

Her eyes narrowed to slits; she didn't believe me. "Alexa … tell Deion to stop being a gentleman and fuck me until our juices are dripping down my legs."

Alexa's robotic voice chimed in, "I'm sorry I do not understand the directive."

When the music kicked back in, I closed the needless distance between us. Reaching for her hair, I massaged a strand against my fingers. "Our safe word is pineapple."

"Locking it in." Sloane tapped her temple.

Our next kiss was slow and deliberate settling into the fact that we could take our time. Savoring every kiss, gentle bite, and the sensation of her tongue running along my neck. I sunk my nose into her mass of hair while she nibbled on my earlobe. There was a hint of a floral, fruity, musky scent overtaking my nostrils. The fragrance working in tandem, both strong and sensual and my body had a visceral reaction to it. My penis was now extended to full capacity and butterflies tickled my stomach at the possibilities laid before us.

Sloane broke free and heeled off her sneakers before removing her matching, leopard-print yoga pants and top. My eyes overtook my face as I tried to commit her features, which before now I'd only imagined, to memory. There was a huge, colorful tropical flower tattoo on the left side of her thigh which wrapped around to her butt cheek. And the freckles and moles that dotted her face traveled to her hips and soft stomach.

With confident steps she walked closer, guiding me back until my legs bumped into the couch. Sloane pushed me pretty hard but I'm an athlete and balance is key. She looked up at me with the sweetest pout. Making a second attempt, she shoved me again but I didn't budge. "Could you please," she said.

"What are you trying to do exactly?"

"I'm trying to get you to sit your ass down so I can suck your dick. But if you're not interested." She turned pretending she was going to walk away but my grip on her arm stopped her.

"I'm interested."

"Ask me nicely."

Hooking my thumb under her chin, I tilted her head upward. "Please can you wrap your beautiful lips around my dick." I bit down on the inside of my cheek.

Her eyes sparked with satisfaction. Sloane extended her finger tapping my chest. This time I allowed her touch to sweep me off my feet, tumbling to the couch.

# SLOANE

I WAS JUST A REGULAR LOWER MIDDLE-CLASS COCKTAIL waitress with no real power to change the world in a substantive way. Nothing I did would probably ever make a lasting difference. But in this moment as I knelt before Deion, I felt like the most powerful woman in the world. Pulling off his shorts and boxers to reveal a perfect buoyant dick. His penis was like two extra-long Snickers bars stacked back-to-back.

Planting strategic kisses to his legs and inner thighs I was pleasantly surprised that he smelled fresh-out-of-the shower clean. Let's be real, this man had played three pickup games this morning so I was essentially proceeding at my own risk. His skin had a slightly salty aftertaste, but overall the scent of Zest soap gave me the green light to dive in.

When I licked the crease between his thigh and scrotum Deion grunted. I cast him an irritated eye. If he thought he was gonna act too cool for school when I put his dick in my mouth, he had another thing coming. I would have him screaming my name before I was through. As my tongue touched down on the head of his penis he released a gratified gasp of air.

Working circles over his tip, I rubbed my hands across the well-defined muscles on his abdomen. I removed him from my mouth and dropped lower, sliding my tongue over "uncharted" territory. When Deion didn't object, I centered my attention on his anus, twisting my tongue around the sensitive crinkles. With each lick Deion became more vocal, practically egging me on. Gotta love a man whose sexually liberated. They were always so much fun in bed.

His breathing pattern was a mixture of pants and gulps for air. I slid my tongue upward sucking his balls into my mouth. Deion seeped in a breath. His eyes were fixated on me kneeling before him aiding in his arousal. Easing his dick back into my mouth I moaned as his penis pressed against my cheeks.

Deion gathered my hair into his large hand guiding me over his length. My tongue curled and twisted as I enthusiastically pleasured him. He folded his body over top of mine, his long limbs exploring my skin as he kissed the top of my head before whispering. "You look so beautiful with my dick in your mouth."

Did I have a praise kink? Why yes, yes I did. Tell me I was pretty and that I made your body feel good and I would work harder to satisfy you. I'm certain this could be traced back to my childhood when the only time I was praised was when I was doing something illegal.

Releasing him from my mouth, I let my hands work over his shaft. Deion kissed my lips causing goosebumps to pebble my almost naked body. He collapsed into the sofa cushions, appreciation written all over his bronzed face. I locked eyes with him, fascinated by the way his Adam's apple wobbled when he moaned. The way he bit his lip every time I took more of him into my mouth. The way he fisted the couch pillow whenever I slapped his dick against my outstretched tongue.

Deion stood abruptly causing me to reel backward. He helped me back to my knees directly in front of him, before taking control as I opened my mouth ready to receive him. His touch was gentle yet firm as he navigated my mouth over his terrain. The pad of his thumb softly caressing the side of my cheek as he slid in and out. I was a giver. I always have been. Sharing is caring and I wanted to share my throat with him. Like Auntie Dionne sang, "That's What Friends Are For."

It was clear he didn't realize that I would let him do anything to me at this point. He guided my head, fitting as much of himself as he could into my mouth. When he finally freed me allowing me to breathe, I was a little light headed and shocked. Dreams do come true. Just a few weeks earlier while I lay in bed alone, I'd fantasized about a man who wasn't afraid to take control and who could fill me to capacity, and here I was living my dreams.

Deion practically growled down at me. "Good job, baby. Good job."

Bending low, he baptized my mouth with messy hot kisses before sucking on my bottom lip. My insides trilled at the attagirls causing me to beam. There was something about this man that made me want to please him, and if the tip of his dick touching my uvula sparked joy then I was more than willing to support him. We played off each other with him taking control then releasing it back to me. Even after he was writhing, shaking and tumbling down my throat I continued to lick and slurp, wanting to prolong his stay in Shangri-La.

When I finally released him, he wrinkled his nose. "You missed some." Deion pointed to my face before leaning in.

He licked a spot of wayward come from my cheek. Extending his tongue so I could suck his essence from his mouth. *Yes, this was my type of carrying on.* While we kissed, I massaged his dick back to life because I was not finished with this man yet. He raised my left arm and licked my underarm which caused me to squeal and then melt into a blob at the activation of arousal points, I never knew existed. His unexpected actions just solidified that I would probably be professing my love and calling him daddy long strokes by the end of the night.

Deion scooped me up and deposited me onto the extra-large couch, hooking his fingers in my thong sliding them from my raised hips. Lowering himself next to me, he draped his leg over mine. Our lips collided, his kisses messy and deep. He detached himself from my mouth to suck my nipple through the bra. His hand disappeared in between my legs and his digits explored my folds, causing my breath to hitch as his thumb glided over my clit and down my expanse before sliding inside.

My body contorted as his hand thrust and rubbed.

Deion's eyes were trained on me, his breathing just as labored as mine. As my moans, and forced expletives ricocheted against the walls, Deion whispered in my ear, "You are so soft and creamy."

I wrapped my arms around him trying to anchor myself against the approaching wave. My body arched as I climbed a small wave before crashing to the couch, his lips slamming into mine. There was no time to catch my breath before the next wave of ecstasy caught me in the undertow. Disoriented and shivering, I drove my nails into his back practically begging him to set me free. When he removed his hand I was left in a crumpled pile completely wrecked. Deion flooded my face with kisses, making me blush.

"Spend the night?" he asked, licking me from his fingers.

"With you?"

"Yeah, I'm the only one here so I'm gonna have to be enough."

I reached for his dick, cupping it with my palm. "You are more than enough."

Deion grunted. I watched in a fog as he rose, walking across the room. When he returned, he had a condom in hand. I unhooked my bra tossing it to the ground. When Deion caught sight of my breast he dropped to his knees. He circled his tongue over my nipples till both were wet and erect. He was messy and the feel of his saliva dripping between my breast made me wetter. Which honestly, I didn't think was possible. When he pulled back, I sat up kissing and sucking his chest and torso while he readied the star of the show.

Laying back, I opened my legs wide and the pool of slickness that saturated my slit invited him to make himself at home. As Deion eased his dick inside inch by inch I was worked into a tizzy. Accommodating Deion McCabe was no small feat. His rock hard dick stretched me wide and I grunted in awe as I acclimated myself to his thickness. The first stroke sent me reeling. I could not be held responsible for the things I said or did while this man was inside of me.

With the second stroke Deion blew out a deep breath. He looked at me, his face a puzzle like he didn't expect me to feel this good. For it to feel so right. Deion brushed my curls from my eyes cupping my face. "You are perfection," he said. A smile pulled at the corners of my lips. That was a gross exaggeration but I allowed it under the excited utterance exception. The strokes were no longer slow and refined. He had grown accustomed to my pussy and was ready to show out with deep thrust that had me clawing at the couch.

The words that spilled from my mouth were incoherent and laced with profanity. I called on God, Jesus and Mary Magdalene to get me through this. My pussy was humming and that low, intense vibration was radiating through every part of me. Deion changed positions so I was on top. Not to be outdone, I rode his dick like it was a mode of transportation. My hips swiveled and ground against him.

"Who taught you how to do that?" He breathed out.

"Boyfriend … senior year." I eked out between thrust.

"Be sure to leave his contact information because I'm

gonna need to send him a thank you note. Because this shit …" He moaned against my lips. "This shit will keep me coming back for more."

As you can expect those words made me kick it up a notch, not because I wanted to be picked or was hoping to fuck him again. Although in this moment I couldn't imagine not fucking him again. But it was his adoring gaze it just made me feel special. And that feeling was rare for me.

Deion made me feel soft and delicate. "Do you like how it feels when I fuck you?" I yelled. Yep, I was a soft filthy mouthed angel.

This man had a very particular set of skills, his dick seeking out my spot and hitting it from every possible angle. As his capable hands kneaded and massaged my body, my skin sparked with unfettered desire from his touch. Deion was my new addiction. I bit down onto his shoulder as my ass slammed down on his shaft bouncing like Jell-O before ascending again.

This is the type of dick that elicited vehicular shenanigans. I'm talking busting windows out of cars, late-night drive-bys, GPS tracker type of shenanigans. As Deion drove into me once more I started to wonder if I could fit a tattoo of his name on the side of my torso.

"Daddy please," I begged. Fuck I was a lost cause. Save yourself because there was no saving me. In hopes of restoring my tough as nails image I yelled, "I fucking hate you."

Without missing a beat Deion breathed out, "I hate you too," before his lips collided with mine. He grabbed my waist, flipping me onto my back. From this vantage point his thrust were so deep my senses began to fail. My vision blurred and it sounded like I was in a wind tunnel, but all I could hear was the whirling beat of my heart. My touch failed me, unable to tangibly grab a hold of anything in close proximity. My mouth was dry and rough from grunting and moaning. I buried my face into his armpit and was hit with the refreshing smell of pina colada and coconut like his underarms were on a tropical vacation.

My body tensed as ecstasy tickled my spine and then the sweet release as the tight coils in my belly loosened, jerking my limbs in every direction. You know when you take a fish out of the water and it flops around uncontrollably on the ground? That was me right now, my body convulsing wildly as Deion drove into me deeper and deeper. As my body began to relax, Deion's tensed and he huffed and moaned in my ear, clawing at my thigh as I talked him through it, rubbing his arm until he grew still.

Deion left the room to dispose of the condom, and when he returned my eyes dropped to his crotch. He wasn't hard but the dick was still very impressive. My inside trilled at the memory of his penis in my mouth and I was tempted to get on my knees once again.

"Have you decided to stay? I can order some food and then we can try something new."

"Like what?" I had a laundry list of sexual acts I was ready to perform on this man.

"Dealer's choice."

I stood from the couch, and grabbing his hand I

wrapped it around my neck. Deion massaged my throat before giving my neck a soft squeeze.

"I laid out some clothes for you in my bedroom. Go take a shower while I order the food."

Under the hot spray of the shower head, I could not control my smile. I knew God worked in mysterious ways but having me find out that my boyfriend was cheating and then expressing my disappointment by driving into his car, which then led me to an anger management group with a hot-headed basketball player with bomb dick, a beautiful house, and a bathroom that resembled a spa, was a whole lot of mystic work.

Whatever the cause I was here now and I was going to enjoy my toe curling, leg shaking, pussy throbbing night with the NBA star. And there was free food. Shit, this was a win-win.

# DEION

IN THE MORNING, SLOANE FOUND ME IN THE KITCHEN making myself a smoothie before practice. She was naked from the top up and rubbing her sleepy eyes, almost narrowly missing walking into a side table. From behind, she wrapped an arm around me, her taut nipples grazing my back causing my dick to expand. The muscle memory of what we got up to last night and well into the morning prompting the physical reaction.

I was known for making poor choices, but bringing Sloane home was a choice I would make a thousand times over. She was like a portable generator, her energy shocking me back to life. Since my father's passing, I'd just been going through the motions. Work, eat, sleep. Waking up to repeat the same cycle. Sloane was like an anomaly throwing off my mundane algorithm. Work … get seduced by Sloane's lopsided smile. Eat … laugh uncontrollably at her random and unbelievable stories. Sleep … but only after we'd sixty-nined and she ruined my sheets.

One night and this woman had me weak like I was a

member of SWV. She was unexpected and, like the thief I was pretty sure she was, I never saw it coming.

"What are you doing?" she asked, her voice still raspy.

"What does it look like I'm doing?"

Sloane circled my body until she was standing in front of me. "Come back to bed."

"I can't, I have to go to practice." I hoisted her up onto the countertop so we were eye level. This was my first team practice since being suspended for eight games. I'd been practicing alone for the last few weeks. Occasionally Coach Justus would show up at the gym. Not because he disagreed with my suspension but because we were friends, and he wanted me to know that in spite of me constantly showing my ass, he would always have my back.

"Tell them you're sick." She set her face in a beautiful pout.

Was it weird I was excited she wanted me to stay? With most women when the sex was done, so was I. If a woman was lucky maybe I'd call her when it was late and I was horny for an encore. I wasn't looking to get attached or distracted. But Sloane piqued my curiosity and for her, I had all the time in the world.

"That's not how that works." I leaned in, no longer able to resist, I grabbed hold of her breast circling a nipple with my tongue.

Sloane's body came alive as she slipped her hands in her panties playing with herself. I buried my face in between her breast and licked upward until my lips found hers. Sloane's breath was shallow and she barely returned my kisses, so lost in ecstasy as her body began to shiver. Hooking her underwear with my fingers, I pulled them over her hips tossing them to the floor. Now I had a front row seat of the show.

Rubbing her thighs, I watched intently as her fingers slid in and out slick with her juices. She removed her fingers, pressing them to my open mouth so I could lick them clean before she glided them over her opening, working her clit. Swatting her hand away, I dove in with my tongue, figuring I'd do the extra laps for being fifteen minutes late.

True to her nature, Sloane was vocal and loud just like last night letting me know I was doing a good job and making lewd promises of all the things she intended to do to me and would allow me to do to her. She pressed the back of my head, persuading me to fuck her deeper. And when I did, her legs violently boxed in my ears holding me captive. Just call me prisoner 23654 because I did not want to be released. Sloane ejected a long, satisfied moan before collapsing on the countertop into stillness.

I stepped back admiring the state I worked her into. Her body still convulsing occasionally as she laid lethargic across the kitchen counter. Before I could stop myself, I said, "You should stay." I turned to the kitchen sink washing my face and hands so she couldn't see how desperately I wanted her to agree.

"Like you I also have to work tonight."

"Call out sick." I turned back to face her with a wink.

Sloane slid down from the counter placing her hand

on her naked hip. "Oh so *I* can call out sick but you can't."

"Not the same. When I don't show up to work I get fined."

"And when I don't show up I don't get paid."

"I'll pay you."

Sloane's jaw dropped.

"I didn't mean it like that and you know it."

"I happen to think sex work is a noble profession. But likening me and this to sex work—"

"Stop, I don't have time for this shit. I need to go and I want you to stay." I wasn't going to argue with a naked woman. I was certain I was barely making sense as I tried not to stare at her in all her seductive glory. "And when I get back you will be handsomely rewarded."

"Fabio just gave me my job back. I can't not show up."

"Let me worry about Fabio."

"What are you gonna do ... sign on as the official spokesperson for Enclave?"

"No, I'm just going to tell him you're not coming in tonight and if he wants that commercial, he'll have to be OK with that."

"Just like that?"

"Pretty much." I tapped my chest indicating I was indeed the man.

"If Fabio agrees which I highly doubt ..." Sloane's eyes softened as she nodded her head in agreement. "Then maybe."

"Great," I said, stepping into my slides. "Your car is in the garage."

"What?"

"I asked my assistant to bring it back here last night. There's a shopping center right down the hill." I pulled out my money clip, dropping a few hundred-dollar bills on the counter. "Or you can go home and get a change of clothes to last you the next couple of days."

"Couple of days?" Her eyes grew wide.

I ignored her question. I wanted to spend the next few days with her and I was hopeful once Fabio gave the green light, she'd be OK with sticking around. "I listed you as a guest with security so you shouldn't have any issues getting back in."

"Was this your plan all along. To get me to your place and then turn me into your concubine?" Sloane grabbed the money off the counter counting it. When she realized she had no place on her person to put it because she was still buck naked, she placed it back on the counter.

"No, it's not that deep."

She shrugged. "It seems pretty deep to me you're asking me to stay and all …"

"We both know the sex was good. And we both know we want to partake in more of that shit." I wrapped my hand around her neck and used my thumb to tilt her head so I could kiss her. Sloane's rigid posture melted as she pulled me closer. Reluctantly ending our kiss, I smiled against her mouth. "So is this you agreeing to be my lady of ill repute."

"If I'm gonna be your harlot I can't let you go to

work like that." She nodded her head in the direction of my dick which was pressing against my sweats, begging to be freed.

Sloane pulled me out and worked my shaft with her hands, and I accepted the fact that when I got to the training center, not only would I have to run extra laps, but extra drills were also in my future. As she stroked my member, she teased my tip with her tongue. My body tensed before a shudder overtook me. Sloane's delighted response to my release made me come harder.

When I regained my motor functions, I said, "Thank you."

"Just returning the favor for the kitchen counter action." She winked.

"My brother lives in the guest house out back. Sometimes he'll come this way to mooch food or workout. He's a little bit eclectic and he will talk your ear off." The last thing I wanted was for Sloane to mistake my brother for an intruder and put him in a sleeper hold. Grabbing my smoothie, I headed for the garage. "Be here when I get home in four hours, and don't rob me." I slapped her ass before kissing her on top of the head and jumping into my car.

---

LIKE I ANTICIPATED I RECEIVED AN EARFUL WHEN I GOT TO practice after being twenty minutes late and ran the additional laps. *Was it worth it?* Definitely, Sloane's low raspy moans were still echoing in my ear.

"Are you trying to get yourself benched again before

you even play?" Pratt asked during the Ramblers first water break.

"No, what can I say, traffic was a bitch." I tossed my hands nonchalantly in the air.

"Listen dude, I love you like a play cousin but after your last stunt all eyes are on you. You can't afford to fuck up right now." Pratt pointed his long fingers into my chest. "This is our year. We are going to the playoffs and everyone, including you, needs to stick to the playbook."

Pratt was right, all eyes were on me and I needed to walk the straight and narrow until this whole thing blew over. I'd been suspended for eight games and management was looking for contrition. Some sign I'd learned my lesson. Turning up late and fatigued at my first official team practice since suspension was only fueling the belief I was a lost cause.

And then there were my teammates. I'd let them down and unwittingly set the tone for the rest of the season and some of my teammates were holding a grudge. No one wanted to win a championship more than me. Having earned that gold and diamond encrusted ring on two occasions, I knew firsthand there was no greater high than seeing all your hard work culminate in the ultimate prize, being crowned the best of the best. I wanted that again, not just for me but for the guys on my team.

After practice I gathered the players for a quick mea culpa. "I know I let you guys down and I just wanted to apologize for that. You needed me and for the past eight games I wasn't available to help because of my own stupid actions. I'm sure you've all noticed I've been in a bit of a funk these past few months. I recently enrolled in anger management to deal with some unresolved issues. I'm not looking to make excuses or promises. But I hope over time I can show you all I'm proud to be a part of this organization and a member of this team."

"Just don't attack any more fans this season, that's all I'm asking," Dennis Lowery, a point guard and ten-year vet, called out.

There was a smattering of laughter but still others whose faces told me they were not yet ready to forgive and forget. Which was fine. I deserved that.

"McCabe, Coach wants a word," Klay, the assistant coach, called.

My stomach knotted into a tight fist, even though Justus was a close friend, mentor, and one of the few people I trusted with my life. When my father died, Justus showed up in Houston. He assured me he was available if I needed him, wanted to talk, or was looking to forget for a few hours. Justus didn't have to do that. Honestly, he could have sent a card and a flower wreath and kept it pushing. But him showing up for me was something I would never forget.

Now Coach Chappel was an entirely different person. He was fair but he never held his tongue to spare your feelings. Excuses would not be tolerated and he expected nothing less than one hundred percent. In my opinion Coach wanting to chat was not a good thing. This man had my number, we played golf every other weekend. If we needed to talk we could do it on the green.

I found him in his office. "You wanted to see me, Coach?"

Justus looked up from his playbook motioning for me to come in. "Close the door behind you."

Taking a seat in front of his desk, I waited as he finished scribbling notes in the margins of the pages. "Why were you late?" he asked, closing the overstuffed binder.

"Uh … traffic. Won't happen again."

"Practice starts at eight Deck. You should've been here to turn on the lights seeing how this is your first training day back with the team."

"You're right. No excuses." I rubbed my hand over my knees.

"How are those anger management classes working out?"

"Yeah … great. I'm learning all my anger stems from the fact that when I was younger I wanted a Nerf gun and my parents got me the off-brand equivalent Zerf gun. The foam bullets often got stuck in the chamber and that was my villain origin story."

Coach rubbed the bridge of his nose. "Why is everything a joke to you? You weren't hired for your comedic timing, you were hired for your ball handling."

"Yep, I was just—"

"Shut up Deck. What's this thing on TMZ about a brawl at a nightclub?"

"That didn't involve me, that was an overzealous bottle girl and Chipmunk. Mostly Chipmunk."

"For someone whose ass is squeaky clean you seem to be in the middle of a whole lot of shit."

I threw up my hands in frustration. Damned if you do, damned if you don't. Before Justus was head coach of the Ramblers, he and I were as thick as thieves but with the title of coach, the power dynamics shifted. I think I dreaded being called to his office because this man knew me. We'd fucked a cheerleader together back in the day, you can't get more intimate than that. He knew when I was lying and he didn't tolerate my bullshit.

"Deion, I don't have to tell you how important this season is. You, Pratt, and Lowery are the only players on the team with championship rings. The others look up to you. If you implode the shrapnel will impale the entire team."

I nodded my head. I was well aware of the weight resting on my shoulders. I wasn't the superstar player or the rising rookie, I was the old, reliable workhorse. I'd plowed this exact field time and time again with consistent results. I was expected to be a leader not the hotheaded fuck up.

Justus tugged at his big ass ears. "Management isn't happy with you right now. Your contract expires at the end of the season. If you don't produce, this could be your last year in Ramblers' red." Concerned was etched all over his face.

This was not a surprise to me but hearing Justus say the words still stung. In competitive sports you were only as good as your last win. When you stopped winning, you stopped being useful. If it were up to Justus, he would extend my contract based on proven past performance. But I couldn't expect him to go to bat for me while I was racking up losses on and off the court.

Coach continued, "Train hard, don't miss an anger management class, and keep your fucking nose clean. You know I got your back, but you have to help me so I can help you."

"I hear you I do."

"You're pushing forty. Maybe it's time you consider settling down," he half joked.

"I'm thirty-six so I still have a few years. And no matter how old I get you'll still be older," I teased.

"Shit, I'm over here aging like fine wine."

"Maybe your face but your rickety old man knees are another story."

Justus displayed his middle finger with a chuckle. "Remember when Pratt got married his playboy persona seemed to evaporate."

"People are still talking … they just lowered their voices." Justus knew as well as I did, marriage did not stop Colin from participating in extracurricular activities. I loved Charmise, but prior attempts to warn her only taught me to mind my business.

"Maybe so but as far as management is concerned Colin is a family man. And Thornton and Busch love that all American bullshit. And the press and fans are eating it up. Black love, a Black family, strong bonds to the community. Just last week he was handing out turkeys."

"So what are you suggesting I get married and start passing out honey baked hams?"

"You know as well as I do perception is reality. The

media sees you as a bad boy with a mean left hook. Never mind the fact that most weekends you are holed up in your house watching old timey movies."

"They're called the classics."

"Whatever." He waved my words off. "You need to learn to shift the narrative. Maybe seek out some charitable projects. Show up to an event with a girlfriend and not some random woman who slid into your DM's the night before."

"So fake it."

"I know how important it is for you to keep it real. But that mentality is going to find you without a job. I'm not asking you to be something you're not. I am suggesting you get better at playing the game. Colin knows how to play the game and he has the endorsements and shoe deals to show for it."

Justus sounded like my father. He was always telling me with a little more effort, I could be just as overhyped as Colin Pratt. I didn't care about accolades and awards but money was a real motivator. The last thing I was going to do was shuck and jive but I could smile, refrain from excessive profanity, and do my best to keep my business out of the press for the rest of the season.

# SLOANE

AFTER DEION LEFT, I DECIDED TO HEAD BACK TO MY apartment and grab some clothes, that way I could pocket the four hundred dollars he'd left behind. Now back at his ridiculously huge McMansion, I resembled the kid from *Home Alone*. I'd showered and lathered myself in oils so when he did return, he could make good on his promises.

Naturally while I was waiting, I snooped around a bit. He told me not to rob him. He didn't say I couldn't look in all his closets, under his bed or try on his expensive clothes. The most interesting thing I found was a drawer filled with unopened sex toys. I made a mental note of the ones I wanted him to use on me. This was completely outside of my comfort zone. Men weren't exactly knocking down my door to spend time with them. If this was how the other half lived, I was doing it all wrong. *Was this the staycation equivalent of being flown out?* The thought gagged me.

Opening the slider doors, which disappeared into the wall, I decided to tour his backyard. There was an extended, covered patio with ceiling fans and mounted

TV's. To the right was a kitchen almost as large as the one inside. You could easily cook an alfresco meal in this space. The mini fridge was fully stocked with beer, juice, and soda. I snagged one of the fancy apple juices in the glass bottle, breaking the seal.

"Let's have a real drink," a voice called from behind me.

"It's kinda early don't you think?" I examined the man with dreads who favored Deion.

"What's that saying … it's five o'clock somewhere."

"You must be Deion's brother."

"Ding, ding, ding. Raphael." He held out his hand.

"Sloane." His handshake was lazy in comparison to mine which included a strong grip and a tight squeeze.

"You look familiar. Why?" He opened the mini fridge and pulled out two beers. Popping the tops, he offered one to me.

"Were you at the Enclave a week ago?"

His face pulled in surprise. "You're the trash talking waitress." He cringed as if the full extent of that night came back to him. "Tough luck about losing your job."

"Your brother actually got me my job back."

"Hmm, he loves taking in strays." Dropping into one of the plush patio chairs he scanned the length of my body making me painfully aware I wasn't wearing anything under my robe.

"I guess that explains your living in the guest house." I released a fake friendly laugh.

He smirked. "Let me guess, you have brothers don't you?"

"Is it that obvious?"

"You seem like the type of woman who gives as good as she gets. A skill that is only cultivated over years of merciless ribbing from a sibling."

"I have two brothers."

"I called it." He tossed his arms up in triumph. "Where's Deck?"

"He went to practice."

Raphael almost choked on his beer. "And left you in his home ... alone?"

I shrugged.

"Your skill set must be impressive cause Deck does not like strangers in his space."

His gaze was becoming a bit too *lecherous* for my liking. "Well, I guess he decided to make an exception. It was nice meeting you. I'm gonna go back in." I turned to leave.

"You haven't even touched your beer."

"Like I said it's a bit too early for me."

"I get it. Deck warned you not to talk to me. He's probably afraid I'll swoop in and steal you right from under him."

I doubled back narrowing my eyes. If Deion's brother was flirting with me then there really was no one this man could trust. The sibling rivalry between Deion and his brother was none of my business. I just wanted to ensure I made it crystal clear where I stood. "Umm, sorry to break it to you. But I don't think he has to worry about that."

"Are you saying I'm not your type?" His eyebrow darted up his forehead like he was unconvinced.

"No, I already had the original. Not looking for a carbon copy."

A subtle smile pulled at his lips. "OK you passed."

"Passed what?"

"My brother's famous and there is always someone trying to take advantage of that so I just like to make sure the people he lets into his life are there for the right reasons." His smile was bright and the lewd look in his eyes was replaced with a jovial twinkle.

I allowed my shoulders to relax and claimed a chair opposite him. It would appear Raphael's heavy creeper vibes were all an act to test my motivations. Can't say I blamed him. I'm sure when you're rich and famous it can be hard distinguishing the real ones from the fakers. Shit, I'd done the same for my two brothers with past girlfriends and neither of them had more then two nickels to rub together.

"So Deck got you your job back?"

"Yes. Which was totally unexpected."

"He was pretty pissed at Chipmunk that night. It makes sense he'd try to make things right."

I glanced over at the guest house. "You live in the backyard?"

"Yeah, it's just temporary until I feel comfortable Deck's in a better place."

My brows compressed, settling over my eyes. "Better place?"

"Yeah mentally, physically, spiritually. His aura's off."

"He'd mentioned he was having trouble with his game. Is that because his aura is cloudy?"

Raphael eyes closed midway as if he was deciding what information he was willing to share. "Our dad passed recently. Shit, it's not really recent it's been a year."

"But it feels like yesterday." I understood that pain, no matter how old, had a way of casting a gloomy fog over the present.

"Yeah, it does. Anyway, people deal with that shit differently. And Deck took it pretty hard."

"What about you?"

His expression offered an appreciative smile at the inquiry. "I wasn't as close to our father as Deck. Don't get me wrong I loved him but accepting he was gone came easier for me." He took a swig of his beer. "You ever lost someone you loved?"

My shoulders slumped. "Mm-hum."

Deion was right, Raphael was talkative. What Deion failed to mention was that his brother also had an intense energy and he could see the things I'd successfully learned to hide.

"Then you get it. Anyway, the guest house is pretty nice and I don't have to pay rent ... so it's a sweetheart deal."

I observed the guest cottage before turning to the main house and back again. "Can you see into Deion's house?"

"Are you asking if I saw you get your back blown out last night?"

"Yes." I collected my robe around my neck.

"Nope. The windows are tinted. You can see out but not in."

A wave of relief washed over me. I wasn't ashamed about what Deion and I did, quite the opposite. But this wasn't a peep show.

Raphael jumped out his seat like he'd heard an alarm. "Fuck what time is it?"

"I don't know almost noon."

"I'm teaching a yoga class in a few. It was nice meeting you. Maybe I'll see you again."

As he walked toward the guest house, I shouted, "I doubt it."

Back inside, I made my way to the walk-in refrigerator. I didn't even know shit like this existed. The fridge was bigger than my bedroom. There's rich and then there was whatever the hell Deion was. The massive house with a mini house out back. The pool with a water park sized slide. If you shouted in this house, you could hear an echo. I shit you not that is how cavernous his place was. If you screamed in my apartment all you would hear was the neighbor banging on the wall telling you to keep it down.

The front door chimed, signaling Deion's return. I exited the fridge, carton of eggs in hand, to greet him. But the person who entered the room was not Deion. Instead, a statuesque woman with beautiful copper skin was heeling off her shoes oblivious of my presence. She had a backpack slung over her shoulder and her hair was fashioned in long, ombre-colored braids. When she caught sight of me, she screamed.

"Who are you?" I braced my feet in case I had to make a quick getaway.

"I live here. Who the hell are you?" She glared at me with confusion in her eyes.

Men are assholes. Deion just conveniently forgot to mention he had a girlfriend. I didn't do love triangles and I tried to avoid men who classified their love lives as complicated. Having a girlfriend while sleeping with me made things very awkward. She looked like she'd barely just graduated high school. So he was a liar and a scumbag.

"Listen, I thought Deion was single. I don't fight over dudes." Admittedly, after the shit he'd done to me last night I was tempted to make an exception.

The woman gagged. "He's my father." Her lips curled in disgust.

"You're Destiny?" I asked, coming from behind the kitchen island. From this vantage point I could clearly see the resemblance. She had some of his features; they were just softer, not as pronounced like his rigid jawline and the glint in his brown eyes.

"And who are you?" she asked again, dumping her backpack on the floor.

"I'm Sloane, I'm your dad's … I know your father."

"Where is he?" She walked to the hallway calling for him. "Dad?"

"He's at practice. He said he'd be gone for four hours and we are pressing against that so he should be back shortly."

"He left you here alone?" She scanned the room in disbelief.

"Like Macaulay Culkin." My face brightened, "Hey, I

was just about to make a fried egg sandwich. Do you want one?"

Over eggs and turkey bacon, Destiny loosened up telling me about life in college and navigating dating.

"Boys are just so stupid. Do they ever grow up?" she asked.

"Sorry to be the bearer of bad news but they don't smarten up with age."

"And sex …" She whispered as if someone was going to overhear us. "Most guys just care about getting off, not about making it a fun experience for the both of you."

"I'm a firm believer in not faking orgasms. If the sex isn't good I don't fake it. I'm not going to carry on like Meryl Streep to soothe his ego. Let him know the sex is bad. Heckle him."

Destiny laughed. "Like a comedian."

"Yes." I pretended to jeer some imaginary partner. "You suck! Go back to your day job. You'll never work in this vagina again."

Destiny folded in laughter wiping at a tear. "Ugh, I wish I could."

"Listen, you're young so you should focus on school not looking for Mr. Right. Your twenties are to be lived out loud and in 5k techno color."

"And your thirties?"

"That's when shit gets very real. Mostly because at that point people expect you to know what you're doing."

The garage door opened to that familiar chime. Deion found us in the kitchen with a concerned look on his face. "Destiny, what are you doing here?"

"It's winter break, Dad." She jumped up from her stool and kissed her father on the cheek.

"Damn, I totally forgot." Deion snuck a glance in my direction. I got the sense he was uncomfortable with his two worlds colliding.

"Don't worry I won't be here long. I'm headed to LA with Harbor for a few days."

"Cool. I see you met Sloane."

"Yeah, she made me breakfast." Destiny rinsed her plate off in the sink. "And we had some fun girl talk."

Deion narrowed his eyes. "Girl talk, aye."

"Don't worry I didn't teach her about police scanner codes and smash and grabs." I reassured him.

"What's a smash and grab?" Destiny asked.

"You are not old enough nor will you ever need that type of information."

Destiny shrugged. "It was nice to meet you Sloane." She gave me a hug before disappearing to her room.

"She's nice. I see why you're proud."

Deion stole the half-eaten strip of turkey bacon from my plate. "Is that my robe?"

"Yes." I smoothed my hand over the collar of the black and gold fabric. "How was practice?"

Deion hooked his shoulders grabbing an apple from a nearby bowl. "I had to run extra laps because of you."

*Was this a case of buyer's remorse?* This morning he'd begged me to stay but maybe now he was regretting that decision. Raphael and Destiny, both seemed surprised I was left to tool around his house all alone.

I'd been anxiously waiting for him to return but all that excitement was now tempered with uncertainty.

Deion continued, "I'm gonna get my daughter situated and then I'm going to watch some game footage." He rolled the apple to the tip of his fingers before catching it. Which was pretty cool.

"Do you want some company while you watch? I can make us popcorn."

"No, I'm good" he said, exiting the room.

# DEION

"She's nice," Destiny said, walking into her closet.

"Well don't get used to her she won't be here long."

Destiny returned to her bedroom with a duffle bag. "You know Dad, it would do you good to hang around people other than Uncle Rafi and Chipmunk."

"I have tons of friends."

"Female friends?" Her eyes slammed into me.

"I have a few of those too." I tried to be as transparent with my daughter as possible. While she would always be my baby girl, she was also an adult and our relationship was evolving.

"Well Sloane seems like a keeper."

"Why because she can tell funny stories and cuss like a sailor?" I moved a pillow shaped like pink lips and sat on her bed.

"No, because she's not vapid or conniving like some of the other lady friends I've met."

"Why is everyone trying to get me to settle down?"

"Because you're old," Destiny said without a hint of humor.

"Old? I'm only thirty-six."

Destiny pointed to an imaginary watch on her wrist. "Yeah, tick tock."

"I happen to like my solitude."

She rolled her eyes.

"So what is this LA trip?"

"Just a weekend with some friends, no big deal.

"Who all's gonna be there?"

"Daddy, I'm an adult."

"You're twenty. Who all's gonna be there?"

She released a protracted exhale. "Harbor, Denny, and Lo. You remember Lo."

"Where are you staying?"

"Uhm … we have a hotel reserved."

"No hard drugs. No unattended drinks." I wagged my finger in her direction.

"I know." She shook her head at my reminders. "I'm also packing my chastity belt so I don't get assaulted."

"That's not funny. It happens every day."

Raising a daughter was probably the scariest thing I'd ever done. First, I had Destiny when I was sixteen, and didn't know the first thing about babies. After she was born, I started to realize just how infuriating being born with a Y chromosome could be. People telling me all the things she shouldn't do because she was a girl. My mother suggested I avoid enrolling her into sports because it would make her too manly. I didn't listen and Destiny was offered several full ride scholarships, settling on UNLV so she could be close to her old man.

Then there were all the dangers beyond my control. Things as a man I never had to worry about. Like walking home alone late at night or leaving my drink unattended at the bar. Having a child was like ripping your heart from your chest and watching it stumble around trying to navigate the world. I wanted to protect her but I knew that I wouldn't always be there to slay the dragons.

"Dad, it's gonna be fine, trust me. And if anything goes down, I have my mace and a wicked right hook."

That was my not so little girl. I'd taught her how to fight. I showed her how to perform donuts in my Porsche. But most importantly I taught her to never settle for less because she deserved the world. It felt like it was only yesterday when I was a lanky kid with a struggle mustache holding my daughter in my arms for the first time. In that moment I knew I needed to get my shit all the way together. My father's advice was one I'd never forget. "It's not about you any more Deion. You have this baby to look after now. You made one mistake by not using protection don't make another by neglecting your flesh and blood."

"Call me when you get there. And text me the address of the hotel."

"Done and done. Now shoo Harbor will be here to pick me up in like ten minutes."

After Destiny left, I sat in my home theater watching highlights of prior matchups with the Miami Heat in preparation for our game Friday evening. My conversation with Justus was still running on a loop in my head. Everything Justus said was valid. After years of being reliable, I was becoming less and less like the person you could count on to score the winning basket when the team was down by three.

My childhood was idyllic. I never wanted for anything, except that Nerf gun. My parents were loving and maybe a bit overprotective. But they supported my dreams, and taught me to be compassionate and empathetic. And as my basketball skills grew, my father taught me to never take those gifts for granted. In spite of all that, I'd grown to become a smug son of a bitch and your stereotypical basketball bad boy.

Maybe because regardless of how hard I worked, people still saw me as Morris McCabe's son. Every accomplishment and accolade was compared to his. When I won my first championship at twenty-seven the conversation wasn't about my hard work and dedication. All the press wanted to talk about was my father's legacy and how when he was twenty-seven, he already had three of his five rings to my one. My father's shadow was large and imposing and no matter how well I performed I could never get out from under it. I was always playing catch up. And how was I expected to compete against a career as illustrious as my father's? He was among one of the greats. There was Chamberlain, Magic, Jordan, and McCabe.

When my father passed last year the pain and grief just seemed to amplify my undesirable behavior. I wanted to be a better person, but my fuse had grown short from years of being lit. And now my game was suffering. You can be an asshole when you're throwing up numbers. Not so much when your "nothing but net" hot hand turns to nothing but air.

I released a long sigh dreading what was next. I'd been hiding out in this theater for the last two hours.

Yes, I invited Sloane to stay but that was before practice and the concern on my teammates face. It was clear that the team was counting on me and the jury was out on whether I was going to be able to step up. The talk with Justus also did very little to assuage my fears that I was letting everyone down.

I was being a bad host and I needed to find Sloane and try to salvage the rest of this day. Exiting the theater, I fully expected her to be gone. I checked the garage and her car was still there so that meant she hadn't left. Walking to the other side of the house in search of her, I found Sloane in my den talking on speaker phone.

"What do you mean you don't wanna go to Florida? You've been looking forward to this trip all year."

"It's far," a boy's voice replied.

"Yeah, but you'll get to see your Grandma Rosa and Grandpa Earl for Thanksgiving. They've missed you."

"Why can't you come with me?"

"Because I have to work, Ace. And your father doesn't want me tagging along to his parents. We've already talked about this."

"But Dylan and Brice get to spend Thanksgiving with their moms. Plus, it's the holidays and you shouldn't be alone."

"What did I tell you about comparing yourself to others, huh?"

"Not to."

"Remember I can't give you everything but …"

"But what I get is more than enough."

"More than I ever had. Your grandfather was big on the minimalist lifestyle before it was even a thing."

"Mom, he gives me five dollars on my birthday. He's a cheapskate."

"Do you miss me a little?" The tone in her voice surprised me; it was soft and vulnerable.

"Maybe a little."

"I miss you tons. I don't miss your stinky cheese feet though." A laugh sprung from her throat.

"My feet don't stink."

"The smell from your feet could knock out a small rodent."

Ace laughed on the other end.

"Get off the phone and get your homework done."

"Alright. Love ya."

"I love you, more."

I crept away from the door reapproaching with a loud cough. I didn't want her to think I was eavesdropping. "Hey," I said entering the room.

"Hey." She pulled herself to her feet from her spot on the carpet. "I was just coming to look for you. I'm gonna head out, clearly you're busy and I can still make my shift for tonight."

"I don't want you to leave."

"Deion, we both know what this was."

I pulled my face into a frown. "Oh yeah, what's that?"

"You got to have sex with a bottle girl from Enclave and I got to have sex with a basketball player. An aging basketball player ... but still."

Clearly the sex haze from this morning had worn off because mean ass Sloane was back.

"You don't think I've fucked a glorified cocktail waitress before?"

Her head snapped back. "That was rude."

"Rude, you just called me an aging basketball player."

"I was being honest."

"So was I." My eyes slammed into her.

"Wow, cocktail waitresses do not offer the level of service I provide. Do you realize how skilled you have to be to facilitate the needs of different customers in a large group all expecting a specific experience. I help people make memories and forget about the real world if only for a little while. Customers leave having had a good ass time." She pinned her arms across her chest.

I think I hurt her feelings. Which was weird because up until now, I didn't know she was capable of feeling anything but rage and sarcasm.

Walking over to where she stood pissed and dejected, I said, "Sloane, I want you to stay."

"Well, you're not acting like a man who wants me to stay."

"How can I make it up to you?" I asked, grabbing my dick through my shorts.

Sloane's gaze followed my hand but she didn't take the bait, instead reaching into her purse pulling out a stack of papers. "Sign these," she demanded, thrusting the stack forward.

I reached for the pages of printed black and white pictures of me, giving them a dubious eye.

"Did you print these yourself?"

"Yes, you're out of ink by the way."

"What is this for?"

"It's for my son."

"Your son needs twenty autographed photos of me?" I flipped through the stack.

"And his friends." She lowered her lids sizing up my gullibility.

"Your son's very popular."

"He gets that from me."

Making my way to the desk in the den I opened a drawer pulling out a stack of color photographs I used for signing events. With a sharpie in hand I sat down to sign, making the first one out to Ace and the rest with just my signature alone. Shit, based on the stuff she did to me, I would sign a warehouse full of merchandise if she asked.

Sloane possessed the type of pussy that toppled empires. The type of goodup that started turf wars. Her box was so fire I would literally invest in a business venture if she asked me. Leasing a spot for a nail salon or shoe store or whatever the latest .com fad was. If I had to sign a few autographs so her son could hustle his classmates, so be it.

With the beginning of a cramp in my left hand, I held out the signed photos.

"Thank you." Sloane pushed my keyboard aside to sit on the desk directly in front of me. Lifting her leg, she offered me her foot.

Accepting, I slowly massaged it. "Uh-hm. I know I asked you to stay and then I was a complete asshole when I got home—"

"Classic dick move."

"I'm trying to apologize."

"Whoa, I get a foot rub and an apology?" Her face relaxed into a smile.

"Yeah, and this dick in a minute."

"So what's wrong? Why are you so stressed?"

I rested my eyes on her face. Did I really want to get vulnerable with the woman who would most likely laugh at me and offer advice like "Man up and don't be such a pussy? I decided to risk it.

"Basketball is all I know. I've been doing this shit since I was five. And I'm … I'm just starting to realize my best playing days are behind me. And that terrifies me."

"I get it. I used to participate in gymnastics and I was good, really good. But it got expensive and my dad was bad with money like it would be funny if it wasn't so tragic. So I know what it's like to see your dream slip through your fingers. But at least you got to live it. Shit, thirteen years is a long time in any competitive sport."

"Fifteen." I corrected her.

"Even better. And for you the dream doesn't have to be over. This could be the start of something new. You're smart enough you could be a head coach. Or a sports announcer you definitely have the smile for it." She ran her hand across my mouth. "If Charles Barkley can do it so can you."

Her optimism caught me by surprise. "But what if I just wanna play ball?"

"Well then your game needs to reflect that because right now you're playing like a dude who would rather be anywhere but on the court."

I appreciated her honesty. In my line of work most people around me hyped me up, and made excuses for my bad behavior. But Sloane was different. While she understood my point of view, she didn't allow me to deflect. She was right, if I wanted to play basketball I needed to stop phoning it in, and get my head back in the game.

"What if I'm no longer good enough?"

Sloane leaned in grabbing my chin. "Listen carefully. Because I'm only gonna say this once. Are you listening?" She shook my chin.

"Yes."

"You're a good player. I actually think you're a better all-around player than your father. If you're not ready for your career to end then prove it." The pad of her thumb softly stroked my cheek.

Her words caused my pulse to quicken its throb. Hearing this woman I barely knew say she thought I was a good player flushed my face with appreciation.

"How difficult *are* you?" I asked, bringing her perfectly manicured foot to my mouth.

"What?"

"How… difficult … *are* … you?" I asked, again but this time I sucked her toes between each word.

Her breath hitched. "Like, on a scale of one to ten?" Air eked from her lungs.

"Yeah." I undid the sash on her robe to reveal her naked flesh.

"On a bad day maybe a thirty-seven."

"And on a good day?" I stood pulling a condom from my shorts before removing them.

Sloane's eyes dropped to my nether regions and she shrugged off her robe. "I don't know, on a good day maybe I'm at a twenty-four, twenty-five."

"I can handle that," I said, before spreading her legs wide and slowly sliding into place. Yep, Sloane had that good good and with each thrust I lost all common sense.

I CALLED OUT FROM THE SPORTSBOOK FOR THE SECOND DAY in a row, convinced by Deion's long strokes to shirk my responsibilities and play house with him. Couple that with the hall pass Deion got me from the Enclave this felt like a mini vacation. After waking me up at five in the morning with a hard dick and insatiable appetite, he was off saying he could not be late for another practice. This left me alone in his house which was close to ten thousand square feet. I only knew this because I Googled the specs last night while he was in the shower.

While he was away, I searched for ways to occupy my time. In his private indoor basketball court with the letter M etched into the hard maple, I practiced my free throws. I'd reclined in the oversized leather seats in his home theater and watched a few episodes of a true crime series. And now I was submerged in his deep soaker tub which I'd filled to the brim with bubble bath soap and bath bombs I'd found in his bathroom cabinets. I was born into the wrong family because the rich bitch lifestyle better suited my disposition. The last few days had been the most relaxation I'd gotten in a long time.

My cell phone rang from the teak bench next to the tub, reaching for it I eyed the unknown number with caution. If it was a bill collector, I would tell them what I always told them. I could put something on it but I wasn't able to pay in full at this time.

"Hello?"

"Hello, hi is this Sloane?"

"Who's asking?"

"It's me, Destiny."

"Who?"

"Destiny, Deion's daughter."

"Oh hey Destiny, what's up." I'd forgotten I'd given her my number. At the time I was just being nice, when she suggested we exchange phone numbers I never expected her to use it.

"Is my dad there?"

"No, he's still at practice."

"Oh thank God." I could hear her let out a rush of air on the other end.

"What's going on?"

"I was robbed. My wallet, my phone, all my money. I found your number in my jacket pocket on the napkin you wrote it on."

"Are you OK?"

"No, I'm freaking out. I'm in LA I don't know anyone and Harbor ditched me."

"Your friend?"

"Yeah, she met this guy and ran off with him."

"OK, well … head back to the hotel."

Destiny's voice creaked as she stuttered out her words. "We didn't exactly have a hotel. Last night we crashed at a dude's house we met at the club. We were supposed to meet up with some of Harbor's friends from college today and stay with them for the rest of the weekend but Harbor is MIA and she's not answering her phone."

"Where are you now?"

"I'm in some shady diner off the highway."

"Ok, I'll call your dad and let—"

"No," she shouted.

"If my dad finds out he'll kill me. Like cedar or birchwood casket kill me."

"OK, so what are you gonna do, kiddo?"

"Could you come and get me?"

"Uh …"

"I know it's a lot to ask and if I had any other options I would utilize them."

Leaning over the lip of the tub, the gears in my head turned. Vegas to LA was a four-hour drive one way not including traffic. There was no way I could pick her up and get her back before Deion returned home. But I couldn't leave a young girl in an unfamiliar city. Shit.

"OK … let me think. I'll just buy you a plane ticket." Granted the money in my bank account was practically nonexistent after paying all my bills but I could swing a Southwest Wanna Get Away ticket one way.

"My license was in my wallet."

"Destiny, why do I get the feeling you're not telling me everything?"

"I told you my purse was stolen and—"

"Yeah, yeah, yeah Harbor ditched you with no transportation, no hotel, and no money." I released an irritated sigh. "Maybe we can RideX you home." Do you have the app connected to your phone?"

"Yes. But my phone was also stolen."

I rolled my eyes. "OK, I'll request the car from my phone." I pulled up the app. "What's the address for the diner?" Destiny fed me the address and I tapped the pickup and return information into the app. When the price popped up as over fifteen hundred dollars, I swallowed hard. I knew the amount in my checking account down to the penny I didn't even have half of that amount sitting in my account and that included the four hundred dollars Deion provided for clothes and toiletries the other day.

Ignoring my lack of funds, I tapped the payment button anyway hoping it would process and I could just deal with the overdraft fees later. My phone dinged with the message notifying me that the purchase could not be completed.

"When did your purse get stolen?" I asked, trying to buy time so I could think through our next step.

"Sometime last night."

"Last night? And you're only now calling for help. Destiny are you fucking kidding me?"

"I didn't know it was stolen at first I thought it was just with another group of friends."

"Where pray tell are all these friends now that you need them."

"I didn't know them they were Harbor's friends."

"Listen the RideX isn't gonna work it's too expensive."

"I promise I'll pay you back when we get home."

I cleared my throat. "I appreciate that but I don't have access to that kind of money."

"Not even an advance from a credit card?"

"No, some people work paycheck to paycheck Destiny."

I could hear her soft sobs on the other end of the phone.

"Don't cry. Tears never solve anything. Sit tight. It's gonna be a few hours but I'll come and get you."

"Thank you, thank you, so much." Destiny squealed, before rattling off the address of her location again so I could type it in the GPS on my phone.

"I'll be there as soon as I can." I reassured her before disconnecting the call.

After washing the suds from my body, I got dressed. Heading to the guest house, I thought I could enlist her uncle to come through with the save. I banged on the door for five minutes but there was no answer. If Raphael was in there he was dead to the world.

I called Deion but it went straight to voicemail. "Hey it's Sloane, I need to run an errand and I'm not sure I'll be back before you. Just wanted to give you a heads up. What do you want to do for dinner? How about Thai? I could go for something spicy. I'll talk to you later. Bye."

I wasn't a snitch but when we walked into the house later this evening Destiny was going to have some explaining to do. My only goal was to head to LA, collect Deion's child, and return her home safely. Her entire story seemed dodgy, but when I was her age I didn't make the best decisions and if I had a "get out of jail free" card I would've used it on more than one occasion.

In the garage, I rubbed the keys to my Honda in my hand before looking at the other fast cars parked next to it. I mean I was going to pick up his daughter and I'm sure if he were here he'd want me to take the most aerodynamic vehicle, and based on my calculations it was the lollipop-red Lamborghini with the suicide doors. Settling into the creamy leather interior, I connected to the Bluetooth because a road trip required music to cruise to. I selected the playlist with DMX, Future, and XYZ Baby and zoomed off.

As I made my way down the freeway, I started to second guess my choice. Maybe jumping in a car and speeding to Los Angeles wasn't the best option. I was hopeful Deion would see this as me helping his daughter out of a jam and not me trying to conspire to conceal information from him. Turning up the music, I reassured myself it was a long way there and back which would allow for plenty of time for Destiny and I to get our stories straight.

# DEION

When I returned home, Sloane was still out just as her message predicted. I also noticed she'd opted to take one of my cars instead of her own. Two days ago, that would have raised red flags, but this afternoon I shrugged it off. Only Sloane could make me brush over the very real possibility I'd just been robbed.

After a shower and quick lunch, I answered some emails and paid a few bills all the while steady eyeing the clock anticipating her return. It had been two days but I'd grown accustomed to having her around. Some people have a way of making you feel like you'd known them your whole life. Sloane laughed loudly finding humor in damn near everything, she slurped her Pho while expressing how good it was after each spoonful, and she initiated naked dance parties after sex. She was stress free when everything else in my life was complicated.

When I was with her, I didn't have to take myself too seriously. And the constant uncertainty noodling in the back of my brain was reduced to a low hum. Don't get me wrong, she was an asshole but so was I, so maybe that's what was drawing me to her. I wanted her to stay beyond the next few days. Which was a weird thought. Sloane had a life and a kid. I couldn't expect her to press pause and focus all her attention on a needy ball player with daddy issues.

Now at six o'clock Sloane had been gone for hours and I was getting antsy. What if she was stranded on the side of the road somewhere, smoke billowing from the engine after drag racing down Las Vegas Boulevard. Reaching for my phone, I decided to call her to confirm she and my car were OK.

"Hello?" Sloane answered the phone offering me mild relief. The bass from the car's surround sound system made it difficult for me to hear.

"Where are you?" I yelled.

"What?"

"Where are you?" Mid scream the music stopped.

"Umm … I'm just leaving LA."

"LA Fitness or the LA Gentlemen's Club?

"No, LA as in City of Angels."

"What the hell are you and my car doing in Los Angeles?"

"Well technically we just left LA."

"Sloane, you drove my car to Los Angeles with gas prices stacked at close to eight dollars a gallon?" Wait did she just say we? So she went on the joyride of the century with a plus one.

"Yes, but I can explain."

"The fuck you better. And who is *we*?" I plunged my fingernails into my palms trying my best not to call the Lambo Bandit out her name.

"It's a funny story really … so boom I was chilling at the crib when I got a call and—"

"Did you steal my car?"

"Really?" Her incredulous tone smacked me in the face through the phone.

"You don't get to be offended by that question. You are literally in another state with your hands wrapped around the wheel of my car."

"Actually, the car is on cruise control so I'm not using my hands."

"I'm calling the cops. Do you even have a valid license?" My voice was growing nasally as alarm began to settle in. I'd invited a beautiful woman into my home. She'd lulled me into a false sense of security with the rocking of her hips and the animated stories she'd weave to help me fall asleep. The minute I let my guard down she stole my car. I didn't even know where she lived. Shit, was Sloane Kaplan even her real fucking name?

"I'm not a thief."

"Says the motherfucker who's riding around in my whip."

"Fuck you Deion." The line went dead. I stared at my phone in disbelief. *Did she just hang up on me?* She was MIA in my car and has the audacity to be mad at me for calling her out. I called back only to be sent straight to her voicemail. *Hey its Sloane don't leave a message.*

"Sloane, if you don't call me back in the next five minutes, I will call the cops. My car has a tracking device and a kill switch. Test me if you want to." Ending the call, I tossed my phone on the couch.

With thirty seconds to spare her number flashed across my phone screen.

"Sloane—" I spat out her name like it was a cuss word.

"Daddy."

"Destiny, is that you baby?" I sunk into the couch my heart pumping a mile a minute.

"Yes, Daddy it's me."

My stomach dropped. Was this worse than I initially feared. "Are you OK baby? Did Sloane hurt you?"

"Daddy chill Sloane helped me."

"What?" My nerves were hanging on by a single frayed thread. If someone didn't start providing answers I was going to unleash the gates of hell.

Destiny explained a nonsensical story about being robbed and then ditched, which ended with Sloane riding in on a candy red horse. I had the sneaking suspicion Destiny was not telling me the whole truth but the interrogation could wait.

"Put Sloane back on the phone."

"I'm here." Her voice was "you're dead to me" cold.

"Look—"

"You have some major trust issues," she interjected.

"OK, let's not pretend you're completely trustworthy."

"I've given you no reason not to trust me. In fact, I've been a model house guest."

I didn't have a comeback for that. "Where are you?"

"Barstow."

"Do you need me to come meet you? I could purchase plane tickets."

"No. We're already halfway to Vegas."

"OK, see you when you get home." There was a long silence on her end. "You know you could have just led with the Destiny information. It would have saved—" The line disconnected. I would chalk it up to bad reception and not Sloane hanging up on me for the second time in a row.

When the garage door opened a few hours later I didn't even give Destiny a chance to fully step into the door before wrapping my arms around her, squeezing her tight.

"I'm sorry, Daddy."

Pulling away I looked my baby girl in her eyes. "You're grounded."

"What? Daddy I'm twenty you can't ground me."

"You may be twenty but that shit you just pulled shows you lack maturity."

"That's not fair. You told me yourself you did dumb shit all the time when you were my age. The biggest one, having me when you were only sixteen."

"I went through all that dumb shit so you wouldn't have to."

Destiny looked to her getaway driver for support. "Sloane, tell him he's being unreasonable."

Sloane lifted a blasé shoulder. "I don't want to have anything more to do with this." Brushing past me she headed out of the room. She seemed tired and pissed and she was due an apology but I needed to deal with my daughter first.

"If you haven't guessed she's mad at you."

"Maybe if the two of you had just been honest no one would be mad at anybody."

"I understand you were worried. But you acted like a total dick to Sloane. You were rude and condescending."

"I was worried about you."

"You were worried about your car." Destiny spat back.

"I overreacted. It happens when you think you're being scammed."

"You've been playing house with Sloane for the past few days you think you could grant her the benefit of the doubt."

I wasn't going to let her flip this on me. "Haven't I always told you to call me if you need to be picked up from a party? Didn't I say no questions asked."

"Yes, but you always blow things out of proportion. Like you're doing right now."

"Destiny, you went to LA with no plan and a friend that didn't have your back. You're lucky I'm the one restricting your movements and not some shady man in a van. The world is too evil for you to be this naive."

"I'm tired. I'm going to bed." Destiny stormed off.

*Were we allowed to drop twenty-year-old children at the fire station or did that only work for babies?*

In my bedroom, I found Sloane in the shower. Tapping on the glass I asked, "Can I join you?"

"It's your fucking house." She stared straight ahead allowing the water to rain onto her back. Stripping naked, I entered the steamy shower. Sloane ignored me continuing to lather her legs.

"Can we talk?"

"No, Tevin Campbell we cannot."

I forgave her irritated tone. "Thank you for going to rescue my kid."

Sloane finally turned to face me. "You basically accused me of abduction."

"No, I accused you of kidnapping, there's a nuanced difference."

"So you were what … waiting for a ransom note?"

"OK stop acting like we're B fucking FF. I barely know you. And the stuff I do know is kind of sketchy."

Sloane's eyes appeared to bulge as the muscles in her fingers and arms flexed. I braced myself for the real possibility she was about to hit me. Instead, she turned back to the spray of the multi nozzle shower.

"I'm trying to apologize, Sloane. Clearly, I'm doing a piss poor job but I'm trying."

She spun back around almost slipping on the soap suds. I reached out to brace her but she recoiled, steadying herself without my assistance. "You really just think I'm some criminal, don't you?"

"I mean you are on probation." My shoulders bounced only half joking.

There was a glint of pain in her eyes but it quickly dissipated giving way to anger. "Well, you know the way I see it despite all your privilege and fame we both ended up in the exact same spot … forced anger management. You are not fucking better than me Deion McCabe," Sloane yelled.

"You're right," I agreed meekly.

"You think because you're an athlete you can look down on others. Not everyone is born with a silver fucking spoon in their mouths. While you were worried about whether you were going to swim in your heated pool or play tennis at the country club, I was trying to scrape up a meal for four with a single can of tuna and half a bag of egg noodles."

"You are absolutely right," I repeated. I'd been judging her this entire time.

"I didn't want to drive all the way to LA and sit in the thick of traffic for hours. But I couldn't just leave *your* kid scared and stranded. And when you called me you came in hella hot with accusations. You accused me of stealing your car and threatened to call the police. THE POLICE ... ON A BLACK WOMAN. I was doing you a favor and your mind jumped to the worst possible scenario because you obviously think I'm a horrible person. You think you're smarter and better than me—"

"I killed someone," I blurted out.

Sloane's mouth hung open as the shower water pounded against her back. "What does that mean exactly?"

I inhaled a deep breath. What was it Raphael always said about apologies, "Apologies were never intended to fix the past, they're meant to fix the future." I couldn't change the words I said to Sloane when I was upset but I could say I was sorry and offer changed behavior.

"When I was seventeen a friend and I took my dad's Convertible out for a ride. I was coming around a corner and I lost control of the car. I'm freaking out twisting the wheel in every direction trying to regain control. My car slams into an oncoming vehicle and just like in the movies their car somersaults flipping head over end several times. My car crashes into a pole. Me and my friend are banged up pretty bad but were able to walk away. I rush to check on the person in the other car and the car is empty and I look to the street and they are crumpled up in a pile on the pavement." I swallow down the stone forming in my throat.

"They are not OK and they end up being transported by helicopter and flatlining on the way to the hospital because I was reckless. Of course, it was all covered up because I was Morris McCabe's son. I never served any time and just performed some community service which I listed on my college applications as volunteerism and my file was expunged. So I essentially got away with murder. But not a day goes by when I don't see that lady broken and bloody on the pavement. So no Sloane I don't think I'm better than you. I know I'm not."

Tears fell from my eyes as I plunged my face underneath the water in hopes of concealing them. The only people who knew about the car crash were my parents, Raphael, and Justus. I hadn't even shared the shit with my ex-wife. It was always too difficult to explain and the less people who knew, the easier I thought it would be to forget. I was wrong because you never forget something like that.

Sloane's expression while still hyper critical had softened a bit. "It was an accident, Deck, you have to know that."

"Maybe but I made choices and those choices forever

changed the life of that woman and everyone who loved her. Shit like that is hard to let go of." Her family agreed to a large payout, nipping any potential civil lawsuit in the bud before it began. With that my involvement was brushed under the rug and my parents never spoke about it again.

Sloane gave a protracted nod.

"You know you really suck at making people feel better," I said trying to lighten the mood.

"It's like one of my worst qualities. The inability to handle emotions. So you're not the golden boy. I guess we're both guilty of judging the other."

I stepped close giving her what she deserved. "I'm sorry for jumping to conclusions rather than asking for clarification. I assumed the worse of you. Which is stupid because when I'm with you I feel like I'm experiencing the best parts of you. You leave me all warm and fuzzy."

"Warm and fuzzy?" She arched a brow.

"Yeah, it's mostly concentrated in my chest. Anyway, Destiny is one of the few things I don't play about. But I should've worked harder to talk it through before automatically pointing the finger. I think at one point I accused you of child abduction ..."

"You did. That is something that happened."

"Not my finest moment. I'm sorry."

"Apology accepted." Sloane added soap to her loofah and rubbed it against my chest. She said very little, occasionally directing me to lift an arm or turn around so she could scrub my back. Now that the argument was resolved I could feel my libido kicking in.

Sloane was naked and wet and paying special attention to every part of my body.

"Thank you for picking up my kid and bringing her home to me safely." I leaned down kissing her shoulder blade. "And thank you for spending the past few days with me." This time I kissed the expanse between her full breasts.

Sloane's hand found my dick as I backed her into the nearest shower wall. "Are you on the pill or—"

"Nope."

My body tensed at the thought of shooting up the club raw and the possibility of it coming back to haunt me in nine months. I liked Sloane but I highly doubted our ability to successfully co-parent.

"I had an IUD implanted a while back and it's good for years."

Her hand was still stroking my dick which made it increasingly difficult to think. I was being reckless. Damn, with the amount of dumb shit I did on the regular, reckless should be my middle name, Deion Reckless McCabe. Dropping to the bench I'd built special for moments like this, I pulled Sloane on top of me.

My eyes scanned her body with glee as she grabbed hold of me slowly lowering herself into place, seeping in air from the size of my girth. Her slick, wet ass crashed into me while her perfect breast jiggled in a circular motion as her backside collided with my lap before rising just to repeat the frenetic friction all over again.

Sex will have your ass thinking the craziest shit, and right now I was wondering if Sloane was ready to deactivate her dating apps. I wrapped my hand behind her head. "Damn girl, you keep doing stuff like this and I'm liable to invite five hundred of our closest friends and family to watch you walk down the aisle in a cream-colored dress … because who are we fooling with white. As they witness a gaudy display of us promising forever to one another."

"All that because of this?" she asked, taunting me with the movement of her hips in a way that should be illegal.

"At this point I would give you my bank account and routing numbers, on God." I breathed out

She ran her soft hands down my chest and arms, her fingertips unlocking the secret code to my heart.

Nibbling on her ear, I breathlessly whispered, "Move in with me."

Sloane grabbed hold of my face. "Shut up. You're doing too much."

Nodding my head, I bit my lip. *Was I doing too much, because that last part I actually meant.* I didn't have much time to contemplate, before I could process my ill-timed words Sloane performed a subtle position change. Bracing her hands on my knees, she leaned back, her beautiful sepia skin on full display, and rode my dick like I was Seabiscuit.

# 16

AFTER THREE DAYS AT DEION'S HOUSE, I WAS FINALLY BACK at my apartment. I had to admit it was a fun little rendezvous but I knew how these games were played. The next time I saw Deion he would be stricken with amnesia and pretend like none of it ever happened. And I was fine with that, it was an extended one-night stand, he didn't owe me anything.

I barely inserted the key into the lock before Tammie swung her door open in dramatic fashion.

"Where the hell have you been?" Her tone was accusatory.

"What do you mean?" I feigned ignorance like I expected my three-day absence to go unnoticed.

"I ain't seen hide nor hair of you for the past few days."

Opening my door, I offered her a nonchalant shrug.

Tammie followed me inside, closing the door behind us. "Let me guess because it could only be two things. You were arrested or you were with Marco."

I cringed. "Marco and I are over. Like Beanie Babies

and Blockbuster Video." Men tend to end things when you lightweight try to kill them.

"I've heard you say that before." Tammie wagged her bony finger at me.

"Well this time I mean it."

"Then spill the beans. Where were you?"

"I was at a friend's house." I had no plans on telling Tammie or anyone about my three-day fling with the superstar basketball player. Maybe the word superstar was doing too much but the way he sparked all my erotic zones, making my body shake, squirt, and practically dissolve into a hedonistic mist, he could have the superstar title.

"Hopefully this friend was a man because every woman needs a good lay once in a while and frankly you were past due."

At the fridge, I poured us both some juice and I added a little vodka to Tammie's cup because she liked to stay tipsy. "I'm happy to report it has been zero days since my last orgasm," I said, taking a sip of my cranberry juice with an obnoxious smack of my tongue. My face lit up. "I forgot to tell you the best news. I got my job back."

"How'd you pull that off?"

I realized if I mentioned Deion, Tammie would connect the dots to my extended sleepover. "Umm ... I had to eat a big serving of humble pie," I lied. "It doesn't really matter how, all that matters is I finally caught a break."

"I'm happy for you baby. One less thing to stress over."

Tammie was right. I didn't have good luck but the past couple of days I'd been winning. It wasn't lost on me that all those wins were courtesy of Deion. He'd gotten me my job back and treated my body like it was his own personal slip and slide. I had to fight back shivers when I remembered our time together. And I'd even walked away with some Benjamins in my wallet.

"I think this may be the season of Sloane. Maybe the gods that be are finally shining a little light my way," I beamed, which was uncharacteristic for me. I never beamed. I scowled, maybe the occasional smirk, but rarely did I radiate joy.

It was a silly thought, if life had taught me anything it was that pleasure and contentment only existed to make you feel ten times worse when you eventually lost them. The job, a man, that new car. Every now and again God would allow you a glimpse of happiness, because you couldn't always be choking for air while you struggled to keep your head from sinking underwater. My extended one-night stand with Deion was a glimpse of what my life could be like if I wasn't born in a mobile home in Reno and the daughter of a scam artist. But like a perfect hair day, all good things must come to an end.

It was Friday and after picking Ace up from school, we made homemade pizzas and watched the Ramblers' game. This was Deion's first game back since his suspension weeks ago, and he was playing like he had something to prove. He hustled for the rebounds and drained all but one of his three-point shot attempts. Ending the game with thirty-two points off the bench and a win for his team.

Ace was probably wondering who'd charged my battery because I was never this vocal while watching a game I hadn't bet on. I was yelling at the screen rooting Deion on. I wanted him to do well.

"Mom, chill it's just a game." Ace rolled his eyes while I hooted and hollered.

"Can't your mother be excited?"

"About basketball?"

"I just have a newfound appreciation for the sport." I bounced an apathetic shoulder.

"Did you bet on this game?"

"No, I did not."

"Well at least the Ramblers actually showed up to play this time," Ace said, taking a sip of his orange Crush soda.

"Yeah, they did, if they keep playing like this maybe they'll make the playoffs."

"I doubt it. They always find a way to crash and burn." Ace sounded how I normally did. But my close encounter with Deion had left me hopeful. Don't get me wrong, I was still a glass half empty type of gal, but for the Ramblers I was willing to put on my rose-colored glasses.

Truth be told the Ramblers hadn't won a championship in over twenty years. I remember the last time they won vividly I was thirteen and my dad bet our rent money on the Ramblers winning game seven of the finals against the Seattle Supersonics. It was a nail biter, but when they won I never saw my father so happy. To celebrate he took me and my brothers out for a steak dinner at a fancy restaurant we were woefully under-dressed for.

During player interviews, in which Deion credited his awe-inspiring performance to the best week of his life, a fire crackled underneath my skin.

"Are you OK?" Ace asked, staring at me.

"Yeah, why do you ask?"

"Because you're smiling like the clown faced killer from that scary movie you won't let me watch."

Cutting the television off, I fixed my face. Ace and I put away the last of the dishes before playing a couple of hands of poker. You weren't a Kaplan if you couldn't play poker and the last thing, I was going to allow was for my kid to be scammed at the family cookout. After letting him win the last hand because I was feeling generous, I directed Ace to get ready for bed while I cleared away the cards and cans of soda.

*It would be nice to sleep in my own bed tonight.* I lied to myself. Deion's bed was the perfect combination of firm yet soft. It was like sleeping on a cloud that cradled your curves just right. And his bed was so big I could roll over at least seven times before touching the edge. There was a knock on my door. I hopped up assuming it was Tammie asking to borrow a cup of sugar or a bottle of gin. When I looked through the peephole all I could see was a huge arrangement of flowers.

Swinging the door open I said, "I think you're at the wrong apartment, buddy."

The man holding the flowers moved them from his face and smiled. "Looks about right to me," Deion said.

"What are you doing here?" My eyes peeled back in shock.

"I moonlight for a flower delivery service at night," he joked.

"How do you even know where I live?"

"I had my assistant Google you. I love your Twitter feed by the way."

That was a silly question no one was ever hidden. The internet was vast but you could find the bitch who was tweeting reckless at you and send her a live snake if you wanted to. Not like that's something I have ever done. But it could happen.

"What do you want?" Seeing Deion standing in the breezeway of my apartment illuminated by dingy florescent lights, felt unseemly.

"First I was hoping you'd let me in, the flowers are kind of heavy."

I looked back into my apartment. It wasn't dirty but it was small with white appliances, a runny faucet, and a worn rug. A stark contrast from the hardwood, marble, and stainless steel found in his home.

"Deion, it's late and I'm not really understanding why you're here." Was I happy to see him? Yes. Was I happy to see him at my front door? Not so much.

"Whoa, Deck McCabe. Mom, it's Deion McCabe."

"Yeah, I can see that." I turned to Ace who's toothbrush was hanging from his mouth.

"Great game tonight. Some of the kids at school say you're washed up and should be traded or put out to pasture. But I told them you're not the worst player in the NBA. I mean sure you're like in the bottom ten percent but you're not last," Ace announced enthusiastically.

"I see you inherited your mom's unfiltered honesty," Deion said, moving over the threshold no longer waiting for an invitation.

"Oh, thanks for the signed pictures. After tonight's game I can sell them for—"

I loudly cleared my throat hoping to drown out Ace's last words. "Baby it's late, you need to go to bed."

"Can I take a picture with Deck first?"

"It's Mr. McCabe to you. No, some other time."

"But Mom—"

"Ace … bed … now."

Ace's expression turned sour but he knew not to test me. "See you later Dec … Mr. McCabe." Shuffling over to me, he gave me a hug and kiss before heading to the bathroom to finish brushing his teeth and going to bed.

"He's a handsome boy." Deion set the massive arrangement of red roses on the kitchen counter. I didn't have a vase big enough to contain all those flowers. Maybe I could put them in the oversized water cooler I often lugged to Ace's soccer games.

"Luckily, he got his looks from me and not his father. So why are you here, are you missing silverware?"

"No, I missed you." He said the words so matter of fact I thought I'd misheard him.

I scoffed at his statement. I mean let's be real, I was a good time girl but for most men I was forgettable. The only people who missed me were my son and my bill collectors. "What do you want?"

Deion nodded his head pacing back and forth across

my shag carpet his words tumbling out his mouth at a frantic pace. "Tonight's game was … it was like the adrenaline was coursing through my veins … and then I thought about you … everything just seemed to click … you know how that happens … I was on tonight. I was in the zone. I felt it. You know?"

"No, I don't know. You're rambling."

His hands swept wildly as he attempted to explain. "The past few months, shit the past year my game has just been off. Even when I was scoring it all seemed like it was dumb luck and not my innate ability. I tried everything extra practice, acupuncture, hypnosis … none of it worked. And then I met you."

I gasped out a laugh. "Are you high?"

"I know it sounds strange but the past few days with you have been the best days in a long while for me."

My facial features became screwed from disbelief. "Deion, we argued like forty-five percent of the time."

"Did we?" He seemed genuinely surprised by my statistics.

"Yeah, I mean I haven't officially run the numbers but I think I'm in the ballpark."

"What you call arguing I call witty sexual banter."

I reached for the side of his temple, the expression on my face grave. "Did you hit your head? Are you suffering from a concussion? Are you concussed?"

Brushing my hand away, he screamed, "No I'm fine. I'm fucking actualized." He waved his arms like a mad man.

"OK shh, let's try to use our indoor voice." Grabbing his elbow, I led him deeper into the living room and further from Ace's nosey ears. I told him to go to bed but I had no doubt he was standing at his cracked door trying to catch a stray sentence or two. "Go to bed Ace," I called out. My command was followed by the sound of running feet and the creak from Ace climbing into his bed. Turning my attention back to Deion I said, "You know what? I'm happy for you. I'm glad you had a good game."

"I had a good game because of you. The past few days with you were like plunging into ice cold water. You shocked my system back to life."

"Deion, if you wanna have sex again just say it," I whispered.

"No, it's not that. I mean don't get me wrong I definitely want to have sex with you again. Like desperately." He paused long enough with a gaze that made my clit pulsate in the hopes he was ready to make that a reality. "But I'm not here because of that."

"Get to the ask, Deck." My features tightened as I pressed my lips into a flat line.

"OK, I have an image problem." His face was no longer projecting the wide-eyed deer in headlights vibe. "The organization sees me as a liability. The Ramblers are at the end of the rope with me. From the gossip blogs with stories about me shoving photographers or carousing with women. It also doesn't help that my game play has been less than desirable. But that all changed tonight. I need you. I need your energy. I think you're my lucky charm."

All I could do was stare at him in dumbfounded disbelief.

"Say something?" he asked.

"Are you listening to yourself? Hmm. Lucky charm? I'm not a lucky charm I'm the rabbit whose foot got chopped off."

"How do you explain my stellar game tonight?"

I blew out a breath of air. "I don't know Deck, maybe you were well rested. Maybe all the sex we had helped to alleviate some of your tension. Or maybe the fact you were suspended and had something to prove, was the cause. But it damn sure wasn't me."

"Or maybe it was a combination of all those things. But I know you are the common factor. I slept better because you were next to me. All that tension-relieving sex was courtesy of you."

"I'm not your magical negro. And what are you gonna do when the mojo wears off?"

"I don't think that's gonna happen."

"I'm sorry, how exactly do I fit into all of this?" I waved my hand in the space between us.

"I need a girlfriend."

Covering my mouth, I hoped to muffle the laugh careening up my throat. "Who are you B2K?"

"Trust me I know it sounds bizarre. But I have two problems and you're the solution to both."

"I feel like you're trying to go with an Elmer's glue fix for a Gorilla glue type of dilemma."

"Just hear me out, please."

Plopping onto the couch I gave him the floor, but I was already working my mouth into a dubious pucker ready to say no the minute he stopped talking.

Deion took a seat next to me. "In the organization's

eyes it all comes down to optics. Ramblers is old school, they want role model players. The type of players kids stand outside the arena to get a glimpse of. Gone are the days of Dennis Rodman bad boy personas. Ramblers wants the organization to make the news, not its players. So I need a double rainbow type of miracle. You know the saying, those who can't …"

"Teach," I offered.

"No, they fake it. So I'm gonna fake this good guy image and shove it down their throat until it's coming out of their nose."

"What does that mean? You're gonna go to church and say your Hail Mary's before bed."

"Better yet. I'm gonna have the most beautiful woman on my arm. She's smart, she has a dry witty sense of humor. She grew up with brothers so she's not shocked by a little off-color language."

"Wow, she sounds great. Where are you going to find her?" I asked in jest.

Deion's mouth twisted into a sheepish grin. "I already have."

"No," I said, pinning my arms over my chest so he knew I meant it.

"It would only be until the end of the season. July if we make it to the finals or April maybe May if we don't. It's not even hard work. I'm just asking you to pretend to like me, hold my hand, rub my back, look into my eyes adoringly from time to time. And attend a few Ramblers' events and most of the games."

He was acting like he was asking me to loan him five dollars, nothing major. This was a big ask. A big deceitful ask. I would be required to deceive his team-mates, coach, and potentially the public all while pretending Deck was the best thing since the invention of the smartphone.

"Then there's part two and that's more personal." He reached for my hand. "That's just about you being around. Being my peace, being my calm, making me Zen."

Peace, calm, and Zen were three words that had never been used to describe me. Being a man's peace was not my strong suit. I was more like that nagging pebble in his shoe that poked at his sole when he walked, and even after removing his shoe and shaking it vigorously, I was still there. An annoying little reminder.

Deion continued, "You're also brutally honest. Which is something I'm in short supply of in my circle. I know you won't blow smoke up my ass."

"Why would I do any of that? What's in it for me?" I leaned forward, genuinely confused. If he thought I was gonna lie for a few fancy dinners and a Birkin bag he was mistaken.

"Twenty-five thousand dollars."

*Am I hallucinating?* I shut my eyes counting down from ten because I knew when I opened my eyes, I would be alone in my living room. No Deion McCabe, no outrageous offer like something out of a movie. Just me and the ticking from the god-awful cuckoo clock I couldn't bring myself to chuck in the dumpster.

I opened my left eye, he was still there.

"Fifty thousand dollars." He shrugged nonchalantly, raising the price like we were on a game show.

I wanted so badly to slap the buzzer and lock in a yes, final answer, but this was bizarre. "For what exactly?"

"I wanna make it perfectly clear I'm not paying for sex that's not what this is about. But I am willing to pay for your company and your time. And that would require you making yourself available to me whenever I called, wherever I was."

"I have a kid. I can't just drop everything to come see you."

"Bring him with you and I'd only expect you to travel out of town on the weeks you don't have Ace."

"I have a job, Deion. Two of them."

"Quit."

"OK no, what I'm not gonna do is throw all of my eggs into your fucked up papier-mâché basket." This was a fun little adrenaline spike, but my pulse was quickly returning to normal. I can't quit, I have responsibilities. And I'd worked really hard to land the job at Enclave. It was the hottest nightclub in Vegas with celebrities galore which meant generous tips. If I quit, I'd never land a gig like that again.

"Let's be real, do you even like what you do? Hmm, dressing up in short shorts bending and fetching for patrons who are drunk, high, and obnoxious."

"It's an honest living which is more than what *you're* offering."

"I could make a call to Fabio and get you placed on a leave of absence with a guaranteed right to return to your same position at the end of the season."

"You could do that?" I cocked a half-raised eye in his

direction. *Why would he willingly do that for me? He could offer this deal to any single woman and most would jump at the chance.*

Deion moved from the couch to sit on the coffee table in front of me, placing his hand on my knee. "Fifty thousand dollars is more than you make in a year, let alone six months. And I am prepared to deposit twenty-five grand into your account right now."

My eyes took on a faraway quality. After taxes I'd probably be left with thirty-five thousand dollars give or take. That's a lot of money. I could open up a college fund for Ace, pay off my credit card debt, maybe get a new used car. All that just to entertain an entitled basketball player. I'd done worse for less money. Shit I'd done worse for no money.

I wagged my finger at him. "The money is guaranteed whether you win a championship or not?"

"Yes."

"And this is for companionship, nothing more?"

He nodded, the corners of his mouth ticked upward slightly in anticipation of my response.

"You know it would be cheaper to go to therapy," I cautioned.

Reaching for my phone, I pulled up my banking information reading the numbers to him one by one. I watched eagerly as he inputted information into the banking app on his phone.

Placing my hand over his phone screen, I said, "Once you deposit that money sex is no longer an option. It'll be strictly a business arrangement from here on out. Understood?"

"Got it." He brushed my hand away.

*Damn the least he could do was object a little. Make me feel desired and wanted.* I had no intentions of abstaining from sex with Deck, but I wanted to make sure this was less about sex and more about the image and ego part like he said.

"Done." He tossed his phone on the couch.

A minute later my phone chimed. It was a notification from my bank telling me a deposit in the amount of twenty-five thousand dollars had just been added to my account. Taking my total to twenty-five thousand four hundred twenty-two dollars and seven cents. As I stared at the phone my chest expanded like someone was filling it with scorching hot air, making it difficult to breathe.

Deion rubbed my back while I experienced a mini freak out. I'd never seen this type of money in my life and all I had to do was sell my soul to the hot-tempered, tattooed basketball player. Closing my eyes, I talked myself down from the ledge I was precariously standing on. *This is easy fucking money. If this idiot saw me as his mojo whisperer, who was I to bust his bubble. He had a good game and that had absolutely nothing to do with me. But if somehow having me around makes him feel better and play with confidence, why deny him that. For fifty grand I would be his Tony Robbins.*

With my lungs once again filling with air, I turned to Deion and said, "I'm gonna need you to fuck me like the world is ending. I'm talking the seven plagues of revelations, zombie apocalypse, infectious disease type fucking."

"I thought you said no more sex?"

"I lied. I do that. Plus, money makes me very horny. I didn't know that before right now because I've always been broke."

Deion smiled and my breath hitched in my chest. *Why the fuck would it do that?* I decided to push the moment of weakness to the recesses of my brain, leading him to my bedroom to seal the deal.

# SLOANE

WHEN DEION ASKED ME TO PRETEND TO BE HIS GIRLFRIEND I didn't think he meant right now. The next morning Deion contacted the owners of both Enclave and the sportsbook and worked out some extended leave of absence for me. I don't know what he told them or what he promised. But I was officially on leave from both my jobs.

The thought made my stomach turn. I'd been working since I was twelve. As the daughter of Stanley Kaplan I'd learned to never rely on others for your livelihood. My dad lived paycheck to paycheck mostly because once he got paid, he was throwing his hard-earned cash at a woman, the poker table, or slot machines. So the fact that I was relying on Deion to make good on his promise, which now that I was thinking about it I should have gotten in writing, was a bit foolish.

Deion's hand was on my back leading me into the banquet hall at the Wynn Hotel and Casino. "Remember this is a friendly crowd. Consider this your soft open," he whispered.

It was business casual attire but when you're rich and famous nothing is casual. Deion, being a man hadn't really provided much guidance on what I should wear. I opted for a linen dress; it was navy and I think the last time I wore it was to a funeral. My hair was slicked back only because my curls would not cooperate this morning. And on my feet were knockoff versions of a popular slip on mule I'd found at a discount store.

The type of men I normally hooked up with weren't big on dates. I don't think Marco and I went on a single date, but that could be because he was married and worried we would run into his wife or one of her friends. That man broke all the rules while pursuing me. He was my parole officer so any relationship should have been a hard pass. But from the minute I stepped into his office, I knew he was interested. And me being me I decided to use that to my advantage. Who doesn't want a parole officer in their back pocket. The sex was a nice plus, but while I was conning the mark the mark was conning me. A man willing to lie to the state of Nevada had no qualms about lying to his wife and me, his girlfriend for months.

As we moved through the space, I was eclipsed by lanky basketball players so I reached for Deion's hand not wanting to get lost. The weight of his grasp was reassuring. At our designated table Deion pulled out my chair before securing the seat beside me. The waiter wasted no time, I wasn't even acclimated and he was standing at the ready to take our drink orders. Deion ordered a hot tea and I requested a mimosa taking my cue from the woman seated to my right.

Tugging on Deion's suit jacket, I whispered. "What's this event for?"

"It's essentially forced team building and allowing Ramblers' management to sing their own praises."

"So a circle jerk with French toast." I chuckled.

"Exactly."

"Hell must be freezing over because Deion is here on time," Dennis Lowery said, lowering himself into a chair across from us. "Normally you stroll in right after the second course."

"There is a first time for everything," Deion said.

"You may be on time but you've lost your manners. Who's your plus one?" Pratt asked, coming up behind Deion and rubbing his shoulders before taking a seat with his wife next to Dennis.

"Umm … this is Sloane Kaplan … my girlfriend." The way he said it sounded more like a question.

"Girlfriend?" Charmise Pratt, Chris's wife exclaimed. "Since when?"

Deion looked up and to the right searching the ceiling for the answer.

"Remember babe it's been like two months since we met." I offered. This was a lie we'd barely known one another for two weeks at this point.

Deion wagged a finger at me. "You're right, a little over two months."

"And this is the first we're hearing of her?" Pratt squinted his eyes examining my face. Deion claimed Colin Pratt wouldn't remember me from Enclave. According to Deion his teammate wasn't good with faces and he'd been too busy checking out my ass most of the night not my facial features. It appeared he was right. I could sense that Colin was trying to place my face but was coming up empty.

"Well, Deck has always been private," the man sitting next to Deion said.

Deion fidgeted with the collar of his button-down shirt. For a man who wanted to lie to his friends and colleagues about having a girlfriend he wasn't very good at making it convincing. "Yeah, well we just recently made it official."

"Wow, Dennis you may be right. Hell has frozen over and pigs are sprouting wings. Because forever bachelor Deck McCabe has finally settled down," Charmise said.

"Calm down. Let's try not to scare her away," Deion said.

"So how did you two meet?" Dennis Lowrey's wife or maybe she was his girlfriend asked.

It was at this point I realized Deion and I never worked out our back story. Every good lie needs a plausible backstory; it made it harder for people to pick it apart. Note to self, come up with a believable backstory, ASAP.

"How did we meet? Umm ..." Swallowing hard, Deion looked at me.

"That is a very good question," I said. We stared at one another in silence for longer than acceptable.

Deion bopped me on the tip of my nose. "You tell it better, go on."

The corners of my eyes creased as I stared at Deion trying to communicate my irritation without it being perceptible to the others at the table. "We met in anger management," I said with a straight face. He wasn't paying me enough to conjure up lies on cue. Granted lying on cue was my specialty but I wasn't going to bear the blame when this shit didn't work out.

Deion smacked his hand on the table releasing a fake laugh. "No ... baby ... so silly. She's always making jokes."

*Who was this man?*

While those gathered at our table laughed, Deion flashed me an agitated expression. Did he really expect me to have a witty meet cute in my back pocket? For the remainder of the brunch we were masters in the art of distraction. If someone asked us a dating related question we'd find a nonchalant way to move the conversation in a different direction. I was on pins and needles for the entirety of the brunch not wanting to say the wrong thing or blow our cover.

Deion wasn't paying me all that money to make him look like a weirdo. I knew if his peers didn't believe us this cushy gig could be over. Turning to Deion I stroked his beard and planted a kiss on his lips. To my surprise he returned my kiss with an intensity that was far too passionate for our current setting. It was an "I want to fuck you on this table next to the red skin potatoes and poached eggs" kind of kiss.

When Deion finally pulled away all eyes were on us.

"You two are so cute," Dennis Lowery's wife

exclaimed. With a slap to her husband's shoulder she asked, "How come you never kiss me like that?"

"Because you're always complaining about me messing up your makeup," he teased.

As the event droned on I made sure my mouth was constantly filled with food so I couldn't speak. And when the plates were cleared, I pretended to be super engrossed by the video montage of the Ramblers' organization and their charitable activity. It was hard to focus because Deion's arm was draped over my chair and he was absentmindedly fondling my earlobe.

When the event ended and Deion pulled away from the valet, I released a long whoosh of air. "How can I say this in the kindest way possible? That was a shit show."

"I disagree. Was it bumpy in the beginning? Sure. But eventually we found our groove."

"What just happened back there was far from groovy. Why would you ask me to be your pretend girlfriend and then not be prepared with a backstory?"

"I didn't think there would be follow-up questions."

"Of course there would be. How long have you been single? You introduced a woman as your girlfriend the first question is inevitably going to be, how did you two meet. It's kind of a no brainer."

Deion shrugged with an incoherent stammer.

"We looked like idiots. If you want people to believe this you need to be ready with a lie. What's my favorite color?"

"How would I know that?" He slowed to a stop at the red light.

I scrunched up my face and made the screeching wrong answer sound. "Make it up."

"OK … pink."

"Can you at least try to make it believable. It's burnt sienna, geesh."

When the light changed to green, Deion turned into the first available lot. Parking away from the other vehicles, most likely to avoid someone hitting his car with a wayward shopping cart, he placed the SUV in park and turned to face me. "OK so let's come up with a backstory. How'd we meet?"

"It has to be something enviable that gets tongues wagging."

"We met after a fender bender and exchanged information. I gave you a call eventually asking you out."

"I hate it. What about this … we met at hot yoga —"

"No."

I pouted but my face quickly brightened with a new idea. "How about we met on a dating app. After the first date we say our goodbyes, never planning to see one another again. But a week later we literally bump into one another at a coffee shop. After you apologize profusely you buy me a replacement coffee and we sit and talk for hours. The rest is history." I bit my lower lip at how perfect it was.

"Why would I be on a dating app?" He scratched at his beard. "Don't they say it's best if lies are grounded in an element of truth?"

"I tried to tell people we met at anger management."

"No, I don't want to remind people I'm in anger management. New man, new leaf … remember?" He leaned back, his head cradled in the headrest. The soft hum of the radio was all that could be heard as we both silently brainstormed hoping to land on a lie we could both agree on. Deion scrubbed his face finally turning to look at me once again. "We met at a nightclub. It's simple. I saw you from across the room. You were stunning and I couldn't leave without at least saying hello."

"I was stunning?" I rolled my eyes.

"Yeah, grounded in truth like I said."

Did this man just admit he thought I was beautiful? My cheeks grew warm and I shifted in my seat so all my attention was now directed to the strip mall shoppers.

"OK, we met at a nightclub. It's basic but I guess it'll work."

"My favorite color is blue, my favorite food are tacos, and my favorite movie is *The Princess Bride*."

"*The Princess Bride*, huh?"

"Yeah, it's the love story for me." He ran the pad of his thumb across my lower lip.

Opening my mouth slightly my heart raced as he slipped his thumb inside. I worked my tongue around his digit. Deion removed his thumb until the tip barely brushed my lips. My nerve endings all hummed with anticipation. When he finally slipped it back in, Deion fucked my mouth with his large finger and I slurped and sucked his stout thumb like it was his dick thrusting in and out.

My hands floated to the hem of my dress as I desperately tried to shimmy the fabric over my hips so I could sink my hand into my honey pot or better yet feel his hands on me.

"Back seat," Deion ordered.

I kicked off my mules and climbed into the back seat of his car. The windows were tinted well beyond what was legally allowed in the state of Nevada so the only way anyone would catch a glimpse was if they were standing directly in front of the car. I don't know how he managed it with his long limbs, but Deion climbed over the center console and made his way to the back seat. Reaching for the small slit at the bottom of my dress, he ripped it up to my waist.

The unexpected reveal caused me to gasp at his fervent yearning. Within seconds his dick was out, my panties were pushed to the side, and he was slipping inside. And from that point forward I begged for him. Asking him to go deep and fuck me harder. Each request he gladly fulfilled. After several long strokes which left my mouth dry from hanging open in amazement, he pulled out sinking lower. He lapped me up, pulling back my folds to feast. I braced my hand on the car ceiling and rocked my hips over his curious tongue.

Anyone walking past would hear an ear full because I was unable to stifle my moans. Deion was performing sloppy sucking slurps as he mumbled how wet and creamy I was. If I was willing to ram Marco's vehicle with mine, a man whose dick on a good day was adequate, I can only imagine the level of clownery I was willing to participate in to continue to be fucked like this by Deion. I'd witnessed firsthand how good dick ruined women's lives. House foreclosures, repossessed cars, fired from their jobs, credit score jacked. Good dick was dangerous. Good dick attached to a shady man was damn near lethal.

When Deion slid back inside, my walls contracted around his thickness and I screamed out, "Take it … take all of it … every last drop." This relationship may be fake but the orgasm and serotonin coursing through my body was very fucking real.

# DEION

I GAVE MY BODY A BIG STRETCH, THEN SEARCHED UNDER the fluffy bedding to locate Sloane's naked body, pulling her close. We were in Memphis, Tennessee scheduled to play the Grizzlies. Most people would think it takes massive balls to proposition someone into pretending to be your girlfriend. But in actuality, all it took was the ability to swallow my pride and ask Sloane who I'd known for less than a month to help me deceive my teammates, the press, and Ramblers' management.

To make it happen I'd offered financial compensation. Expecting someone to alter their life to accommodate you, no matter how mundane and stressful that life may be, was a huge imposition. Sloane was in need of cash and I needed Sloane. Plus, I'd wasted my money on foolish purchases in the past, like the artwork Sloane called out as ugly.

The Ramblers wanted proof I could be a well-adjusted individual capable of conforming to the rules. And nothing said sheep like appearing to be in a stable, loving relationship. My need for Sloane was dualistic. She helped to shift people's perspective of me. If this beautiful woman found something to *love* then maybe I wasn't all that bad. I was also convinced my improved game play was due to her. Sloane was a boost to my mental health.

It had been two weeks since our agreement, and to my great relief my barely thought-out plan was working. We played five games and only lost one. And that loss against the Golden State Warriors wasn't on me because I scored twenty-five points, with ten assists and seven rebounds. That was the Sloane effect. When I was with her, I didn't worry as much. I was present and focused on the moment, usually admiring the sway of her hips or the wild glint in her mink eyes.

I pressed my lips against her spine, cupping one of her perfect breasts. They were literally perfection and when I told her this, she would always brush my words aside and point out that they were once several millimeters higher or whatever. I noticed she frequently deflected when I'd offer a compliment. If I told her I wanted to bury my face in her thick, auburn curls she would call it a rat's nest. When I kissed her body focusing on the little jiggly fupa that was practically nonexistent, she'd claim it was from her love of beer and lack of discipline and not from the fact her body expanded and changed to create a miracle and bear new life.

We all had insecurities, shit I hated my smile but I got the distinct impression Sloane wasn't used to being praised. So any compliment, especially about her physical appearance, she turned into a criticism. She may only see her flaws, but when I looked at her I was often left in awe. It was practically superhuman the way she was able to lug her suitcases down her apartment stairs, refusing my many offers to help. At five feet five, her body was compact and her size six-foot fit into the palm of my hand. And when I massaged the soles, she would squeal loudly, her face bunched together so you could barely make out her eyes.

I climbed out of bed and headed to the bathroom. At the door I turned and asked, "Do you want to join me in the shower?" I stroked my dick in hopes of enticing her.

"Nope, you need to be fresh for the game."

"I'm fresher than a newborn baby."

"And we don't wanna do anything to disrupt that. Win now and we can fuck later." She shooed me away.

In the bathroom I folded myself into the shower, it was not constructed with a man of my stature in mind. I had to bend so I could wash my hair because the nozzle was too low. "Win now, fuck later." I mimicked her voice. She wasn't wrong … sex with Sloane left my knees weak so it was probably best to hold off until after the game.

A smile pulled at my face as I remembered our flight to Memphis. Because Sloane was a traveling novice, everything was new and noteworthy to her. The first-class seating with complimentary champagne, mini charcuterie boards, and seats that laid flat so you could sleep comfortably. She gushed over the limo that picked us up from the airport, outfitted with a fully stocked bar, television, and all-important privacy divider. Normally I'd just jump into a RideX, but since this was Sloane's first time traveling with me I wanted to make it special.

And Sloane did not disappoint offering a velvety hand job that made me release in under five minutes.

I enjoyed spoiling her. She was doing me a huge favor by agreeing to schlep from one city to the next, living out of her suitcase, and missing time with her family and friends. Yesterday, I was scheduled for practice and she'd be alone for hours so I provided her with money to shop and pamper herself. But I suspected she was pocketing the funds because there were no shopping bags when I returned to the hotel.

After my shower I caught a glimpse of myself in the fogless mirror. I couldn't help but flex. The Deion McCabe from a few years ago was back, and I was playing at my highest level. Tonight, was the first away game in which Sloane would be in attendance. This would solidify Sloane as my girlfriend in the minds of those who mattered the most. Sure, she'd been to home games, but paying for a woman to fly out to watch you play meant shit was serious. It was a flex. I never flew women out. If I wanted to get fucked I could easily find a beautiful woman, in any respective city, willing to sign up for the job. This would send the message that my playboy days were in the past.

When the executives looked at me I wanted them to envision squeaky clean, home by six and in bed by ten. The new Deion McCabe didn't lose his cool. He always turned the other cheek. And he certainly didn't assault fans. If they wanted all American, I would drape myself in the flag, while eating apple pie, and knocking out a quick country two-step.

I was ready to head out, but first I needed to check in

with Sloane for a goodbye kiss. Before every game I'd kissed her goodbye prior to heading to the arena and each game had gone well. So call me Stevie Wonder because I was now superstitious and a goodbye kiss was required. She was in the second bathroom taming her shiny curls. Game time wasn't for another three hours, but players arrived early to change, warm-up, and get their minds right. Sloane would show up right before the game and sit with the other players' significant others.

Because people thought she was my girlfriend, she was granted access to seating reserved for the players' family and friends. Sloane was treated like a VIP alongside the other basketball wives and significant others. This included being escorted to her seat, provided free food and drinks, and security stationed nearby in case a fan from the opposing team got rowdy. And if I was feeling like an imposter before the start of a game, she could meet me in the tunnel and give me a classic Sloane pep talk, which usually included her telling me to stop being a twat.

Sloane looked up at me with her big eyes from her seat at the vanity. "You're a force. You have gold coursing through your veins. Lebron who—"

"OK, are you gonna do that before every game?" She now considered herself my personal hype woman. The Flavor Flav to my Chuck D. And before each game she'd run through these asinine mantras to pump me up. It was corny as hell but I kind of liked it. I guess my love language was words of affirmation.

"I just want you to get your money's worth. You know, fill your cup."

"Consider my cup topped off, thank you." I winked.

"How do you plan to handle Jones?" she asked, fluffing her hair.

"I'm going to play him close, not giving him an inch of breathing room. He's gonna have to work for every shot and every rebound."

"He's fast."

"I'm faster." Leaning in, I planted a long kiss on her lips. The type of kiss that if I didn't have a car waiting for me downstairs could easily morph into something more. Reluctantly pulling away I said, "You look beautiful."

Sloane rolled her eyes. "I'm bloated and my hair looks like a mop head."

*Do you see what she did there?* I needed to break her of that nasty habit. Squatting down, I grabbed her face. "Sloane, when I tell you you're gorgeous, or compliment your intoxicating scent, or note how soft your skin feels don't contradict me. As girlfriends go you are by far the most tantalizing."

Her tone rang like a warning. "Fake girlfriend. Plus, you date models so not likely."

Grabbing her hand, I pulled her to her feet facing her toward the mirror. "Are we not seeing the same thing?" I tapped the glass.

Sloane's gaze settled on my reflection in the mirror. "What do you see?"

"I see all of you. Your flaws and imperfections which

are the things that make you most beautiful." I ran my finger over her forehead. "This scar. Your breast which are two different sizes." I gave the smaller of the two a soft squeeze. Flipping her around to face me, I continued. "Perfect is overrated. What you have going for you is special because it's unique. I've done a lot of things and been a lot of places but I've never met anyone quite like you."

"People do tell me I'm unfuckingbelievable a whole lot." She smirked.

I buried my face into the side of her neck peppering her neck, chin, and décolletage with kisses. Her body melted underneath my hands. Oh the things I would do to this woman if I had the time.

"OK I gotta run." I untangled myself from her. "See you at the game."

"I'll be the one screaming your name at the top of my lungs," she called after me.

In the car on the way to the arena, my phone dinged with an incoming text message.

Sloane: I'm really, really, really glad you picked me to be your fake girlfriend.

Deion: Who the fuck is this?

Sloane: It's Sloane, damn how many fake girlfriends do you have?

Deion: One, but she's a mean son of a bitch.

Sloane: I'm probably PMSing.

> Deion: I like the warm and fuzzy Sloane.

> Sloane: Don't get used to it, fuck nugget.

Through the reflection on my phone, I could see myself smiling like an idiot. Only Sloane had that type of power over me.

> Deion: 🥹

> Sloane: 🤮

When it came to romantic relationships, I'd been there, done that, and was still making alimony payments. By nature, I was a hermit preferring my company over anyone else. During the off season I could go weeks just tooling around my house. The only people I'd come in contact with were my trainer, assistant, and the occasional food delivery guy. How did I go from selective isolation to practically moving Sloane in with me?

On the weeks she didn't have Ace she was at my place, playing Pac-Man in my game room, steaming in my sauna, or fixing us a snack in booty shorts and nothing else. When she cast a brief glance in my direction or leaned her head on my shoulder while we watched a movie, my happiness meter would spike. The weeks she was gone I craved her and had to suppress the urge to call, wanting to hear her deep voice and villainous laugh. She had this warped sense of humor and a wicked attitude. But on odd occasions, she'd drop the facade and it became clear just how delicate and sweet she could be. In those moments I wanted to pull stars from the sky to give to her one by one just so I could see her smile.

Shit with Sloane felt different, maybe because none of it was real.

# SLOANE

THE MEMPHIS CROWD OF CLOSE TO TWENTY THOUSAND fans were hype, and the noise from the FedExForum arena was deafening. When Deck made a basket from three-point range I cheered and screamed loudly. He probably couldn't hear me over the rush of noise but I hoped he could feel that energy he'd paid so much for.

Watching Deion play was different now. Before, he was a recognizable player who'd fallen off. But now … now that I knew him, now that he was making me orgasm multiple times per night, I was invested in him doing well. And being in a packed arena with other people who loved the game didn't hurt, even if most of those people were rooting against the Ramblers.

It was the third quarter and the Ramblers were up by five. "YOU GOT THIS DECK STAY ON HIM," I yelled.

"You must really love basketball or you really love Deion," Charmise Pratt said.

"Neither, I just really love competition."

When I first showed up at a Ramblers' home game none of the other women would talk to me. Maybe they didn't want to waste their time with Deion's newest flavor of the month. But the first few games I attended was reminiscent of me versus the popular girls. Which was pretty much the story of my life. Admittedly, I didn't fit into the basketball "wife" aesthetic. My natural curls weren't tamed and had a mind of their own. I'd never been known as a fashionista. I mostly wore dresses from Old Navy and chucks or ripped baggy jeans I'd thrifted from Goodwill with slides.

On the flip side these women were dressed to the nines for a basketball game. Designer bags, outfits that clung to their curves, brand names from head to toe. Perfectly coiffed hair. Even the natural hair sisters looked like they'd spent several hours in a stylist chair to achieve shiny, bouncy curls that fell in the perfect pattern giving off effortless beauty.

Tonight, I'd tried to step my game up wearing a scoop-neck, lace-up top and the only name brand jeans I owned which were no longer on trend. Deion gave me money to shop but I couldn't bring myself to spend hundreds of dollars on clothes. No one would claim that I was a financial whiz kid, but I knew blowing cash on trendy items was a bad investment. If Deion had an issue with the way I dressed, he never said anything. He was always giving me these ridiculous compliments I knew he couldn't possibly mean.

"So how did you two really meet?" Charmise leaned close nudging my shoulder with hers. I suspected she'd lost a coin toss and was assigned the role of being nice to the new girl while digging for dirt.

"Umm ... at a nightclub." It wasn't a very interesting story but this was Deion's con and I was just along for the ride. So if he wanted to tell people we met at a crowded, noisy club, so be it. "Yep, he was staring at me. At first, I thought maybe we knew one another but when he approached me I realized I'd remember a brother that fine. So we chatted it up and he asked for my number. And then he actually used it." I rambled in hopes of selling the unfamiliar lie.

She took a sip of her ginger ale. "Anytime I've gone to a club with Deion he literally holds up the wall. He is not a social butterfly. I guess he doesn't have to be he's a ball player, women tend to seek him out."

"I suspect being a ball player comes with tons of unexpected perks."

"If you managed to land Deck you must be pretty special. He's not really a people person."

"That's just one more thing we have in common because most people are stupid." I shoved a handful of popcorn into my mouth.

The corners of Charmise's eyes creased before her face lit up. "I like you; you say exactly what you're thinking."

"Yeah, and that often gets me in trouble." I stood clapping my hands loudly. "WAY TO HUSTLE. YOU FIGHT FOR IT." Dropping back into my seat, I took a swig of beer.

"Deck said you and Pratt recently got married?"

"Yeah, we did." Charmise flashed her ring with a diamond so large it was shitting on my entire existence. Her ring was probably the equivalent of a four bedroom, three and a half bath home in Henderson.

"That's exciting."

"And overdue. If I'd let him, Pratt would have kept me on ice while he continued to entertain his side chicks." She delivered the words like it was common knowledge.

My eyes grew wide. I'd read the rumors on social media and there was an incident a few months back where Charmise made a big show of letting everyone know she was single. It included a live social media stunt where she tried to act like she was unbothered and focusing on herself. I never understood why people took their issues to the internet. Those people did not care about you, and most were only watching to have a front row seat to your demise.

"Sounds like love won. He realized you were the love of his life, and the mother of his kids and changed his ways."

She gave me a side eye which told me she thought I was naive. "Something like that. What about you and Deck are you two exclusive or is he free to see other people?"

"Um ..." Once again without a cover story, I had to make shit up as I went along. "It's just vibes right now. We are definitely in the stage of the relationship where we can't keep our hands off one another." This was true. When we were alone, I always found a reason to touch him. And touching often turned into him bending me over nearby furniture and fucking me in a way that only made me crave more. Maybe I was a bit attention deprived, but feeling that man move inside me while his hands explored every inch of my body ... I lost my train of thought, a shiver overtaking my spine as the memory flashed in my head.

"He must be vibing pretty hard to call you his girlfriend with a capital G."

I watched as Deck swatted the ball from an opposing player trying to make a shot, allowing Dennis Lowery to rebound the loose ball. Once again, I stood calling out. "THAT'S RIGHT. GET THAT SHIT OUTTA HERE."

The man sitting directly in front of Charmise and me stood spinning around with fury in his eyes. "Would you sit down and shut up," he yelled at me.

"Are you gonna make me?" I asked, tilting my head to the side. "I bet you're fucking not. I know you're all butt hurt because your team is taking a shellacking on both ends of the court but no need to take it out on me. Turn the fuck around and finish your hot dog, bud. Trust me you do not want this smoke."

I stayed ready. It didn't matter the time or place. People really thought they could just say whatever to whoever and walk away. You know what we need? We need to start punching people again. Sticks and stones can break your bones and words can get your ass whooped. We used to be a proper country and when someone said some grimy shit, their jaw was rocked.

Charmise tugged on my arm pulling me back to my seat. "Ahh, Sloane you can't talk to people like that."

"Yeah I can and so can you. Last time I checked I was grown and if I wanna scream, LET'S GO RAMBLERS, at the top of my lungs, I will."

The man in front of us spun his head like the chick from the exorcist and flashed an icy glare.

"What if he pops off," she whispered.

"For every action there is an equal and opposite reaction." I spoke loudly enough so the man in front could hear me. "Sure that guy could jump up and punch me in the face. But those consequences spin both ways because I could just as easily gouge his eyes out with my fingernails. So what you need to ask yourself is are you tough enough to deal with the consequences. Me … I'm coo-coo for coco puffs."

After I announced to anyone in ear shot that I would set it off in this bitch if a miscreant tried to test me, my shouting went unchecked for the remainder of the game. One thing about me, I would cuss your ass out in a heartbeat. Fuck conflict resolution, sometimes it was necessary to beat the brakes off someone so they knew exactly when and how they fucked up.

And this was why I was in anger management. If Shelly were here she would suggest I speak from a place of reason and not emotions. "Our emotions can deceive us. And in the times you sense your emotions spiraling you should walk away," she always said. That part was the most difficult for me to implement. I was a scorch the earth type of woman.

The game ended without incident, other than the crime scene on the court. The Ramblers won by ten points. As he headed to the locker room, Deion flashed me a toothy grin. My heart stuttered before descending into erratic beats as I returned his smile with one of my own. I hadn't yet drunk the Deion Kool-Aid but I was readying my glass with ice and a bendy straw.

# DEION

When you're in Memphis you do what the locals do. After the game I took Sloane to The Wind Down, a country western bar with generous drinks, dim lighting, and loud music. The goal was to blend in, which was dumb because at six foot five, I rarely blended in. And then there was the fact that Sloane and I were two of the only melanated faces in the joint.

The place was not one I would normally frequent with cowboy hats, wrangler jeans, and men named Brayden and Trig. But a traditional club would be too crowded with people looking to take my picture and hand me their mixtapes. Interesting fact, I've probably been given hundreds of CDs and now in the digital age people would DM me a link to their Tik Tok or YouTube channel. I didn't know the first thing about music and I wasn't interested in cosplaying as a record producer. If you sent me a music link, that was an immediate block.

The other thing that was preventing us from blending in was Sloane's insistence to stand out. I stood on the sidelines while she took her turn on the mechanical bull. As the speed increased she held on for dear life, her thick thighs doing most of the work with an assist from her strong arms. Her buxom body jiggled, causing her breast to bounce and her thighs to quake. More than a few men in the bar watched lecherously, all hoping for an accidental nip slip. How her big ole bitties remained sheathed in her lace-up top was beyond my comprehension.

The back of the electrical bull reared, bucking Sloane to the padded floor in a fit of laughter. She came bounding toward me, all smiles. "Did you see that shit?"

"It was impressive, all of it. Quite the show."

The bull operator handed Sloane a gold medal. "Good job little lady, you rode Warren the Bull for more than twenty seconds and you won yourself this plastic gold medal."

Sloane slid the ribbon over her wild, auburn golden-brown curls until the medal rested on her chest. "You see that I'm a winner."

Handing her back her beer, we clinked bottles before taking a swig. Pressing through the crowd, we managed to find a small empty booth at the back of the bar.

"So I bet a few weeks ago you wouldn't have seen yourself in a honky tonk bar?" I said.

"A country western bar, yes. With you at said bar, no."

"Are you having second thoughts about our little arrangement?" I half teased but deep down I hoped she wasn't regretting this.

Sloane's response was a blasé shrug of her shoulders.

"Since you're my girlfriend now we should probably work on getting to know each other better."

"Fake girlfriend. And you know plenty."

"Do I? I know that you're ticklish, and that you consider sugary cereal a square meal. I know that you were arrested—"

"You don't know that," she scoffed.

"Were you arrested?" I asked, tugging on the beaded bracelet around my wrist.

"Yes."

"OK, so now I've confirmed you were arrested. Do you wanna flesh out those details for me?"

"I was arrested for a *crime*." Her hands performed air quotes when she said the word crime.

"Against a person, property, or cyber?"

Sloane took a long drag of her beer before responding. What she did didn't matter. But I'd trusted her with some pretty personal shit and I was hoping that trust ran both ways.

"Property."

"Theft?"

"Vandalism."

I tossed my hands in the air signaling this game of twenty questions wasn't working for me.

Sloane hissed out a sigh. "I tagged a police station."

"What does that mean?"

"It means that the police are corrupt and when they kill Black and Brown people from my community they almost always get away with it. They lie, they obstruct, they rally the troops, call in the wagons and put on their riot gear. And they treat us like we're the irrational ones. Like our anger is misplaced.

"You know when the trash reaches the top of the can and you push it down to make room for more. That's what it feels like. Like our voices, our pain, our very real and justified concerns are being pushed down, out of sight only to make room for more shit to be dumped on us.

"I went to a protest and maybe I got a little carried away and I spray painted a police station with the word 'murderers.' But it was appropriate because that's what they're doing their murdering us. So I got arrested but because it was a victimless crime I got off with probation." She peeled at the label on her bottle of beer. "Is this the part where you tell me I was reckless and stupid and I have a son to think about?"

"No, I get it. I know what it's like to feel helpless."

Money and fame insulated me from some of the harsh realities that regular people faced, but I remember how the string of officer-involved shootings affected me. How it affects me still. I wanted to do something but wasn't sure what I could do to help. I spoke up in the media when asked but that didn't feel like enough. Being rich may protect me from a lot of things, but I'd been stopped by police on more occasions than I cared to remember, because I was cruising around in an expensive car they assumed was stolen or because I was considered out of place in my gated community, heading to my house. Our tax dollars at work.

Sloane leaned in with a smirk, "You thought it was

gonna be a sexy crime like money laundering or something … admit it."

"No, I would not have guessed vandalism in protest of unjust and corrupt policing systems. I was really hoping it would be something like you selling your foot pics to random men."

Sloane raised a bushy eyebrow. "Is that a crime?"

"I mean it should be. Paying for photos of someone's feet is weird. The internet's right there. Who pays for porn in this day and age?"

"You know I did that once."

"Sold images of your feet?"

"My feet and others." She gave me a shifty smile.

"Hold up." I held up my palm like a stop sign. "You were a foot madame?"

"I was a curator of beautiful feet." She corrected me.

"Ooo you're freaky." A smile pulled at the corners of my mouth. "But I already knew that when you did that thing with the beads the other night."

"Shut up." Sloane checked over her shoulder to make sure no one was ear hustling in on our conversation.

Was she embarrassed, because she struck me as a woman who had no shame. She was unapologetic and politically incorrect. Why would she care if the group of college kids in the booth next to us knew that she inserted anal beads in my ass.

"I want some foot pics." I pretended to sulk. But for real I wouldn't turn down personal flicks of Sloane's manicured and silky soft feet.

"No, I'm retired. Now I travel across the country

with my fake boyfriend, boosting his ego and sucking his dick."

I threw the bottle cap from my second beer at her. This wasn't a fake relationship; it was a relationship of convenience more than anything else. There was nothing fake about our connection. Or the way my body responded when she touched me. Or the weird tug at the bottom of my stomach whenever I smelled her scent lingering in a room she'd just exited.

"What's up with you and your ex?" I asked.

"Which one?"

"Ace's dad."

I just wanted to make sure he wasn't gonna be a problem. I didn't need someone who was still pining over Sloane seeing me as a threat. I was supposed to be on the straight and narrow. And while if anyone stepped to Sloane sideways I would make sure they regretted it, I wanted no parts of a spurned lover. Love made people do strange things.

"Umm, we're cool. He's married and has two other kids. When we first split it was rough but eventually we put our pride aside because at the end of the day Ace is our priority. And him being good, being happy is my most important job. So the fact that his father was a lying cheating sack of shit no longer mattered. We co-parent and he gets to lie to someone else now." She tussled her hair and I caught the scent of warm sweet amber wafting from her curls. "What about you and your ex?"

"Lara? We don't fucking talk. It ended badly and stayed bad."

"Weren't you married for like years?"

"It wasn't always bad but looking back on it now it's hard to remember the good parts because the messed up parts overshadow everything else."

"What were you two fighting about?"

"My cheating, her using me for clout."

It had been seven years since my divorce and all that remained was the damage. I was like a house after a flood. Leaving behind soggy carpets, warped foundation and a damp musty odor that covers everything the water touched. This didn't include the things you couldn't see, the mold behind the walls, damaged wires and gas lines, and appliances that no longer worked.

"Relationships are a mind trip." Sloane unshelled a peanut, dropping the remnants to the floor.

I headed to the bar to get us another round. I couldn't agree with her more. Relationships, at least mine, were never easy. People just assumed that I could land any woman I wanted. Yes I had a semi stable job, because let's be honest right now I was fighting for my career. I had a home, a well-adjusted kid, and I was able to purchase whatever I wanted whenever the urge struck me. That kind of stability was attractive to many people.

Unfortunately, I was attracting the wrong women. Everyone wanted to be famous and being photographed with me or having their name said in relation to mine upped their social media cache. It was all about likes and follows. I was old school, I wasn't into image defining relationships. *I know what you're thinking, ain't you the dude that just paid Sloane thousands of dollars to hangout with you?* Yes, I am he. But that was about basketball, not trending on Twitter.

Back at our booth, I placed Sloane's beer in front of her before taking a seat.

"Do you think this is working?" Her eyes searched my face.

"What … us?"

"Yeah."

"I mean I'm winning." I shrugged.

"Yeah because this is all about winning." Her body was no longer loose and easy, her back snapping into a rigid line.

"Winning is important."

"It makes me sound kind of disposable."

I leaned forward reaching for her soft hand. "How can you be disposable when you are the linchpin to this entire operation?"

She shrugged. "Anyone could do what I'm doing for you."

I vigorously shook my head. "This shit doesn't work without you. *Anyone* … couldn't make me feel the way *you* make me feel."

Sloane's body began to thaw as she rested her elbow on the table and buried her hand in her hair supporting the weight of her head. "How do I make you feel?"

"Full," I said, giving her hand a squeeze. I could say more, so much more, but I thought it best to refrain.

Her eyes grew wide.

"So no this isn't an insert random person here type deal. We're a team."

"A team huh, I tell you your great and you choose to believe it. It's kind of pathetic." She spat out.

"You or me?"

"Both of us." She pulled her hand from mine, locking her arms across her chest.

Sloane was like those Sour Patch candy commercials, one minute she was sweet the next minute she was sour. You never knew which one you were gonna get. I was trying to be nice and she essentially gave me the middle finger. She wasn't the only one who knew how to get pissy.

"If anyone is pathetic it's you. You basically just sold yourself to the highest bidder."

Sloane's brown eyes danced with flames. Grabbing her beer, she proceeded to pour the contents over my head. Jumping from the booth she screamed, "FUCK YOU, DEION."

The college kids next to us pointed and laughed at me, amber ale dripping into my eyes.

"So I tell the truth and you get mad?" I yelled, wiping at my wet face.

"The truth, the truth? The truth is you're the loser who has to buy friends."

Even though the music in the bar was loud, people nearby stopped carousing and turned their focus on the two loud Black people fighting in the back of the bar.

"You have no room to speak. Let's keep it all the way real you're just as fucked as I am that's why you're here."

One of the college kids shouted.,"Yo, get your girl, dude."

Slamming my fist on their table I barked, "Shut the fuck up."

At the same time Sloane ordered him to "Mind your fucking business." Her balled up fist at her hips ready to fight.

Cell phones were out and pointed in our direction, there was no way this didn't hit the gossip sites tomorrow morning. I was trying really hard to keep a low profile, but drama seemed to find me like it was tracking my ass.

Reaching for Sloane, I led her to the outside patio which was decorated with a row of painted toilet bowls that could be used as seating. Sloane paced back and forth, most likely pumping herself up for round two, but I wasn't looking to fight.

"Serious question," I asked. "Do you ever think before you do anything?"

"I do what feels right."

"Dumping your drink over my head felt right?"

"In the moment, yes."

"I'm not using you, you know."

"You kinda are."

"Well then we're using each other. Which makes it a wash." I sat on a floral painted bowl.

"I just don't want to be treated like something you can just throw away."

"Have I treated you like that? Hmm? Have I made you feel that? Because if I have, I apologize."

"No, but I know it's coming."

"You don't know shit."

Sloane let out a chuckle.

I pinched the brim of my nose. "What?"

"It's just funny. You saying, 'You don't know shit' while literally sitting on a crapper."

I concealed a smile, that *was* funny. "Do you want out? Do you wanna end this?" I silently prayed that her response would be no.

"Deion—"

"If you want to walk away it's cool. And you can keep the initial twenty-five thousand." Once I made that offer, I regretted it because admittedly I was making it easier for her to call it quits.

She answered my question with one of her own. "Is that what *you* want?"

"I'm not interested in forcing you. I want you to want this as much as I do."

"I do." Her voice was meek. She was probably embarrassed to admit that she wasn't ready for this to be over.

Standing, I walked over to her, stopping inches from her face. Tilting her chin with my thumb, I said, "Be sweet for me."

Sloane's cold gaze started to thaw when my hand slid down her neck. She lifted to her tiptoes but I kept my lips just out of reach. I wanted to make her work for it. Climbing on top of a green toilet bowl, her lips now hovered over mine. Despite my best efforts Sloane always managed to be in control.

Giving my beard a rough tug she said, "I don't wanna be sweet." Her lips slamming into mine.

I don't know if her brown matte lipstick was laced with acid but when I kissed her it was like my mind lit up in technicolor making everything explode and pop in unnaturally bright shades of pinks and reds. My hands danced up and down her back before coming to rest in her plush curls.

"Eww, this isn't your bedroom," a woman said from behind us.

Sloane pulled her lips from mine. "Fuck off," she said with a hiss.

Showing my support, I flashed my middle finger at the brunette with the razor sharp bob, whose face turned red before she stomped back inside.

Whiskey Wild's "Shit Kickin Boots" started to play and Sloane sang the song word for word at top volume like it was autobiographical. She jump from the top of the bowl and her body swayed and jerked to the twang-infused tune.

When she finally returned to where she left me standing so she could perform her impromptu concert she planted her hand on the back of my neck and guided my head to her level. Sticking out her tongue, she licked the dried beer from my face.

"You owe me make-up sex," she whispered.

# SLOANE

DEION LEANED BACK ONTO THE HEADBOARD WITH ME standing over him while he ate me out from behind. I folded my body forward at the waist until my face met his erect penis, taking it into my mouth.

"Damn girl you're flexible as fuck," Deion muttered as his tongue slid from my clit to my anus.

He grabbed hold of my legs pressing me closer so he could suck every fold. Each swipe of his tongue across my clit made me want to suck him harder. I lowered my head taking more of him in. When I started to gag and had to pull him out, Deion slapped my thigh in protest. Diving back in, I worked his tip, my tongue curving around his member.

With his dick throbbing in my mouth, my legs grew weak. A warm sensation flooded my core and my knees buckled as an orgasm ripped through my body. Deion held on to my clit far too long and my ecstasy shifted to mind-numbing nirvana. My body convulsed and shuddered, but I never released his dick from my mouth. I wanted my lustful moans to vibrate against his shaft. Let's call this paying it forward, the moans he was pulling out of me were humming against his dick, intensifying his satisfaction.

When I collapsed to the bed Deion gave me no time to recover. Scooping me up, he walked over to the bedroom's mirrored closet door. He hoisted me upward, his chest against my back. With a hand on either thigh, he spread me open wide so my legs almost resembled butterfly wings in the mirror. I wrapped an arm around his shoulder and then used my free hand to guide him inside. Once he was in place, our bodies worked in tandem.

Sex with Deion was fun. It was unpredictable. I never knew what to expect; every thrust was different from the one that preceded it. Deion wasn't afraid to try new things and he didn't clench his butt cheeks if I got too close. He was sexually astute, his primary goal ensuring it was pleasurable for both of us. Like a mind reader, he knew when to be gentle and when to toss me around like a rag doll.

My head rested against him as I watched the action in the mirror. He was so strong and his face was serious as his reflection stared back at me. I couldn't look away. I wanted to experience this man with all my senses. And the visual feast of witnessing his thick, hard dick thrust out before burying deep inside me was almost too much for me to bear. Deion kissed my shoulder and an unfamiliar emotion settled in my throat.

This man made my body feel good. He made *me* feel good. "Deion …"

His eyes focused and settled on me. "Are you OK?" he asked mid thrust.

No I was not OK. I was confused. But all I could say was, "Don't stop." I grabbed his neck bringing his lips to mine.

"You feel so soft and wet, Sloane. You always feel so good."

My head was dizzy and my senses were frayed. "I know that this is pretend. But it feels very real. It feels real to me," I confessed.

"Everything you're feeling is legit. I'm not fucking pretending."

I'm certain it was just words one says when their balls deep in pussy that is dripping and throbbing, but for the next few minutes, I was going to let myself believe. I needed to feel his weight on top of me. Unhooking my arm from around his neck, I tumbled to the carpet laying on my back. I opened my legs wide inviting him to join me.

In one smooth motion he lowered himself over me slipping back inside. I draped my hands over his back, running my fingers down the length of muscles. Like a greedy lover I over indulged on his full lips, kissing and sucking to my hearts content.

"I'm happy we met," he said in a low-pitched murmur.

"No one is happy after meeting me," I countered.

"I guess I'm the exception." He brushed the hair from my face, kissing my collarbone.

Lifting to my elbow I asked, "Why are you being so nice to me?" I was too far gone and tangled up in these newfound emotions.

Deion pulled out and rested on his knees. "Because I like you and you deserve it."

"I don't deserve any of this." I was a bit of a self-saboteur if you hadn't guessed by now. I told you men didn't love me. That was a lie. I didn't allow people to love me. And when they did, I pushed them away.

"Let me show you what you deserve. Is that OK?"

I nodded meekly.

Deion found my clit with his wet and warm tongue and all the negative thoughts were silenced. After he slipped back in he showed me exactly what he thought of me with intention behind each stroke. My body buzzed with energy as he swam laps like his name was Michael Phelps. When his fingers intertwined with mine, my soul floated from my body and watched from above as this sweet simple gesture sent me crashing into a violent release which left me clawing at his back and twitching uncontrollably. I was in la la land but when Deion groaned over top of me, my soul locked back into place.

His orgasm was close. I rocked my hips, his thickness rallying me close to the edge once again. "You're my good little slut," I said. With those words Deion shivered and bucked, his hands digging into my waist. I went tumbling right alongside him. This orgasm wasn't as intense as the last one but it was the nicest surprise.

When he regained his composure, his cool smile returned and he swore, "I'm only a slut for you."

AFTER WORKING UP AN APPETITE, I WAS SEATED CROSS legged on the king-sized bed next to Deion in a hotel robe, rocking side to side as I took a bite out of my meat lover's pizza.

"Do you want some of my salad?" Deck asked.

"No, who orders a Cobb salad for a midnight snack."

"It's good stuff, not heavy."

"It's psycho behavior. Them leafy greens are not gonna sop up all the alcohol swirling around in your belly."

"You worry about the heartburn you'll be dealing with in an hour and stay out of my plate."

Deion's cell phone dinged. Reaching for it he looked at the face before tapping on the keyboard on his screen, a slight smile playing at the corners of his mouth.

"Hot date?" I asked, hoping my tone sounded unbothered because I was. I was just asking the question to move the conversation forward, nothing more.

"The hottest … my mom. She texts me sweet dreams and reminds me to say my prayers every night."

"Awe, that's sweet and creepy at the same time."

Deck raised his middle finger playfully, pressing it into my forehead. "What are you too gangsta to text your parents?"

"I receive all types of text messages from my dad but none ever wishing me sweet dreams. His texts are usually asking for money or trying to talk me into some absurd get rich quick scheme."

"Sounds like a character," Deion said, before shoving dry veggies into his mouth. No dressing, just healthy vibes.

"He's not a character, he's a criminal."

I don't think my father ever held a real job for longer than a few months. He always did something stupid and got himself fired, or he just stopped showing up all together. My dad was the type of man who didn't do well with authority and wanted to be his own boss. The problem with that was he was lazy, always choosing the easy way out.

He stole a bunch of knockoff designer bags and then tried to sell them to a cop. Arrested. He tried to breed dogs in his apartment, two huskies. Yes, I said huskies in the Las Vegas heat. Both were removed from his care because two full grown fifty-pound huskies in a one bedroom apartment isn't humane and it was against the leasing agreement. Down three thousand dollars with no huskies to show for it.

"What about your mom?" Deion asked.

My lip curled. "The woman who gave birth to me split when I was eight so there's not much to say about her."

"Damn … I'm sorry."

"Don't be. Shit happens to everyone." I wasn't looking for pity. In fact I despised it. Maybe because I'd been pitied all my life. Poor Sloane, her mom up and left leaving her with her no-good daddy. Poor Sloane, her father is a drunken, belligerent weirdo. Poor pathetic Sloane, she's such a smart girl, too bad she turned out just like her no-account father.

"So your dad raised you."

"'Raised,' is a strong word. Let's just say he managed

to keep us alive." I pulled a piece of sausage from the cheese and popped it into my mouth.

My dad was the type of father who would let us jump off the roof into the pool. Or have us wait in the car while he played at the tables. That's how I learned all of those card tricks. Sometimes we'd tag along with him to some late-night party. Where the men and women were loud, obnoxious, and inebriated. At one of those parties a man with a curled beard taught me card trick manipulation and sleight of hand. I would later use the things I learned to make quick cash. It was also a great party trick. You know, pick a card, any card type shit.

"And your brothers? What do they do?"

"What's with all the questions?" I asked, tossing my crust back into the box.

"I'm just making conversation."

"Yeah well it's giving interrogation. Real FBIish if you know what I mean."

"Feel free to chime in and ask me a question at any time," Deion said, taking a drink of his room temperature water.

I learned fairly early on Deion was superstitious. I'm talking about wiping the soles of his sneakers for good luck. At the Rambler arena he always bent to touch the brand logo in the center of the court, a flaming basketball with claw marks, before the start of each game. Then there were the quirky food preparation and decor habits. When he arrived at a hotel, he unpacked everything like he was moving in and not passing through. You know, just weirdo behavior.

"Where does your family live?"

"My mom's still in Houston where I grew up. My dad passed away a year ago."

"I remember hearing about your dad's passing online. I'm sorry."

"Don't be. Shit happens to everyone." He raised an eyebrow as he threw my words back at me.

"You and your dad were close?" I asked, repositioning myself so I was now sitting in between his wide-open legs, staring into his face.

"He was my best friend." Deion puckered his mouth. "You probably think that makes me a bitch baby or something."

"Being able to love your dad doesn't make you a bitch baby. It makes you lucky."

"Don't you love your dad?"

"My dad … I just don't think loving people is his thing."

"I didn't ask you if your dad loved you. I asked you if you love your dad."

Chewing on my bottom lip all I could offer was a wishy-washy shoulder. "How'd your father die exactly?" I recalled the stories and tributes in the press after Morris McCabe's passing, but now in front of his son I was drawing a blank on the cause of his death.

Deion cocked a half open eye in my direction. Probably deciding if he was going to let my non answer slide. "Covid."

"Covid? That's been over for years."

"It's not over, people just stopped caring about it."

Shifting closer I ran my hand down his tattooed arm,

uncertain of what to say. I wasn't good at making people feel better. Actually, I had a real knack at making people feel worse.

"You were right I was lucky, my dad was great. Even when I fucked up time and time again. The car accident, having Destiny at sixteen. He always supported me. Sometimes his love was tough but I deserved it. It's not easy finding people who truly believe in you. But my dad always did, even when I wasn't so sure myself."

Deion really was an open book. I believed there was nothing I could ask that he wouldn't answer. I'd learned at an early age it was best to keep your business out the street. It prevented nosy neighbors and visits from child protective services. If I'd mentioned when I was ten that I was essentially taking care of myself while my older brothers were out late at night helping my dad steal cars, it would have definitely brought unwanted attention.

But something about Deion's transparency was refreshing. I bet he wasn't fighting a gnawing pain in his chest and stomach like I was, which my masters from WebMD University told me was most certainly an ulcer caused by holding onto toxic shit. His honesty made me want to return the gesture and before I knew it I was saying thoughts I never expressed out loud.

"I remember the day my mom left. She said she'd be right back; she was just going to Target to pick up a few things. I begged her to let me tag along but she said I'd slow her down. I thought she meant at Target, not in life. When she didn't return of course we were all worried, we thought she'd been kidnapped or was in some ditch somewhere. But then my dad started noticing things were missing. Half her clothes were gone. The jewelry box with cubic zirconia rings and manufactured gems was missing. She always told me that jewelry box would be mine one day."

Deion sat quietly rubbing the pad of his thumb across my palm.

"My dad was upset at first. But in true Stanley Kaplan fashion he pushed it down and hid it away. And we weren't allowed to talk about it or her. He chucked all her pictures. I managed to save a few and we just moved on. Sometimes it feels like I made her up."

I stole a glance at his face to see if he was horrified or eyeing the exits.

He looked at me and said, "Your mom leaving wasn't your fault."

"I never said it was." My chest caved in as my spine bent.

"I know I was just saying."

Biting on the inside of my cheek I added, "People don't just up and leave for no reason though."

"I'm sure she had a reason but none of those reasons were you."

I'd bet my last dollar that the primary reason for my mom leaving was my father being a neglectful prick. But I'm also sure me being a needy brat who asked stupid questions didn't help matters. I scratched at my leg deep in thought, so when the pillow hit me across my temple I was caught off guard. Reeling backward, I fell onto the bed trying to man myself with a plush weapon of my own while taking incoming fire. Grabbing a pillow, I swung hard making contact with Deion's long torso.

He was now on his feet in a defensive posture. Rolling from the bed, I swung wildly until my pillow connected once more. Deion allowed me to get off a few extra hits before snatching the feather filled pillow from my grasp. Swooping me in his arms, he dropped me to the bed, being mindful of my head as I shouted in protest. He unraveled the belt of my robe and with an indulgent kiss to my lips, he trailed kisses over the length of my body. Down my neck, running his tongue under my boob before circling the nipple and areola. Deion French-kissed my armpits causing me to giggle. Next was the side of my stomach before sinking his tongue into my belly button. He lifted my thigh planting kisses from my knee to my ankle. With my feet in his hands, he paid close attention to each little piggy, including the one that cried wee, wee, wee all the way home.

All I could do was receive, my hands grasped at the silky soft bedsheets as a series of moans escaped my throat. This man seemed passionate about three things. His family, basketball, and pleasing my body. When Deion finally licked my warm and dewy center, I accepted the title of the luckiest woman in the world.

# DEION

CHRISTMAS IN VEGAS CAME WITH LITTLE FANFARE. THERE'S something about stepping outside to seventy-degree weather that makes the thought of roasting chestnuts less appealing. On Christmas Day the Ramblers were in Arizona, another city that brought out my inner Scrooge. I hated playing games on Christmas Day, especially away games. I'd rather be in Houston with Raphael, Destiny and my mother right now but I was in Footprint Center lacing up my Jordans.

To make things worse Sloane wouldn't be in attendance cheering me on. She was spending Christmas with Ace and when I offered to fly them both out she declined. I get it, every family has their traditions and apparently Sloane the least traditional woman I knew was all in when it came to decking the halls and Santa coming to town. Before the start of the game, I decided to video chat with her, virtual support was better than none at all.

"Merry Christmas," I said when she popped up on my screen.

"Merry Christmas. How's Arizona?" The sincerity of

her smile caused my heart to pitter patter with thoughts of her missing me and being genuinely happy to see my face.

"It doesn't feel like Christmas and the twinkling lights wrapped around the palm trees aren't helping. Did you get my gift?"

Her eyes narrowed and she shook her head. "You didn't have to do that."

What I did was gift her one of those fancy designer purses all the players' significant others carried. Knowing Sloane, she'd probably sell the purse and dump the money in her savings account. For Ace I got a MacBook, a tablet, and software since he had a new found interest in graphic design.

"What about Ace did he like his gifts?"

"He loved them. But you don't have to buy me or my kid gifts." This time her expression was a smidge softer.

I tugged at my beard, secretly wishing it was her hand grabbing hold. When Sloane fondled my beard, I turned into Pavlov's dog salivating after the slightest tug of my facial hair. "Had it ever occurred to you that I wanted to?"

"I got you something too." She offered her eyes darting around her living room.

"Really, what?" Liar, liar pants on fire.

Dropping the phone, she bolted from the couch. The sound of doors opening and closing and the creaking of cabinets let me know she was searching for something, anything to pass off as a well thought-out gift picked especially for me. When she returned, she held up a statue of a Black Santa with chubby cheeks. My jaw unhinged as my brain tried to process what I was seeing.

"It's a Santa gnome," she beamed, giving the monstrosity a shake. "You said it didn't feel like Christmas."

"Wow. Thanks?"

"I got it from a garage sale. It's vintage."

Something about Santa's eyes were menacing, his toothy smile slightly twisted. It was off putting and weird, just the kind of gift I would expect from Sloane.

She poked out her bottom lip, which caused my pulse to spike. "You don't like it?"

"Am I supposed to?"

"Ouch." She hoisted her middle finger into the camera.

"Are you serious? I thought this was one of those white elephant gifts that are intentionally horrible."

Sloane's right eye twitched. Did she genuinely purchase jolly St. Nick with me in mind? That statue was without a doubt the worst gift I'd ever received. He resembled a Chucky doll. I wouldn't be surprised if it came to life at night and tried to stab me in my Achilles heel. This red-suited freak cast in ceramic would be found posted up next to the swimming pool with my dead lifeless body floating underneath the surface.

"I love it. I can't wait to get home and put it in the yard for everyone to see. If nothing else it'll scare away potential intruders."

Sloane chuckled. "OK, I admit I'm not the best when it comes to gift giving."

"It's the thought that counts. I don't understand what you were thinking, but it's cool. I can honestly say no one has ever given me anything like that before."

"Just keeping you on your toes, sir."

When a woman called you sir that was code for, *I want to gag on your dick.* I don't make the rules, that's just how this shit works. And the next time I saw Sloane I was gonna give her exactly what she wanted.

"You definitely have me on my tippy-toes," I said.

Sloane set down the Santa from hell and leaned in close so all I could see was her face. "You're a unicorn and tonight you're gonna go on that court and you are going to gouge any player who tries to get in your way with your rainbow horn. Because no one can stop you …"

Sloane gave the best pep talks. I loved the one where she compared me to Darth Vader. It was clear she'd never watched a *Star Wars* movie because in her retelling Darth Vader was the hero. She had a unique way of getting me pumped for the game. I don't know if it was even the words so much as it was words coming from her.

Initially I thought she was blowing smoke up my ass, but after a few of these talks, it felt genuine. I believed she had faith in me and my abilities and wanted me to succeed not because of the money but because she cared. Maybe she was just a good liar but she had me hook, line, and sinker.

"Repeat after me. I am a unicorn."

With a quick sweep of the locker room I leaned close to the phone and whispered. "I'm a unicorn."

"I don't believe you. I AM A UNICORN!" She shouted into my earbud.

Fuck it. "I AM A UNICORN!" I screamed out like I was Tom Cruise in *Jerry Maguire*.

The heads of my team members turned in my direction, as I waved in embarrassment.

"Now scream that you have a thick throbbing horn and you're ready to unload."

I sawed out a mirthless chuckle. "Nope not gonna do that one."

Sloane's face disappeared from view as she dissolved into laughter.

"A-hole," I called out.

When she finally stopped guffawing her skin appeared to glow and her eyes held a twinkle. "Have a good game, Deck."

"Tell Ace Merry Christmas."

"Will do."

"Alright, love you …" Both our faces bore the same expression: total, unmitigated, shock. What the fuck did I just say? Fumbling with my phone, I disconnected the video call.

# SLOANE

DEION WAS ALREADY UP AND DRESSED MOVING AROUND IN his walk-in closet, which was bigger than my bedroom and bathroom combined. I was curled in a ball still under the covers in no rush to move from my comfy side of the bed. Several weeks had past and the Ramblers were on a winning streak. Initially, I thought Deion's musings of me as his good luck charm were ridiculous. But after several outstanding performances, I was starting to think maybe he was right. Maybe I was his magic elixir.

If nothing else I was definitely getting lucky in the sex department every night. After a win, Deck would be high off the adrenaline from the victory and he would worship my body like a man of faith. And when the team lost, he worked out his frustrations with deep, hard thrust and love bites that left an impression. I'd always hated the feel of being sore after a workout but being sore after you were contorted into positions you'd never heard of, was my type of physical fitness.

Returning to the bedroom, Deion called my name. "Sloane."

I didn't answer, pulling the pillow over my head to drown out his voice.

"Sloane, wake up." Before I could stop him Deion was pulling at the bed linens until my naked body was exposed.

"It is entirely too early for the bullshit, Deck." My throat was dry and my voice raspy.

Deion glanced at his phone. "I need you to come with me to this Ramblers event tonight."

Sitting up, I narrowed my eyes. "What type of event?"

"Black tie, formal, mandatory."

"And you're just telling me now?" I smoothed my hand over my head scarf.

He was stuffing a pair of shorts and sneakers into his gym bag. "I was trying to get out of it but no such luck." Deion tossed a card in my direction.

Climbing from his extra tall bed I threw on his robe before turning the business card over in my hand. "What's this?"

"It's a card for a boutique. Ask for Ashley. She'll help you pick out a few dresses and get them tailored to fit. My credit card is on file so you should be all set." His tone was nonchalant like this was perfectly normal.

He'd just given me the green light to go shopping at a fancy store on some Pretty Woman type shit. Rich people were too trusting. I would never let someone run up the bank on my dime. Granted I didn't have many dimes to spare, but still.

"So you want me to get a dress?"

"Dress, shoes, undergarments, whatever you need to

make the look work." He scanned his phone preoccupied by *Sportscenter's* coverage of the Ramblers.

"OK." I bit my lip to conceal a smile.

Deion placed his phone in his pocket, his eyes now trained on me. Ambling over, he wrapped his massive hand around my neck. His palm was slightly rough from the almost healed callous on his skin. "Just a few things, OK. Nod in agreement."

"Yeah, sure just a few things," I said, sweeping my head into a long arch.

"I'll pick you up from your place around seven."

"It'll probably be hard to recognize me in my ten-thousand-dollar gown," I joked.

Deion's eyes didn't even twitch at the proposed price tag. He kissed my neckline before planting one final kiss on my lips. "See you later."

"Have a good practice, baby."

The corners of his mouth twitched as he resisted the urge to smile. After fake dating for close to three months, I knew he loved terms of endearment. Baby, sweetie, pookie, daddy.

"Be good." He gave my ass a quick pat.

"You give me ten minutes and I can show you just how good I can be." My hands dipped into his sweats working his semi chubby into its full thickness.

Deion seeped in a lungful of air. "Pineapple."

"What?"

"It's our safe word, pineapple."

I pulled my hand from his pants. "You don't feel safe right now?"

"No, not with your hands stroking my junk. I have to go. I can't be late."

"And I'm not stopping you," I said, dropping my robe.

"You are evil. You're an evil woman." He paused like he was considering his options. "I have to go. Tell me you'll miss me."

"Every second," I said, watching him practically float out of the room.

I want to tell you that when he left I hopped in the shower and went about my day. But instead, I crawled into his side of the bed and buried my face in his pillow so I could be surrounded by his soapy clean scent. Your girl was down bad. He'd been gone all of two minutes and I already missed him. I didn't even recognize myself.

This situationship found me doing things I vowed I never would. Last night I roasted a whole chicken, with crispy potatoes and seasonal vegetables. *Pause ... because I don't think you heard me.* I cooked food for a man. And then I watched eagerly as he took his first bite. When the satisfied moans of approval hit my ear, I smiled so broad my cheeks started to hurt. It was like I'd been body snatched and replaced by a dumb bitch.

This wasn't a relationship, and when the season ended so would we. I should be riding the wave and enjoying the vibes and perks. Not learning how to make quiche because they were Deion's favorite breakfast food. My relationships always ended, eventually. It had with Ace's dad, with Marco and with all the other men

I'd dated. This shit with Deck wasn't the exception to this well-established rule.

My head was in the clouds when I needed my feet to be firmly planted on the ground. Flipping the black-matte business card over from Luxe Boutique, I ran my digits over the raised lettering. I could tell by the feel of the card underneath my fingers this place was high end. A bit of anxiety snaked its way around my body. Deion said this was a formal event. He really should have reviewed other options before picking me for this gig. Nothing about me was formal or understated. I was bold, loud, and often times crass. Fortunately, one thing I did know how to do was play a role. Whether it was the talkative woman at a car auction or bursting into tears at a gambling hall when I was nine so my dad could swap out bad cards.

I agreed to this so I needed to show up and show out. Pulling back the covers, I jumped out of bed and performed the cha cha slide all the way to the shower.

---

I invited Charmise to come with me to the boutique because I didn't know the first thing about fashion or picking a dress appropriate for the occasion. When we entered the building, I already sensed I didn't belong. The store dripped rich bitch energy and my faded jeans and coffee stain T-shirt were giving the complete opposite.

"Are you sure we're in the right store?" I asked.

"Yep, Luxe is known as the place to go when you want to turn heads."

Luxe was in an outdoor mall with lush greenery and extravagant fountains. This was the type of place where stay-at-home moms met up for a quick bite and some retail therapy. The problem was most of the retail spaces were woefully outside of my budget. I'd lived in Vegas for years and I didn't even know this shopping center existed. Granted I was a long way from my neighborhood. In this part of the city almost all the cars were luxury and the homes expensive.

"Welcome to Luxe, can I help you find something in particular?" a young woman with long, wavy blonde hair asked.

I have to admit I was surprised by the warm greeting. I was expecting to be ignored. "Hello, I'm looking for Ashley."

"Ashley is finishing up with another customer so it'll be a few minutes. While you wait can I get you a beverage?"

"What are you offering?" I asked.

"We have water, flavored seltzers, or if you're feeling celebratory, we have champagne."

"Ding, ding, ding. Champagne for her and a seltzer for me," Charmise said, a huge smile sweeping across her face as she rubbed her very pregnant belly. The young lady left to fetch our drinks and we found seating by the window. Charmise turned to me, "Stop looking like a deer caught in headlights. You're the girlfriend of a rich basketball player. You need to get used to being spoiled."

Yeah, no that wasn't going to happen. I would never get used to someone buying me nice things or flying first class. And seeing how this was a temporary arrangement I would never have to.

"I'm not really used to the white glove treatment."

"I get it. I grew up in a town with three stop lights. So living in a huge house with a nanny and chef still blows my mind."

"How'd you go from that to all this?" I asked.

"When you're from a small town the first thing you want to do is escape. After high school that's what I did. I worked a couple of odd jobs and partied at night. I caught the eye of a few players and men with deep pockets and started getting invited to the VIP events and flown out to exotic destinations all expenses paid. After a few years of living my best life I met Pratt. I was pretty and he was rich with an ego that needed stroking, we were kind of the perfect match," she joked. "We fell fast and he promised to take care of me. And I thought I'd hit the jackpot."

I was finding Charmise's story was fairly common. Beautiful woman meets an athlete, quits her job, and then dedicates the rest of her life catering to his needs. I couldn't imagine trusting someone enough to permanently walk away from my sources of income. Love was unreliable and fickle it shouldn't be anyone's plan A.

The store clerk returned with our drinks and I immediately tipped back my glass. This neighborhood and its inhabitants were way out of my comfort zone. I was grossly out of place and I was certain everyone else was thinking the exact same thing.

"I have a confession to make," Charmise said, her eyes creased at the corners like she was sizing me up.

"OK." I eyed her suspiciously.

"I didn't expect for you and Deion to last this long. Truthfully, I thought after the Ramblers' charity brunch I'd never see you again. I also didn't anticipate liking you this much. So I'm hoping my next words don't fuck up our budding friendship."

I took another long sip of my bubbly, bracing myself for what she was about to say. Maybe she knew Deion and I were lying about our relationship. Shit, was she about to call me out in this fancy boutique that served your champagne in glass flutes and not plastic?

"Deion and I slept together. It was a long time ago before me and Pratt. But I wanted you to know."

I pressed my palm to my chest. "Is that it?"

"Yeah."

I nodded thoughtfully. "That's cool. I'm not tripping off of something that happened before Deck ever met me."

I understood that basketball circles were small and relationships were bound to overlap. The way some of these women's gaze would frost over whenever I approached I just assumed Charmise wasn't the only one he'd been intimate with.

Charmise breathed a sigh of relief. "Thank God. I just know how some people can be. Truthfully, I'm super territorial about my man but more often than not he has me out here looking stupid." She rubbed her belly with a rueful nod.

I decided to completely ignore her implication that

Pratt, even after marriage was still less than faithful. Deion told me stories about Colin that made my blood boil. And if Charmise and I got any closer it would be difficult not to share the details with her. "Does Pratt know about Deion?"

"No, his ego couldn't handle that. Like I said it was a long time ago Deion was playing for the Utah Jazz and neither of us had met Colin yet."

"What happened between you and Deck?"

"We hung out for a few months and I wanted more but Deck wasn't interested. Don't get me wrong he was fun to be with, he made me feel special, and the sex … well you know."

"Mind numbingly amazing. Yeah, I definitely know."

"Ever since his divorce Deck hasn't been a commitment type of guy. That's why we were all so surprised when he announced you two were dating. But they say it just takes the right woman to change a man forever. And Deion seems to be certain about you."

A ridiculously beautiful woman approached us. Her hair was cut into a flowy long bob and she wore a stylish monochromatic pants suit that accentuated her russet skin. "Hello, I'm Ashley. You must be Sloane." She stretched out a perfectly manicured hand.

Standing, I encircled her hand with mine. "Yes, Deion said you'd be able to help me find an outfit for tonight."

"Anything for Deion." Ashley sized me up, tilting her head to catch a glimpse of my ass. "You're curvy. This will be fun. I think we should go with something bright. Your skin tone is beautiful and a bold color will really pop."

I helped Charmise to her feet and we followed behind Ashley as she perused the racks, selecting several items for me to try on. She didn't ask for my input, she just flipped through the dresses at lightning speed. With little hesitation she plucked up pink, red, gold and coral dresses from the rack.

When I exited the fitting room in the first selection, a form-fitting yellow dress, Ashley once again examined me with a critical eye. "I love the color but the cut is wrong." She shooed me away with her hand.

Second was a cream-colored number that made me feel more virginal than vixen. The last outfit was a gold ruched dress. When I stepped out of the dressing room, Charmise gasped.

"Is that a good gasp or a bad gasp?" I asked, pushing my curls behind my ears.

"It's a damn I didn't know you were stacked like that gasp. Why do you hide your body underneath these raggedy baggy jeans?"

Ashley shoved her hands down the top of my dress adjusting my boobs before handing me a pair of strappy heels with the distinctive red bottoms. "Try these on."

When I checked myself out in the full-length mirror, I had to admit I didn't look half bad. If, fingers crossed, my hair cooperated tonight I could actually pass for one of these pampered basketball spouses.

"I think we have a winner," Ashley said. At the register she checked me out and just like Deion said everything was on him. Ashley handed me the garment bag. "Deion wanted me to tell you La Perla is a few doors down and he has a package waiting for you to pick up."

I'd heard of La Perla, the lingerie shop but I'd certainly never crossed the threshold. A blush flushed over my face. This man sure knew how to make a woman feel special, new dress, new shoes, and new panties. My underwear was more about function than sex appeal. If a man was down to fuck, cotton drawers were not going to stop him.

After returning home with a gold dress, high heels and a gift of several pieces of lingerie, some practical and some other naughtier bits I could only assume were for Deion's eyes only, I was greeted by a makeup artist and hair stylist both posted outside my apartment. It would appear my Julia Roberts' moment wasn't over.

My experience with a glam squad was my friend Olive who worked at the MAC store. She would add the glittery stuff to my eyelids and help me achieve the perfect cat eye. Tonight's event must be pretty important if Deion was hiring a team to beautify me. After a facial and the best shampoo I'd ever experienced, you know the kind where they hit every itchy spot on your scalp while massaging your cares away, I was a clean palette for the stylist to work on. It took two hours of poking and prodding. My face was something out of a magazine, pores erased, skin flawless and blemish free and my nose was contoured in such a way to diminish my unmistakable African American features.

My curly locks were slicked straight with a sheen and bounce like I was in a *Dark & Lovely* commercial from the '90s. I can't remember the last time I'd straightened my hair and I was now in the mirror whipping my head back and forth admiring the volume and body. By the time Deion knocked on my door I was questioning everything, the slutty dress, the shimmer I'd added to my neck and shoulders and the contoured nose I fixed to closer resemble the original schnoz I was born with.

# DEION

WHEN SLOANE OPENED THE DOOR, I BARELY RECOGNIZED her. I was used to seeing her in ripped jeans and tank tops. Her dress hugged her voluptuous curves, highlighting her perfectly rounded ass. It wasn't my favorite part of her anatomy but it was pretty fucking close. Her skin shimmered even under the dull living room lighting. And her hair was sleek and straight flowing past her shoulders. I preferred it curly and wild just like her, but this was a nice change.

"Wow," I said, reaching for a strand of her sun-kissed locks. "You look …" I pressed my fingers to my mouth offering a chef's kiss.

Sloane tugged at her dress. "Ugh, I probably shouldn't have gone with the gold dress. I look like a plastic trophy."

"You look like a fucking Goddess."

She made a face indicating she wasn't so sure.

Circling around her, I pressed Sloane's ass into my lap so she could feel Deion, Jr. hardening from just the sight of her. With my hand under her breast plate I drank her in. She smelled different, a soft floral sweetness that made my mouth water.

Turning, Sloane smoothed my tie. "You look nice." Releasing me, she went for her purse stuffing random items inside. "Tell me more about this party. How important is it?"

"Grover Thornton will be there."

"Who?"

"Ramblers's venerable owner." Every year, right after the holidays, the organization threw a party. I think they waited until the end of January because it was cheaper. This year's event was at Thornton's estate.

"Got it. I'll make sure to turn up the Kaplan charm." She tossed her overnight bag in my direction before pushing me out the front door, locking it.

In the car on the way to the event, I had one last surprise for Sloane. "Here." I pulled a red box from the pocket on my driver's side door and handed it to her.

"What's in the box?" Sloane offered her best Brad Pitt from *Seven* impression. "It's too small to be a head." She gave the box a shake. When she pulled back the lid, the diamonds made her eyes glimmer.

"It's just a small token of my appreciation." My knuckles gripped the steering wheel as I snuck glances in her direction trying to gauge her response.

Sloane eyed me suspiciously. "Are you hysterical? Small token my ass. Are these real?" She was breathless.

"Yes."

The whites of her eyes were visible. "Deion—"

"Shut up. Shut up and take the gift."

Sloane stared into the box her hands trembling. "It's

too much." Her voice was hushed so I don't know if the statement was intended for me.

"Try it on." I encouraged her.

She removed her necklace which she probably got from T.J. Maxx and replaced it with twenty carats of radiant, round diamonds.

"If I wasn't nervous before I am now. This jewelry probably cost more than everything I own." She admired herself in the flip down mirror.

I'd known Sloane for three months and in that time she'd never asked for anything. That was the weird thing about her; it was like she had no expectations. Some people were conditioned to go with the flow. It was my suspicion Sloane had been burned one too many times so she just stopped reaching for anything beyond her grasp. I wanted to show her she could have more.

I turned right and drove the two-minute journey up a long and winding driveway. Placing the car in park, we stepped out and I handed my key-fob over to the valet attendant. Thornton's estate made my spot look like a trap house. I'm talking about palatial living, indoor pool, tennis court, and a guest house which was just a normal sized house that could comfortably host a family of five with separate bed and bath for each.

Sloane clung to my hand, her head on a swivel as she observed the water features and ornate light fixtures. When you entered the home there was an impressive staircase, like something out of *Gone with the Wind*. A server offered us champagne and Sloane eagerly grabbed a glass and drank the contents in one long gulp.

With a squeeze of her hand I said, "Hey."

"Yeah."

I pressed my forehead to hers. "You're a unicorn. Ain't no one at this party got shit on you. You are one of a kind just like that Santa troll you bought me."

"It was a gnome."

"It was demonic." With a tug I added, "Come on. Let's go find Pratt and Charmise."

---

AFTER DINNER WE FOUND OURSELVES IN THE STUDY WITH floor to ceiling book cases and plush arm chairs. Sloane and I were posted up at the peripheral of the crowd listening as Thornton compared basketball players of yesteryear to the players of today. Sitting on the arm of a chocolate leather sofa, I nodded my head and faked a congenial smile. I was ready to go, having reached my fill of the bougie shit before the third course.

"They don't make players like they did back in the day, Ewing, Jordan, Miller. Today's players just want the endorsements and the social media hype." Grover Thornton's booming voice filled the room. The attendees all nodded in agreement, lapping up every word. Which was typical any time Thornton spoke. People didn't contradict him they cosigned his words. This man lived in an echo chamber. His beliefs always mimicked back to him with little to no correction or divergent views.

I sensed Sloane shift her weight leaning forward from her hidden seat on the couch tucked next to

Lowrey whose large mass obstructed her view. "Are you implying today's players don't have heart?" Sloane asked. Causing me to freeze in place.

Thornton turned to her, sizing her up. "That's exactly what I'm saying, sweetheart."

"Pretty fucked up coming from the owner of a basketball team. You don't think your players are just as hungry to win as those old school cats? You don't think they pour out their souls onto the court every single night?"

"I'm sorry, who are you? Thornton stiffened his glare and the corners of his eyes creased.

"I'm Sloane Kaplan of the Nevada Kaplans. And I think it's pretty wild to make a blanket statement like that. Your players work hard to make you rich. You should be a little more appreciative."

It was good while it lasted because I was about to get fired. Thornton would most likely crack the top ten of Forbes richest people in a few years. He and Michael Jordan were the only two Black professionals to own a majority stake in an NBA franchise. Grover Thornton was rarely subjected to ideas or thoughts contrary to his own. As such he was often the loudest voice in the room. But he'd never been in the same room as Sloane Kaplan.

"I appreciate winning. And the Ramblers are due a championship," he said.

"If I were one of your players, I'd find it hard to produce for someone who just saw me as a means to an end."

"I hate to break it to you pumpkin but winning is

what we are here for. The NBA ain't no kiddie league where everyone gets a participation medal."

"My name is Sloane not pumpkin and no one is looking for a fucking medal, but the occasional good job would be nice."

"Hey, let's get some fresh air." I stood hoping Sloane would follow.

Thornton's gaze settled on me. "I should have known this mouthy beauty was with you. Make sure Sloane ..." he said her name like it was a dirty word, "understands we prefer players's girlfriends to be seen and not heard."

Sloane stood with a deep throated laugh. "I can make a *scene* if you want. I don't know how to break it to you gramps but it's a new day and women are allowed to work outside the home and have independent thoughts."

The murmurs in the mahogany walled study were almost deafening.

"Maybe we should go for a walk." I suggested reaching for her hand but she shook me off.

"I'm sure Deion is so glad he brought you to this event tonight. Maybe he should have outfitted you with a muzzle." Thornton took a slow drag of his dark liquor.

Sloane's hand settled on her hip and her stance was reminiscent of the night at Enclave and the scuffle with Chipmunk.

Clearing my throat I said, "I vote that we agree to disagree. We don't all see this topic the same way and that's fine. We can disagree without being disagreeable." I barely recognized myself, anger management had me seeking out resolutions rather than leaning into conflicts.

"Wise words Deion since you're skating on thin ice," Thornton said, sharing a chuckle at my expense with others in the room.

Sloane took several steps forward. "Do you even realize that this season Deion is leading the NBA in both rebounds and assists. And let's not forget that he's coming off the bench and posting twenty-five to thirty points consistently per game."

My head flinched as Sloane ticked off my accomplishments. I didn't know she was paying attention. I thought she was mostly showing up to the games for the corndogs and beer.

"I'm sure Deion is a joy to be around off the court but on it he's a hot head and unpredictable."

"Deion hasn't missed a game, other than the ones he was suspended from, in his three seasons with the Ramblers. Deion McCabe is the man that gives your team the much-needed pep talks to hustle harder and pull out a win. Deion is the guy who stays on the court shooting around with the rookies so their ball handling improves. Number twenty-seven is the reason you have a viable chance at making the playoffs and maybe all the way to the finals. Any prick with money can own a team. But do you acknowledge your players and their sacrifices?

"You speak in lofty terms about your love for the game. But it sounds like you're more focused on profit. Basketball isn't about hefty paychecks, it's about heart. Deion is dedicated to this team even though you don't believe in him. He shows up for the Ramblers every fucking day. I've watched this man sacrifice sleep rewatching game footage working out the best way to defend an opposing team.

"Did it ever occur to you that if you took a vested interest in your players maybe their output would be better. When Deion's father passed there was nothing from upper management, not a card, not an email, not a phone call … nothing. And you really expect players to hustle hard for you when you don't give a fuck about them. And then you have the audacity to fix your mouth and call Deion out as some problem child. In my humble opinion you're the motherfucking problem."

Grover Thornton was speechless. Mouth agape, eyes bulging, balled fist with no comeback in sight.

"I think I'll take some of that air now," Sloane said, brushing past me toward the front door.

All I could do was smile like an idiot and excuse myself from the room. "So nice seeing you all again," I said with a slight bow before turning on my heels and following after Sloane.

Her red bottom stilettos clicked with determined steps down the paved driveway. "Look, I know what you're gonna say but, I have a low tolerance for assholes. And that fucker Thornton is a textbook case."

"He's a son of a bitch." I scratched at the back of my neck.

"You're probably regretting the life choices that brought you to me. I know this night was important and I know I fucked it up. If I had a time machine I would go back to last week and play the Powerball with the winning numbers and then I'd time trip to this evening and fix this," she said, tugging at her bottom lip.

"Not gonna lie, it was awkward." I scrubbed my face.

"I'm sorry Deck." Sloane reached for my hand but pulled back, instead taking a seat on the ledge of the massive fountain with two naked cherubs that spat water. "You can tell him I hit the open bar one too many times."

It had been a long while since someone had gone to bat for me. If my father was at this event he would have cussed Thornton out too. The fact that Sloane defended me with such passion was the nicest surprise. She pretended not to care, but for five minutes she ethered Thornton and was my staunch advocate.

Sitting next to her I rubbed her knee. "Did you mean that shit you said in there? About me, I mean."

"Yeah, of course I did. Deck, you're an amazing player. You've been distracted." She poked me in my ribs with her long fingernail. "But when you show up you show the fuck out."

FUCK! I was unable to remove the silly grin from my face. This woman, this woman was everything I never knew I needed. She was the missing ingredient. You know when someone's cooking and they're constantly tasting the soup, or stew, or sauce trying to figure out what's lacking? That was me, my life was devoid of an essential element and I'd smack my lips after giving it a taste and decide I needed to buy a new car, throw a party, or go on an exotic trip. But no matter how many ingredients I added to the stew, shit was always still bland and flavorless.

Sloane was like a spice rack. I'm talking Lawry's Seasoned Salt, Old Bay, and Sazón all rolled into one. And when I added her to the mix she turned everything up a notch. I was falling for this woman like I'd just tripped down a long flight of steps, just tumbling head over feet over and over again.

"How'd you know all those stats about me?"

"It's my business to know about you. You're my fake boyfriend, remember?" She wrinkled her nose playfully.

*Yeah, I remembered.*

"Do you wanna swing by Fatburger? Because I'm still hungry, those small ass plates weren't hitting on anything," I asked.

"A strawberry milkshake sounds amazing right now."

Standing, I intertwined my fingers with hers before making our escape toward valet.

# SLOANE

ALL MAGNETS HAVE A NORTH POLE AND A SOUTH POLE AND opposites attract, so when we're near one another my north pole finds Deion's south every time. How we made it home without wrapping his car around a tree I would never know. I don't know if it was the milkshakes or the moonlight. But as we cruised down the partially deserted streets to his place my mouth cruised up and down his shaft.

Deion's breathing was erratic as my warm, wet mouth left a puddle in his lap. Pulling into his driveway, he put the Mercedes in park. "Get out of the car Sloane." His voice was rough and edgy as he commanded me.

By the time I exited the vehicle Deion was half naked, stripping his clothes on the pavement at a frantic pace. I turned so he could unzip me from my dress. Deion kissed my shoulders before freeing me from the tight ruched garment. Directing my steps, he led me to the front lawn. Pushing hard he knocked me to the grass.

"Was that too rough?" he asked.

"No." I was already tugging off my fancy new undergarments.

Dropping to his knees, he bit at my flesh leaving mouth-sized love bites along my body. "Is this OK? Tell me if you want me to stop."

"It's good, it's all good. There are nothing but green lights."

Turning me onto my stomach, he entered me on the well-manicured lawn outside his home. The fullness of him drove deep as his hand pressed on my back pushing me into the wet grass. Heat ignited in my core as Deion's other hand firmly smacked my ass with authority, like he knew it was his. The subtle tingle of pain made me cry out before biting down on my lip.

Deion was in full control and I let him use me. Now on all fours his fingers stimulated my clit while back shots propelled my body forward before slamming back down on his shaft. Reaching around I grabbed for his thigh. I wanted him to drown in me.

I don't know if The Ridge had neighborhood quiet hours, but my loud moans which echoed through the night air alongside the very dirty talk we were engaged in, was probably gonna get him fined by the home-owners association.

"Yes Deck, just like that. It feels so good," I cried out.

"Make that ass dance for me."

Just call me Savion Glover because I twerked my ass over his dick.

Adjusting our position, Deion flipped me onto my back, his entire body sinking into mine. With my fingernails I branded his wide back with scratch marks. The warmth from his breath danced across my face as he spread my legs wide, thrusting at an angle. I tried to sneak kisses between pumps that made my eyes water with ecstasy.

"Don't stop fucking me," I begged and ordered in the same weak breath.

Deion slung my legs over his shoulders and his dick found uncharted territory, a part of me that had not had the pleasure of his thick veiny member. His dick was impressive and I'm not just saying that because he was actively hitting my spot which triggered mini pulsating vibrations throughout my body. It was the kind of dick that could be cast in clay and used for dildo manufacturing. *Get your very own NBA all-star in the palm of your hand. Our nine inch Deion dicks are warm to the touch and will leave you satisfied every time. Put it anywhere for unmatched pleasure.*

"OH MY GOD!" I screamed as the pulsating vibrations turned into sonic booms that rolled up my thigh before exploding inside of me. Everything went silent as my body convulsed and tensed. Lost in a stupor I couldn't tell you if Deion came or not. I remember the words "I fucking love you," being uttered but I couldn't tell you which one of us said it.

When I finally returned to my senses, I shivered now painfully aware of the prickly wet grass underneath my ass. Lifting me from the lawn Deion carried me into the house. In the shower his touch was gentle as he washed dirt and grass from my body. Night and day from the man that had just shoved my face in the sod and slapped my ass until it turned red.

In bed he made me his little spoon, his strong arms wrapped around me as his thumb absentmindedly circled my nipple. Other than the dust up with Grover Thornton this had been a day I would always remember. The fancy clothes and pampering and this brilliant necklace which I'd had Deion place back around my neck once we got out of the shower. And on top of all that I was getting paid while this man was spoiling me rotten. I'd do all this shit for free.

"What do you want from me, Sloane?"

"I want everything you have. But I'll settle for what you're willing to give," I joked.

"You shouldn't have to settle for anything."

I hoisted a lazy shoulder. "I'm used to it."

"Just because that's the way it's always been doesn't mean that's the way it has to be."

I turned so I could see his face. *Where was this coming from?* "Don't do that. Don't promise things. We had an agreement. Don't make me want for more."

Deion cupped my face in his hand. "What if I want to give—"

"Please Deck." I pressed my finger to his mouth. "Please. Just this. I'm happy with just this."

I'm sure his intentions were good. We'd just had really great sex and he was in his feelings. Sex did that, it clouded your judgment and would have you believing that someone was your soulmate because when you were together, you breathed heavy and made funny faces. I didn't need declarations of love or plans for the future. I was content with living in the moment with the understanding that, like all things, this fake relationship had an expiration date.

"OK, just this." His roan eyes were delicate as his lips touched down onto mine.

# DEION

SLOANE SLEPT PEACEFULLY NEXT TO ME BUT I WASN'T SO lucky. Leaving the bedroom, I retrieved our forgotten clothes and set her cell phone at her bedside along with a bottle of water because she often woke up thirsty in the middle of the night. *My fake girlfriend doesn't want to be my real girlfriend. What does that mean?* Was I reading this situation all wrong? I thought she liked being with me. But maybe this was just a business transaction with sex being a fringe benefit.

In less than a month I'd professed my love to Sloane and she ignored it both times. Settling back into bed, I tried to get some sleep. Tomorrow was Sunday with no Ramblers games and no practice. Hopefully, Sloane and I could spend the day together, maybe pick up Ace and go play mini golf. I wanted her to want that. But it appeared she was fine with the randomness of whatever this was.

Shutting my eyes, I attempted to block out the adverse thoughts. I was being naive. This was nothing more than an exceptional lay. Sex with Sloane was without a doubt the best I'd ever had, I mean by leaps and bounds. Sloane was vocal telling me exactly what she needed. She made me work for it, often teasing me until I was begging for release. Most importantly, she didn't kink shame me. Nothing was too weird. When I asked her to stroke me with her feet, she didn't bat an eye. After expressing my desire to eat off her body she ordered sushi, stripped naked, and allowed me to savor strategically placed maki rolls between eating her out. I could not lose this woman.

I awoke to the shrill piercing noise of Sloane's chosen ringtone. It sounded like a howler monkey. Sloane stirred next to me fumbling for her phone in the dark.

"Hello?" she answered, her voice sounding dry. Good thing I left that bottle of water for her. "Who? … What has he done now?"

My ears perked up thinking something may be up with Ace.

"No, don't call the cops. I'll be there." Sloane sprang up searching for clothes.

This sounded serious.

"Monty, I said I'd be there, just give me thirty minutes."

Whoever was on the other end must have agreed because Sloane ended the call rushing to the bathroom.

Pulling myself up from the bed, I followed her, finding her taking a piss. "What's going on?" I asked.

"It's my father." She yawned, rubbing at her eyes.

"Is he alright?"

"He's about to get his legs broken." Flushing, she headed to the sink to wash her hands and splash water on her face. "Is my overnight bag still in the car?"

"No, I brought it in."

Brushing past me she found the bag in the closet, pulling items from it she got dressed. "Can you call me a RideX?"

"No, I'll just drive you." I offered, turning on the closet light.

Sloane squinted her eyes adjusting to the brightness. "It's late. I can't ask you to do that."

"I'm not just letting you leave the house in some strange car at one in the morning," I said, pulling on sweatpants.

"Deion, I can handle this." She sounded tired and in no condition to be alone.

"I'm coming with you." My tone was final. I wasn't going back and forth on this.

It was obvious from her rigid jaw and pursed lips she wanted to object. Sliding into her off-brand Uggs, she acquiesced.

In the car, Sloane fed me directions until I pulled into a parking lot miles away from the strip. The lot was half empty with a small group of questionable individuals hanging outside smoking. A sign overhead hummed softly as the lights flickered. The sign should have read Fates Casino but the letter E was burned out so the neon sign glowed Fats Casino. Exiting the car, we made our way to the entrance passing by a couple who were stumbling toward the shady motel a stone's throw away.

Inside, the cold air laced with nicotine slapped me in the face. It was darker inside than out and it took a minute for my eyes to adjust. Reaching for Sloane's hand, I followed her lead. We moved past a bank of slot machines and across the gaming floor with gamblers slumped over tables or counting their dwindling chips. Sloane stopped at large wooden double doors guarded by a man that was more fat than muscle.

"Can you tell Monty that Sloane is here?" she ordered gruffly.

"Who."

"Sloane, Stanley's daughter, he's expecting me."

The broad backed fella communicated with someone through an earpiece before opening the door and letting us through. We traversed a long hall at the end of which was a steep staircase. At the bottom of that staircase, we were confronted with another door and a final security check that included a pat down before gaining access to the inner sanctum. This room was ten times darker and smokier than the main floor. It also offered a stale, cool dampness as if mold had set in.

"You're late," a short man, with a pageboy hat and a polo shirt that was several sizes too small for his belly, said.

"What can I tell you, there was a shit ton of traffic," Sloane lied.

"You enlisting security now?" The hobbit pointed in my direction. "Sloane I've known you since you were a little girl no need for the lanky muscle."

"He's my ride. I don't need a bodyguard. I can whoop your ass all on my own."

Monty kissed his teeth. "I'm sure you could, sweetheart."

He gave Sloane a lecherous stare that caused my

blood to boil but I remained quiet.

"Where is he?"

Monty made his way to the back of the room where a man was propped against the wall bleeding from his head.

Sloane gasped, shooting Monty an icy glare. "You beat him up?"

"Like I said you were late."

Kneeling, she cradled her father's face. "Dad it's me. Are you OK?"

"Baby girl, where you been hiding?" His voice was labored and his right eye twitched with every breath. "Come to … you come to bail your old man out?"

Standing, Sloane's gaze slammed into Monty. "How much?"

"Five thousand."

"Dollars?" I said, my tone incredulous.

"No five thousand beanie babies. Where the fuck did you get this guy?" Monty coughed out a laugh.

Grabbing her arm, I pulled her across the room. "Sloane you are not about to pay five thousand dollars for your father's fuck up."

"When did I ask you for your advice, hmm?" She tilted her head with a cold stare.

"This is suspect. How do you know Monty's on the up and up? Maybe it's not five thousand dollars. Did you ever stop to think he could be lying to you?"

"My dad's bleeding from the head, what other options do I have? Like what … do you want me to review the books … conduct a gotdamn audit?"

"I just don't want you getting swindled."

She released a mirthless laugh, "I'm Stanley Kaplan's daughter my whole life has been one long con." Wrestling her arm from my grasp she walked away.

"Can I write you a check?" Sloane asked.

"No sugarface, Kaplan checks are no good here. Thank your father and your brothers for that."

Her shoulders rounded into a heap. "Okay I'll just have to move some money from my savings to my checking account. It should just take a minute."

Clearing my throat, I pulled out my black card and handed it to Monty.

"No, absolutely not." She pressed a hard palm into my chest. "I'm not asking you to do this, I have the money. I don't need your help." When she made no headway with me she turned to Monty. "Don't swipe that card."

"Too late." Monty handed me back my card and even provided a receipt. "Pleasure doing business with you as always."

Sloane's head jerked from Monty to me. The expression on her face was perturbed and I braced myself for an expletive-filled tongue lashing in which she called me all types of descriptive and colorful words. But she did none of that, with a long swipe of her head she focused her attention toward her father, struggling to help him to his feet. Stepping in, I placed my arm around him supporting his weight. Back at the car Sloane appeared depleted. All the fight she had in that dark, smoky room evaporated.

As I started the car Sloane meekly said, "I will pay you back. I promise."

# SLOANE

My father was belligerent the entire drive home. Like we didn't just save his ass from a trip to the ER. At my apartment complex, Deion helped as we struggled to get my dad up the stairs while he sang his rendition of "Fuck the Police" by N.W.A at the top of his lungs at three in the morning. Safely inside my apartment, Deck deposited my dad on the couch while I pulled out the first aid kit to attend to his wounds.

"Sloane, who the hell is this negro and why is he so tall?"

"He's my friend," I said, removing the cap from the rubbing alcohol bottle and squirting some on a cotton ball.

"Well, I don't like the way your friend is eyeballing me."

"My *friend* just paid your gambling debt." I pressed the cotton ball to his temple and took great satisfaction when he grimaced in pain.

"I was doing just fine before you showed up," he said, through clenched teeth.

"Just fine? Just fine? I found you in a crumpled heap on the floor."

"Maybe you should have left me there." He snapped his fingers at Deion, like douchebags do when they're trying to get a waiter's attention. "Hey Chewbacca, make yourself useful and pour me a drink."

"I'll get you some water," Deion said, heading toward the kitchen.

"I don't want no water. Pour me a glass of vodka. Sloane keeps a bottle of the cheap stuff in the fridge."

Deion shot back, "It's water or you can die of thirst."

"He's an asshole," my father whispered under his breath so only I could hear.

Turning his attention back to me, my dad started to do what he always did, make hollow promises. "I know I've let you down baby girl but I'm gonna pay you back every penny I swear."

My father owed me far more than the five thousand from tonight. I'd been bailing him out for years never once seeing a dime of my money returned. Correction, one time he gifted me two tickets to the Anjeni concert front row seats. I don't know who he scammed to get them but I gladly accepted and Tammie and I had a blast singing and dancing our hearts out.

Deion returned with the water and my father accepted it with a scowl before guzzling it down in one long gulp.

"If it's alright with you I think I'll crash here tonight," my father informed me.

The alcohol, adrenaline, and other illegal substances were wearing off, and as I pressed the bandage to his forehead his body slumped, his eyes drooping closed. Removing his shoes, I retrieved a blanket from the linen closet and spread it out over him. This string of actions were like muscle memory to me. I lost count of how many times my dad would come home wasted when I was growing up. He could barely walk straight as he'd stagger into the front door. After fussing at us he'd eventually pass out on the couch and I'd take off his shoes, pull or push him until he was laying on his stomach and cover him with a blanket.

When I was younger, I feared he wouldn't come home and when I got older, I started wishing that he didn't. My daddy never hit me ... well once when he caught me kissing Jason Evers from down the street. But other than that he never laid a finger on me and still I lived most of my childhood in fear of him. Even now as an adult he scared me, although it was painfully obvious he was a pathetic old man with addiction issues.

After washing my hands, I pulled Deion into the bedroom. Retrieving my check book from my sock drawer, I cut Deion a check for five thousand dollars. Unlike my daddy I paid my debts, unless you were a bill collector then you could rot in hell.

"Don't worry about that," Deion said.

"I'm not a mooch. Take your money." I shook the check in his face.

He took it, folding it in half, he shoved it in his pocket. "Is your dad always like that?"

"What? Drunk, pitiful, and combative. Yes, those are essentially his three moods."

Deion removed his slides. I didn't realize this was gonna be a sleepover but I didn't object because the last thing I wanted was to be alone, with my father or my thoughts. I'm sure Deion was asking himself what he'd gotten wrapped up in. My father was a strong, abrasive personality. If Deck thought I was bad, my father was ten times worse.

Calls in the wee hours of the night were not uncommon. Sometimes it was a call from my father, excited because he'd hit the jackpot or was cashing out his chips. Those calls were often followed shortly after with some sob story about that windfall being suddenly gone. My father would blame some outside force because it was always someone else, never Stanley Kaplan. Unlike my father, I knew I was the problem and I owned it. My asshole behavior was baked into the cake. So if you didn't like chocolate cake filled with putrid cream filling, a bitter after taste, and colorful ratchet sprinkles on top you were out of luck.

I moved around my bedroom pretending to fold clothes and rearrange items on my night stand.

"Are you OK?" Deion asked, following my every move like an undercover cop.

"I'm fine." I brushed my hair, which was now half straight and half frizzy, from my eyes.

Deck's face was lined with concern. It threw me for a loop because I was used to people looking at me with pity, not compassion. I was tired. So tired of pretending this was normal and I was OK. *It's no big deal that my father's a total fuck up. It didn't matter that he forgets every birthday. And that he only praised me when I was doing something illegal. It was perfectly fine that I couldn't count on anyone but myself.* A sorrowful moan crawled up my throat and slid out of my mouth catching both Deion and I by surprise.

Cupping my hand over my mouth, I tried to stop the years of hurt and disappointment that I'd stowed just underneath the surface. My body shook violently as I attempted to regain my composure. All it took was one tear, my eyes twitched as I dared not blink because if I did, the tears pooling at the bottom of my lower lid would spill over. When Deion stood, presumably to console me it was game over. Tears ran down my face like a dam no longer able to hold back the strong current.

Deion attempted to pull me into a hug but I pushed him as hard as I could like a rabid dog who was cornered, snarling at anyone who got too close. "Please don't. I can't ... please ..." I managed to cough out between sobs. Even though I rejected his touch I wanted so badly for him to hold me and make promises we both knew he couldn't keep. Instead, I sunk to the carpet, tugging on my lower lip as my emotions got the better of me.

Dizziness and tears made it hard to see. My thoughts were scattered and even when I tried really hard to focus, all I could feel was an emptiness so pronounced it seemed to claw at my chest with a consistent pang. The sobs ripped through me with such intensity, breathing was now difficult.

Deion sat next to my heap of flesh on the floor.

Extending his hand to me again, he begged, "Please baby, just let me help you through this."

It was clear he had no intention of leaving my side like so many others had in the past. That's a lie, most of my ex's fought hard to be with me but I pushed them all away. I was good with the laughs, I was great with the sex, but it was their need for me to open up and be vulnerable that I couldn't stomach. Why open yourself up to hurt when you can just start over again. Clean slate.

I didn't want Deion to leave and so for the first time in a long time I did the unthinkable … I trusted him. Crawling onto his lap I buried my face into his chest. The tears were now coming faster than I could wipe them away. Deion's embrace was like a well-worn over-sized sweatshirt immediately offering comfort as his imposing palm rubbed my back. He just held me as I lost my shit on the bedroom floor, tears staining his T-shirt. Deion didn't say anything in an attempt to make me feel better. He just let me dwell. Dwell in the hurt, pain, and disappointment until I fell asleep from exhaustion in the kindness of his arms.

THE LIGHT FROM A NEW DAY CAME MUCH TOO FAST FOR MY liking. By my estimates I'd only gotten two hours of sleep. Sweeping my hand across Sloane's side of the bed, I found it empty. I'd never witnessed Sloane cry, not that I didn't think she was capable of emotion, but she walked around like the school bully ready to pummel any kid that looked at her sideways.

In anger management we're learning that anger is often a guise for unprocessed hurt. Anger is used as a coping mechanism to shield us from experiencing our true emotions, like fear, vulnerability, and disappointment. When something doesn't go as planned, we lash out with violent words sometimes with fist, or in Sloane's case a car.

Last night I felt a bit useless because she was hurting and I desperately wanted to make it better. The way Sloane's life was set up it was clear she was expected to be strong all the time for everybody. I just hoped she knew she didn't have to play the Karen White role and be the superwoman for me. She could be soft and unsure and I'd love her regardless. Because I was falling in love with her. Honestly, I wasn't falling anymore I was fully in love. Like Jodeci's "Forever My Lady," nah scratch that my love was deeper more rooted than that it was more like Lenny Williams, "Cause I Love You." That soulful stick to your ribs type of love.

And I'd probably end up begging and whining just like Lenny over this woman. A still voice whispered, *she's the one.* The declaration caused me to jump from the bed hoping to escape the unfamiliar thought. I stepped into my sweatpants, finding Sloane's check in my pocket. Ripping the check I placed it on her bedside table. Her money was no good with me, especially when I knew it was in limited supply. After draining the main vein, I found Sloane and her father in the kitchen. Stanley was stabbing at his eggs with his fork.

"Morning," I said, looking over to Sloane who would not meet my eyes.

"Well hot damn. I thought you looked familiar last night. I was just too twisted to place it," Stanley said.

There was discoloration and swelling around his eye from where Monty's fist had connected with his face.

"Dad, this is—"

"I know who the fuck this is. D'Money McCabe. Number twenty-seven for the Pistons, Timberwolves, and Ramblers," he said with a click of his tongue.

"Nice to meet you, sir."

Sloane handed me a plate with eggs and two toasted slices of Ezekiel bread which I suspected she'd purchased just for me because she didn't fuck with that healthy shit.

"Is it? Because I vaguely recall you grumbling while loading my drunk ass into a car last night."

"Glad I was able to help." I sat on the couch. The stench of booze escaping from Stanley's pores was a deterrent and I did not need to get any closer.

"Hmm," Stanley scratched at his salt and pepper beard. It was more of a struggle beard, because it was sparse in places. "Did Sloane tell you about me?"

"Yes, Dad I told him you're addicted to booze, cards, and loose women." Sloane moved around her small kitchen placing items back in the fridge.

Stanley's response was to suck his teeth while patting at the pockets of his jeans. "You seen my cigarettes, baby girl?"

"No, I have not and there is no smoking allowed on the premises."

Next to her father Sloane came off as an upstanding law-abiding citizen.

"So what, are you and number twenty-seven having a sleepover?"

"He's an acquaintance."

"Nice to have acquaintances with deep pockets." Stanley's eyes flickered over me like Bugs Bunny in the cartoons when he spots an oasis in the desert.

"I'm gonna call you a RideX," Sloane said.

Stanley moved from the small dining table in the kitchen to sit next to me on the couch, assaulting my nostrils with the scent of Newports, sweat, and Hennessy.

"Just like you I've built a reputation for myself in

this city. And just like you, that reputation ain't worth shit." He tagged my shoulder with his hand.

"Dad, chill."

"Did she tell you your ball handling sucks?"

"Stanley." Sloane's voice sounded like she was on her final warning.

"Well shit, someone has to tell him because it's clear the coaches aren't. And I heard he graduated from Duke with a 2.9 so he may not be able to comprehend the articles that outline all the ways his game could improve."

Stanley's intel was incorrect. I graduated with a 3.4, which was respectable for a man who was juggling school work, a toddler, and an active social life.

"Yes, she has. It's actually one of the first things she told me."

"That's my girl. Where's my hat?"

I watched from the balcony as Sloane walked her father to his RideX and made a big fuss telling the driver to take Stanley straight home with no stops.

She reentered the apartment apologizing. "I'm sorry, I know my dad can be …"

"An asshole?"

"I was gonna say douche but asshole works just as well."

"Have you thought about getting your dad into treatment?"

She counted out a list on her fingers. "One, treatment costs money. Two, the patient has to want to get better. Three, my father is entirely too old and too stubborn to learn any new tricks." She disappeared into the bedroom and I took the last few bites of my toast.

I was probably simplifying things too much. Sloane was right and she knew her father better than I did. Stanley Kaplan gave off big scorched earth energy. The type of person who would make everyone pay for forcing him into a treatment center he didn't want to be at. But I found it hard to believe he wasn't exhausted from always disappointing others and himself.

Sloane stormed back into the living room, her hands balled into fist. "What's this?" She opened her hand to reveal the ripped check.

Hoisting a blasé shoulder I said, "Come on, Sloane."

"Deion, I don't do charity. I'm not some exercise in philanthropy that you get to just write off."

"I'm trying to help."

"I don't fucking need your help," she yelled, tossing the torn check in my face.

My shoulders took a nosedive as I watched the pieces fall to the carpet like confetti. "Damnit Sloane, I'm not the fucking enemy."

"You just think you can throw money at any problem. Your father's a junkie … send him to rehab. You need a girlfriend so you can pretend you have your shit together … you'll just buy one of those too."

"OK when exactly did you climb onto this high horse because the last time I checked that *money* was being deposited into your checking account."

Was this the same woman that made me pay one hundred dollars a pop to talk to her months ago at the club? Trust me I respected her hustle. That hustle mentality is what inspired this fake dating gig in the first place.

Standing and venturing closer but far enough away so she couldn't punch me I asked, "What do you need from me?"

"I can take care of myself. And you have to let me. I don't want to rely on someone who's just passing through."

"What if I'm not passing through? I don't know, maybe I'm looking for a place to call home."

"Deck, I'm a thirty-four-year-old single mom who lives paycheck to paycheck and has to pretend I no habla inglés when bill collectors call. That is not the foundation you build a home on."

"Maybe I'm looking for a fixer upper."

Sloane's brows knitted as she placed her hand on her hip. "People buy fixer uppers for dirt cheap and then flip them selling to the highest bidder."

Tossing my arms up I surrendered. "I just like being with you and I want to continue to do that as long as it's OK with you."

Her stiffened back appeared to curve, her lips no longer in a tight wad. "I guess," were the only words she was willing to offer.

Moving closer, I leaned in until my nose was resting on the top of her head. Her hair smelled slightly of cigarettes from our time in the casino. "Not everything has to be a fight. I want to take care of you because it makes me happy. Because what I feel for you is ..." I forced the words to die in my throat. Sloane didn't respond to flowery words or declarations of unwavering love. I wrapped my arms around her determined to show her. Show her how much she meant and how much I cared until she could no longer deny it.

"Thank you," she said.

"For what?"

"For sticking around despite my best efforts to push you away."

"I'm a glutton for punishment." Tilting her chin until our eyes locked I said, "Hey, grab an overnight bag for Ace. Let's pick him up from his dad's and head back to my place. We can watch movies and BBQ or I'll have my assistant grab us some food."

Sloane's hands were underneath my shirt, her long fingernails giving my back a good scratch. "Can we get donuts?"

"Sure, we can stop for donuts. I'll even let you pay," I teased.

"Umm, no habla inglés."

# SLOANE

"AND WHY DO YOU THINK YOU GOT SO MAD?" SHELLY, THE anger management group leader asked.

"The coach wouldn't play my kid," Glen said. He was a bear of a man whose anger issues landed him in jail.

"So you beat up the pee wee league coach?" I asked.

"My son is good and deserves to play."

"Your son is eight and you overreacted."

"Oh, I'm sorry, should I have tried mowing him over with my car like you?"

Shelly clapped her hands. "Enough of that. Remember this is a no judgment zone. We're here to help each other, not attack."

"Sloane, isn't wrong," Deck announced from the other side of the circle. "We all ride hard for our kids, I get that. But most of these coaches work for little or no pay. In the pee wee league, it's more about learning the fundamentals and the importance of being a team player."

A subtle smile played across my face. We love a supportive king.

No one in group knew about our arrangement or that just an hour before I arrived Deion's dick was so far down my throat, I struggled to breathe. When we were at group, we pretended we didn't know each other. I don't think there were any rules forbidding fraternizing outside of meetings like with other groups but we were attempting to keep our real life business out of the gossip blogs.

Which was probably a futile task. Pictures of Deion and I were posted on social media sites and sports blogs with headlines like "Rambler Nation in Love" or "The Baller and His Cocktail Waitress." When I agreed to pretend we were an item, I failed to consider the publicity. The stories quoting sources close to the couple. And the paparazzi pictures of us doing mundane tasks like grabbing a frozen yogurt or attending a friend's party. One story even made mention of Ace. Which angered me. I thought kids were supposed to be off limits.

I don't think either one of us anticipated how hard the media outlets would run with this story. Maybe because it had been a minute since Deion was photographed with the same woman. Or maybe it was the fact I was a cocktail waitress. A lot of the online coverage was calling it a Cinderella story. I wasn't sure if I should be flattered or insulted. Whatever it was, this fake love affair was gaining traction.

After group, Deion ambled over to my car, his strong confident strides ignited the bundle of nerves in my pants. "Are you all packed?" he asked.

My fingers twitched as I resisted the urge to touch him. "Yes."

We were headed to All-Star Weekend in Houston, Deion's hometown. The past few months of stellar game play coupled with mostly positive media coverage, landed Deion on the All-Star team for the West. This honor was decided primarily by the fans. Deion's plan of being the player who fought hard on the court and loved harder off it was working.

"Is Ace excited?"

"It's all he's talked about."

"Are you excited?" He reached for a strand of my hair rubbing it between his fingers before quickly dropping his hand and taking a step back.

I would only offer a coy smile. You needed to keep men on their toes. If you let them get too comfortable, they'd often take you for granted.

"My mother's looking forward to meeting you."

My heart dropped with a clunk, mothers were my kryptonite. Ace's grandmother hated me because I refused to baby her grown ass son. I wasn't interested in raising an adult. And a romantic relationship shouldn't be like a second job. I'm not working all night and then coming home to cook and clean while the able-bodied male lounged on the couch playing video games.

"You told your mother about me?" My brows knitted in confusion.

"Kind of had no choice seeing how pictures of you at games and us at events are all over the internet."

When Deck invited Ace and I to All-Star Weekend it wasn't an automatic yes for me. For the most part I'd been able to keep Ace out of the spotlight and brush aside his questions. If I went to the All-Star game without Ace he would hate me forever so I sat him down and was honest with him. And by honest, I mean I told him a sliver of the truth. Deion was my friend and I was helping him to improve his self-esteem which also helped to improve his game play and because we were seen together often, some media outlets and fans assumed we were dating.

Ace was smart for a ten-year-old and Deion had spent the night on more than one occasion. My son had to suspect there was more to the story but he took my explanation at face value and was rewarded with a trip to Houston and primo seats to all the events over the long weekend.

"Well hopefully I don't disappoint her." When I signed up for this I didn't know I'd be meeting and lying to mothers.

"You don't ever disappoint." His hand fell to the waistband of my yoga pants. "Follow me home." His voice was deep and raspy and his eyes looked at me like I was standing in this parking lot completely naked.

As much as I wanted to go from anger management to physical therapy, I had some errands I needed to complete. "We leave in five hours and I still need to finish packing and grab a few toiletries."

"Make a list, I'll give it to my assistant."

"No, I've gotta go. I'll make it up to you tonight."

His creamy gaze dissipated as he backed away.

"I'll text you when we're on our way to your place," I offered before jumping in my car and pulling away.

I made a quick stop at the grocery store and then headed to my father's mobile home park. This community was actually one of the nicer ones. Well maintained and clean. Each trailer was painted a bright, bold color like something out of Candyland. Parking my car in front of my dad's shamrock-green trailer, I grabbed the groceries and knocked on the glass of one of the large windows. It took Stanley several minutes to open the door.

"Well look who came slumming." His tone was harsher than usual. "Where's your boyfriend?"

I pushed passed him and choked on the stale smoky air inside his unit. Setting the groceries on the counter, I walked through the narrow trailer, opening windows to allow for ventilation.

"This place is a mess," I said.

"I've been busy. We can't all have maids and butlers to look after us like you."

"Chet said you almost got arrested the other night."

"Almost doesn't count. I talked my way out of it that's all that matters."

"Dad you are too old for this shit."

"I'm not afraid of a little jail time. Shoot, they lock me up and I can visit your brother."

My oldest brother, Stanley Junior, but we all called him Lee, was in jail for check fraud. He deposited fake checks into random accounts and then attempting to make purchases before anyone caught on. It was stupid and he'd left a paper trail a mile long and was now serving a three-year sentence in the Southern Desert Correctional Facility.

"I don't think Lee is interested in babysitting his father in prison." I opened his fridge and just as I suspected, it was empty with the exception of a half-eaten sheet cake and a case of those flavored quarter waters Chet, Lee, and I would drink when we were kids. "What, are you just living off of sugar, liquor, and cigarette fumes?"

"I was planning on making a store run today," he protested.

"Well, no need to bother I got you some frozen dinners and ramen noodles. And a jug of water." I pulled the jug from one of the bags unsealing the top. "Drink it all and when you're done fill it up and drink some more."

My father complied, draining half the jug before wiping his lips with the back of his hand. "I was scrolling through the internet and seen a picture of you and that ball player. You were all dressed up and your neck and wrist were sparkling. How long have you two been a thing?"

"It's not a thing. Like I told you Deion is my friend."

"The way he had his arm wrapped around you it seems like he's interested in more."

"Stanley, you know how the gossip sites can be. They see us together and then jump to conclusions and claim we're an item. I can assure you we are not."

"So you're not dating, because the caption called you his girlfriend?" His eyebrow inched up his forehead.

"Like I said assumptions are not facts." I moved around his tiny kitchen putting items away. I wasn't discussing Deion with him.

Stanley rubbed his whiskers. "Fact, you showed up

at Monty's place with Deion. Fact, Deion paid my debt making things square with me and Monty."

"Yeah, until you screw that up again," I murmured under my breath while adding canned goods to his bare cabinets.

He inched closer to me. "Fact, I may have been drunk and bruised but I distinctly remember being loaded into a fancy car with all the bells and whistles. And lastly the next morning Deion came slinking out of your bedroom. That's a whole lot of coincidences."

"Drink more water," I ordered.

"You think I care about you and some loser NBA player?" he spat out.

"He's not a loser. And you have no place to call other people out. You're an old man whose entire life has been one failure after the other," I snapped back.

"Not my entire life." He brushed his fingers across my cheek.

I pulled away but my frustration was ebbing. "I got your favorite ice cream, Rocky Road."

Stanley choked out a laugh. "The irony is not lost on me."

Despite my best efforts a smile crept over my face. "Ace and I will be out of town for a few days so don't get into any trouble."

"Where are you headed?"

"Just an impromptu road trip. We'll probably visit some national parks." I couldn't tell my father about the All-Star game. If I did it would confirm his beliefs about the nature of my relationship with Deion but more likely he'd try to wrangle his way to Houston claiming he was Deion's father-in-law to be.

---

DEION RENTED A PRIVATE JET TO FLY US TO HOUSTON. Private jets cost upward of five thousand an hour. I knew because I Googled the information before takeoff. When Ace wasn't staring out of the windows, he was showing Destiny how to capture a scorpion without getting stung in the Animal Crossing game. Raphael was dead to the world, spread out in his seat with a sleep mask and earphones on.

"When's the last time you played in an All-Star game?" I asked Deion whose long limbs were stretched out and crossed at the ankles.

Deck rubbed the back of his neck. "I won the three-point contest three seasons ago. But played … that would be a never."

"It's OK if people are late to the Deck show, they have their tickets now and you are not disappointing them."

Deion leveled up these past few months. He worked hard in the gym and was constantly reviewing game highlights. I could listen to him talk for a full thirty minutes about dribble pacing, guarding the cylinder, and the help side of the court before my eyes glazed over. But it was clear his pilot light had been reignited. He was having fun again and it showed on the court.

He was an aggressive player, fighting for every ball. Deion was the type of player who sacrificed his entire body for the game and that left him with a knee he had to ice every night and a curved pinky finger he never allowed to properly heal. He was posting big numbers and teams were scrambling trying to find a way to defend him. On Game Center the other night Surge DeVoe from the Sacramento Kings said the player he studied the most before a head-to-head match was Deion McCabe.

For some reason Deck attributed his new found positive notoriety to me. Which was a silly belief because all I was doing was flying in private jets and schmoozing with rich, entitled men who seemed to get off on me calling them out. After the dinner at Grover Thornton's home, word traveled fast in the basketball community about the woman who left Thornton speechless. Because of my stunt Deion was on the owner's permanent shit list. He'd also gotten his ass chewed out by his coach.

What Deion accomplished these past few months was all him. His hard work, his newfound optimistic outlook, and him actually listening and walking away with useful takeaways from our anger management classes.

Wrapping my hand around his, I gave it a squeeze. "I'm proud of you, Deck."

His eyes slammed into me, his body stiffening as he took in my entire face. "Is this altitude getting to you?" he teased me.

Pulling my hand away, I shoved him playfully before securing my earbuds in my ears and closing my eyes for the remainder of the flight.

When the plane touched down, I pulled my phone

from my purse, with airplane mode disabled my cell was flooded with notifications.

I clicked on a text message from Chet.

Chet: Listen I don't know what's going on with you and that basketball player but Dad talked to a reporter from Vegas 411 and now he has dollar signs in his eyes.

I pulled up the website for Vegas 411 and the first article was an exclusive interview with the father of NBA superstar Deion McCabe's girlfriend.

Stanley Kaplan, the patriarch of the Kaplan family, had sold me the fuck out.

# DEION

FROM THE WAY DESTINY AND ACE REACTED TO OUR HOTEL suite it was clear they approved. We were staying in the heart of Houston. I picked this place because it was walking distance from the Toyota arena with restaurants and shopping in close proximity in every direction, which would keep Sloane and the kids entertained while I was at practice or fielding promotional interviews. Then there were the pools and spa resort downstairs for quick relaxation.

The room was large with three bedrooms and full living quarters with a kitchen and dining area. Concierge service was available twenty-four seven with room service or whatever else we might need delivered directly to our door. I'd also scheduled some surprises for Sloane. I wanted her to feel how much I appreciated her and my way of expressing it was by flexing my purchasing power. Raphael was in a room a few floors down, because I did not want his adult activities around the impressionable youth.

My phone dinged in my pocket. It had been a deluge of notifications since we'd landed. Something about an interview Sloane's father gave to Vegas 411. As we taxied to the gate, Sloane's big brown eyes practically pleaded for my forgiveness. I squeezed her knee and told her we'd talk about it later. She spent the ride to the hotel reading the interview and the way her hand was balled into a tight fist, I got the impression Stanley had a lot to get off his chest.

Ace ran from room to room announcing the first thing he saw. "There's a fridge with all kinds of candy, chips, and drinks. The curtains in the bedroom open and close with the touch of a button. There's a pool on the balcony. A POOL."

I'm glad Sloane agreed to bring him along. I knew he'd get a kick out of this four-day weekend. If he got this hype over the room, wait until I introduced him to Aldridge Mosley, the NBA phenom everyone wanted a piece of. Destiny always tagged along for All-Star Weekend since she was a little girl. Even when I wasn't playing, All-Star Weekend was dedicated to some of the best in the league and celebrating our collective love of the sport, was always a good time.

While Sloane settled into our bedroom, I convinced Raphael to take Destiny and Ace off our hands for a bit. He complained but seeing how I'd paid for the jet and his room for the weekend, he owed me.

"If you're under twenty-one follow me." Raphael announced wrangling the kids out of the suite.

When Sloane reentered the living room their absence was the first thing she noticed. "Where's Ace and Destiny?"

"They headed downstairs to check out the hotel with Raphael."

Sloane gave her head a slow thoughtful nod. "Listen Deion … my dad—"

"He talked to the press. How bad was it?"

"He doesn't know about our arrangement. It was mostly him sharing made up stories from my childhood and claiming you're the son he always wanted. Which is fucked up because he has two sons."

I scrubbed my face.

"I should have seen this coming. If there is money to be made Stanley will be first in line and he'll willingly use his children as pawns if need be."

I bounced my shoulders. "What's done is done. Can't cry over spilled milk."

"I warned you I come from a long line of scam artist. And we are always on the lookout for the next grift."

"Does that include you?"

"Sometimes. I never claimed to be perfect."

"When did I say I was looking for perfect?" I slipped my hands in my pockets. "I trust you with my life."

Her brows slammed together. "Are you stupid?"

"No, but I am crazy about you."

She shrugged off my words. "I'm sorry about Stanley. I'll talk to him."

"I've met your father, remember. I know he's not easily controlled. Don't let your dad's little stunt ruin our trip. We're gonna have a good weekend." I was not going to lay the sins of the father at her feet. Plus, Stanley's interview was benign and in all honesty it helped to support our lies. To hear Stanley tell it I'd met my girl-friend's eccentric father and we'd become fast friends. "Raphael and the kids should be gone for another forty-five minutes. He wanted to give us time to talk."

"Forty-five whole minutes. Wow."

I bridged the gap between Sloane and I in two long strides. We clawed at one another's clothes, frantic for our bodies to connect. Lifting her upward, I hoisted her legs over my shoulders, anticipating the taste I French-kissed her engorged lips. From the first kiss Sloane's body soared backward and I balanced her weight while she writhed in the air. It wasn't long before she expressed her appreciation, it started out soft as her breathing changed from a low delicate hum to a stut-tered exhale. Gaining tempo as I swiped my tongue over her folds, greedily swallowing her juices which now soaked my beard.

When I dipped my tongue in and out of her warm center Sloane began to sing, her voice elevated as she called on heaven in disbelief. Backing up, I braced her against a wall to prevent her from falling from her sacred perch. I loved the way her body responded to my touch and it made me work harder to make her come. She rotated her hips and ass while my tongue flicked her clit, working in unison to bring her a much-needed release. The last thing I wanted her thinking about was her flake of a father or the media's obsession with our relationship. All that mattered was us in this moment. I wanted to suck and fuck all of her fears and anxiety away until her thoughts were so carefree she practically floated.

Sloane's leg twitched uncontrollably while verbally reinforcing I'd hit the right spot. "Yes, Deck, just like that, right there." Her hand stroked my head as a deep guttural moan crawled up her throat. I held her closer and she shook and cussed her way to ecstasy.

When she fell silent, I helped her dismount. The trance-like gaze in her mink-colored eyes told me she was ready to return the favor.

"Thank you," Her voice was as smooth as velvet. Lowering my head, she tasted me and herself at the same time. Her hand found my dick and she began to stroke me slowly.

Leading her to the bedroom, I draped her over the loveseat and fucked her from behind within an inch of her life. I performed deep thrust which left her babbling and incoherent. Wrapping my hand around her neck, I applied delicate pressure, tightening my grip with each pump. The way Sloane begged for me sent shivers down my spine. But she didn't have to beg because my dick and my heart were all hers.

Sloane's body crumbled underneath mine, exhausted from my urgent thrust. I hooked my arm through hers, pinning her in place against me. Sloane's jaw dropped open and she emoted love sounds like I never heard before. I kissed her back as she gained her second wind bucking her pussy over my shaft.

"I love being inside you," I moaned.

Sloane's core contracted around me. With one final thrust we both crashed into euphoric release until we tumbled to the floor. When her eyes uncrossed, she examined my face and gently tugged my beard.

"Are you alright?" I asked planting kisses along her jaw line.

The glint in her eyes was diffused and dreamy. As if she was still caught up in our love-making haze. "Is it weird that this fake relationship is better than all of my real ones?" She asked.

"Maybe because there isn't any pressure. We're just allowed to enjoy one another."

I wanted to tell her everyday could be like this. That nothing needed to change when the season ended. If she let me, I'd pamper and adore her, I'd support Ace and make sure they wanted for nothing. But Sloane warned me once that she didn't want promises. She just wanted the moments. This moment with our limbs entangled while she combed her fingers through my beard. This would have to be enough.

---

THE FIRST FULL DAY OF ALL-STAR WEEKEND WAS A BLUR. While Sloane and the kids enjoyed the NBA sponsored events, I was busy going from practice, to photo ops, to press events. At the final presser of the afternoon, I was in a panel interview with other players from the West Coast team, currently fielding questions about my improved game play.

"Deion, after this past season many counted you out as a serious ball handler. But this year your stats have consistently gone up, causing some to reminisce back to the Deion McCabe Timberwolves era. What do we owe to this resurgence?"

My relationship with the sports media had always been a contentious one because in my opinion, the press was on a gotcha mission. Constantly shining a light on my mistakes and rarely highlighting my success. *He's not like his father,* was a phrase that was synonymous with my name. *Deion McCabe, he is nothing like his father.* When it's a big time athlete the press gushes over them to the point of embarrassment. Workhorse players, like me, who sacrifice their bodies to the game, diving for balls, fighting for rebounds, hustling to the other end of the court to line up a dunk or alley oop, we're often an afterthought.

Because I was producing, people were taking notice and the press had to cover it. But that didn't mean they had to like it. That reporter just essentially said, "You were a trash player and now you're less of one. What happened?" The old Deion would have given him a piece of my mind, but the new, warm and fuzzy, Deion just smiled and answered his disrespectful question.

"I realized I needed to focus on the basics. Unfortunately, I allowed myself to get distracted by the wrong things. Situations that were beyond my control both on and off the court."

"What helped you find that focus, was it meditation or your faith?" another reporter called out.

I lifted a lazy shoulder. "It's been a combination of things, my teammates, creating a routine—"

"Did the new lady we've seen on your arm the past few months play any part in that?"

I let out a nervous chuckle. Talking about Sloane was always awkward because while we both agreed to the lie, I didn't want to push her further into the spotlight than she was comfortable with. Should I lean into it or play it cool? As far as everyone in this room was concerned, she was my girlfriend. The press was always in search of a sexy story angle even in sports. And Sloane, with her thick thighs, and smoldering smile made for a great story.

"Umm, yeah definitely she's one hell of a motivator that's for sure." I decided it was best to keep things neutral.

"Has Sloane helped you cope with the passing of your father," a voice in the back called out.

My Adams apple wobbled. "Ultimately time is helping with that but I won't deny it's nice to have a person I trust in my corner. Someone I can talk to when it's gets kind of dark."

"Your father was your mentor, isn't that correct?"

*There were three other guys on the panel why were all the personal questions being directed toward me?*

"My father was a mentor to a lot of people. For me he was my role model and my guide. I looked to him for wisdom because he'd been down this road before but mostly because he was my pops and my success and well-being was his priority."

"It's been over a year since the Legend Morris McCabe passed. What do you want to say to his fans all across the world?"

I scratched at my beard. "Morris McCabe wasn't just an amazing ball player he was a great man. I'm not saying he was perfect naturally we bumped heads from time to time. But if I inherited a fraction of his kindness and work ethic, I'm a lucky man."

"If your father was here today, what do you think he would say?"

My throat was raw with emotion. I didn't anticipate these types of questions. I'd never shied away from talking about my father with fans because they missed him just as much as I did. And in a way it was cathartic to hear them reminisce about his signature spinning dunk or the time he crossed over Pippen and shot an effortless three pointer to win the finals.

I cleared my throat. "Uhm … if my father was here today I hope he'd tell me he was proud of me." I tugged at the brim of my ball cap to shield detection of the moisture cresting my eyelids.

On the way back to the hotel I felt the weight of the past few weeks settling in on me. Since pushing this dating lie, my life was like a bullet train. Photo shoots, parties, enthusiastic fans who were waiting outside of the arena to get my autograph, not Pratt or one of the other players, but mine. If my father were still alive, I'm certain he wouldn't approve of the lie. He always told me my greatness came from within. But I secretly believed my success was intrinsically tied to the McCabe name and not my own God-given talent.

Was Sloane the key to my current success? No, not entirely. Maybe her true impact wasn't even ten percent. But when I was with her, I experienced a sense of calm I hadn't in a long time. And it wasn't because Sloane was level headed and Zen it was because she accepted me for exactly who I was. She wasn't repulsed by the dark and murky corners of my heart. Never once did she suggest I change who I was and I loved that for me. This past year everyone including myself thought I was broken. With Sloane's help I was realizing I was actually evolving and oftentimes growth is painful and scary. My father was gone and I was finally learning to be my own man.

My phone rang, pulling me from my thoughts, it was Raphael. "What's up?"

"Hey, are you good?"

"Why wouldn't I be good."

"I'm getting notifications on my phone about your emotional interview."

"There was no emotional interview."

"The interwebs are claiming you were crying."

"I didn't cry. I got a little choked up is all."

"Well if you need to talk. I'm here, Sloane's here—"

"Yeah, yeah, yeah. It's all good. Are you coming to dinner tonight?" I asked.

"With Mom … no."

"Come on man, I need you there."

"For what?"

"I just need you to help me divert some of the attention away from Sloane."

"So you want me to be the punching bag?"

"Yea, tell Mom you're thinking about moving to Belize or that you just met this awesome woman named Becky."

Raphael laughed. "That would send her over the edge."

"You know how she gets and Sloane isn't like other women I've dated."

"Yeah, because you're not actually dating her."

"It's complicated."

"No it's not, it's a verbal agreement with financial compensation."

"I just need all hands on deck. Your mother is nosy and she always has a tone to her questions. If she says the wrong thing Sloane's gonna call her out."

"Well truth be told, getting called to the carpet could do Mom some good."

"She's grieving."

"We're all grieving. She's just doing a piss poor job of it."

While the words were harsh, he wasn't wrong. Mom and I had that in common. Since my dad passed our mother had become clingy. More than normal. Growing up she was a stay-at-home mom. The type of mother with a color-coded calendar who drove me to basketball practice and Raphael to track all while squeezing in a manicure before picking us up and taking us to swimming lessons. Her family was her life.

She found joy in bragging about us. *Raphael is going to nationals and Deion made the high school basketball team and is playing as a starter which is rare for a freshman.* When we moved out, her energy shifted to my dad but now that he was gone, she was rudderless. I told her she needed to take up a hobby or go back to school, but she was content poking her nose in her children's business to our great dismay.

"Come to dinner, my treat. I need your level head."

Raphael released an agitated breath. "Your treat? Mom's cooking."

"Even more reason to come. You know you can't resist Mom's smothered pork chops."

"If I go you're introducing me to that cheerleader."

"No dude, I'm not playing matchmaker."

"All I'm asking for is a simple 'Have you met my brother.'"

Rolling my eyes, I agreed. "Fine, I'll introduce you but that's it." This wasn't the first time my brother asked me to hook him up with a cheerleader or reporter. Usually doing so got me burned when Raphael ghosted them and they came to me looking for answers.

"Good looking out." I could hear the smile in his voice and I didn't blame him, the cheerleader in question was fine as hell.

"So you'll be there?"

"Yes, and I'll keep Mom distracted."

"Great, a car will pick us up at six."

Back at the hotel I was hoping to get some downtime before we headed to my mother's house for a home-cooked meal. When the elevator doors opened Russ Howard the Houston Rocket's head coach stepped out.

"Hey Deck. It's good to see you again." He extended his hand giving mine a firm shake.

"I thought you hated these types of things?" I joked.

"I do, but I'm contractually obligated, seeing how we're the host city."

"You guys have had some tough breaks this season."

"We have. But once Marsh is all healed up we'll be looking to make a go at it next year."

"Don't tell me you're already giving up on this season, it's not even over."

"Between you and me. Marsh will need all summer to be at one hundred percent. So, unfortunately the Rockets aren't viable this year."

"Sorry to hear that." A chill coasted down my spine. Injuries were part and parcel in any professional sport but you never wanted to hear about a player being side-line due to one.

"But you … you've been out here playing like a beast. Isn't your contract up with the Ramblers at the end of the season?"

"Yep."

"Are you fielding any offers?"

"I've always believed in keeping my options open."

"Houston could be a great fit for you, Deck. You could play out your career where it all started."

Not gonna lie, that was my dream. To play my remaining seasons in my hometown. I probably had two, maybe three good years in me. Plus as a local, Houston fans have always shown me love.

"You offering me a contract?" I laughed.

"I'm offering you a sit down with general management. Maybe we could make some things move."

I pulled my face in surprise. "You have Brenden's number if you're serious."

"So you'd consider it?"

"Hell yeah I'd consider it. I'd be close to family and I could finally get some decent barbecue."

Jerry slapped me on the back. "I'll make some calls,"

he said before heading in the direction of the hotel lobby.

I started this year with a suspension and calls for me to retire and now I was dealing with several organizations interested in extending an offer. I was a strong wingman and teams were taking notice. I made superstars like Colin Pratt look good. I got them the ball and protected them in the paint. The plan was to keep my options open and run the bag all the way up. That meant sticking to the plan ... eating right, practice, and my secret weapon, Sloane.

# SLOANE

Wearing the most conservative outfit I could find and with my hair slicked back into a sleek bun, I fidgeted with my neckline while Deion's mom was off making us drinks. At lunch I'd hardly touched a bite, too preoccupied with tonight's meeting and now sitting at the table my stomach was making obscene noises.

Deck squeezed my knee. "Drink some water, it'll help with the grumbling."

"Is it that loud?" I whispered.

"Oh my God yeah. Like a freight train." He smirked.

Of course, he was joking but his words didn't help to calm my nerves. His mother was going to hate me and there was nothing I could do about it. Meeting the mother of the man you were pretending to be madly in love with was completely normal ... not. Deion could save all the pretense and just tell his mother the truth about us. He claimed she would never understand. I just knew she was going to come in here and immediately call bullshit since she knew Deion better than I ever could.

The dining table was something out of a Pinterest

board gold utensils, linen napkins and chargers. She even had personalized place settings and a postcard sized menu. If she went all out like this for a simple family dinner, I could only imagine what a party would look like.

Deion mentioned she had a ton of time on her hands since her husband passed. But from the size of this home most of her time was likely spent keeping things tidy. During the quick tour Deion provided, I was escorted from room to room and marveled over how much house this was for one person. I also noticed that there were reminders of her late husband everywhere. Pictures, trophies, framed magazine covers. Parts of this home were more like a memorial than anything else.

"I dare you to move the centerpiece just an inch," Raphael said to me.

"Normally I'd be down for a little mischief but I'm gonna sit this one out."

With a shrug, Raphael took it upon himself shifting the floral centerpiece slightly to the left so it was no longer perfectly centered. I liked Raphael, he reminded me of my brother Chet but with baby of the family vibes.

When Deborah McCabe and Destiny returned with a tray of drinks my back straightened. She looked like the type of mom who would swat you on the hand mid-sentence never spilling her drink. Serving up the refreshments, she paused the corners of her eyes wrinkling as she narrowed them. Setting the tray aside, she adjusted the centerpiece until it was perfectly centered.

Deion and Raphael tried to stifle a laugh.

"It's so nice to have both my boys home. I'm sure you can understand Sloane being a mother to a son. Boys are just different."

I would never admit it to Deion but I was getting strong Stepford Wife vibes right now.

"Yes, boys are fun."

"I'm sure your son keeps you on your toes." She pointed to Ace.

"I grew up with two older brothers so there isn't much I haven't seen. Gushing head wounds from rough housing. Sneaking their little girlfriends in when my dad was gone. Almost burning down the apartment trying to test some experiment. My brothers prepared me for Ace."

"Sounds like your brothers were rambunctious."

"They were left to their own devices. We all were, so we had to find ways to entertain ourselves and that often involved innovation. Like a homemade slip and slide that left me with a black eye." I was rambling and oversharing which was characteristic of me when I was nervous.

"How'd you make a homemade slip and slide?" Deion asked.

"Garbage bags, a water hose, and dish soap for extra slip." I winked.

"So what do you do for work, dear?" Ms. Deborah asked passing the carrots. They were the fancy kind that resembled miniature carrots and it was coated in a sweet glaze.

"I'm a cocktail waitress."

The muscles in her jaw worked into a circle before she plastered on a smile. "Ohh, good for you."

"She's really good at it," Deion chimed in.

"Serving drinks?" Although Deborah's tone was upbeat, it was clear by her pinched expression that she didn't think a cocktail waitress was good enough for her son. Shit I could probably have a doctorate degree and she'd still find fault.

"It's more of a curated experience. People are looking to have a good time, most are on vacation and she helps them make memories." Hearing Deion talk about me like I was saving children in the NICU was sweet.

"Did you go to mixology school for that?"

"No, I don't mix the drinks. I just serve them. But I do make a really mean bloody Mary with olives, lemon, a piece of cheese and a pickle." Bringing my hand to my mouth I gave a chef's kiss. "It's to die for."

"I can cosign that," Raphael said nodding his head in agreement.

"So your job just allows you to travel with my son to all the games?"

"Umm … not all the games." I corrected her.

Deck chimed in, "Yeah she's kind of on leave from work right now."

"So she's unemployed?"

"No … no. She's got a job, she's just taking a break."

Deborah interlocked her fingers. "So who's supporting her while she takes this break?"

The table was silent with the exception of Ace who'd tuned out the adult conversation focused on devouring his meal. It was bizarre to watch Deion fold in front of his mother. He was always in control but his mother's valid questions turned him into a bit of a child. This man texted his mother good night each day, I should have suspected I was dating a mama's boy.

"I'm not a gold digger," I finally said hoping to appease her valid concerns.

"I never said you were dear."

"Yeah, but you're strongly implying."

"I just know when people see Deion they see dollar signs. And he is generous to a fault." She leaned in, lowering her voice. "Prime example is his ex-wife."

"Well when I first saw Deck I didn't see dollar signs. Initially, I thought he was an asshole. And while my assessment was correct, I soon learned he was more than just an egotistical athlete, he was also a kind soul. Is he generous, yes, but not because he's naive. He's just genuinely a nice guy. And he makes me feel special everyday not because of the things he buys me but because of the way he treats me."

Deion's eyes grew soft as my words sank in.

"If you haven't noticed, I'm kind of obsessed with your son." I stroked his cheek.

Deion planted a toe curling kiss and as always when his lips touched mine I was unable to resist. So at the dining table in front of his mother, God, and my ten-year-old son, we tugged at each other like two love struck teenagers. When he pulled away, he had the silliest look of contentment on his face.

"That was gross," Destiny said.

"Nah it was sweet … and kinda gross but mostly sweet," Raphael countered.

"I vote gross," Ace added.

Deborah's nose curled in disgust. She didn't approve of the kiss or the glint in Deion's eyes when he looked at me. Who could blame her. On paper I was a mess, no job, a ten-year-old son, no real prospects to speak of. But what I lacked in financial fortunes I made up for with a plucky can-do attitude. I had to ask myself why would Deion bring me to dinner when he knew his mother would disapprove?

After dessert the conversation turned to the future. "Have you talked to Brenden about next season?" Deborah asked.

"It's looking good. Lots of teams are interested."

"Interested in what?" I asked, stealing a scoop of cookies and ice cream from Ace's pizookie dessert.

"Adding a shooting guard to their team," Deck said.

"Wait, I thought you were trying not to get traded."

"No, I'm trying not to get fired. At this point I'd sign with the Alaska Sea Otters if they were interested."

"But you're doing so well. Why wouldn't the Ramblers re-up?" I asked.

"I don't know. Maybe they will but I've gotta be flexible."

"New York would be nice," his mom said. "And there's not really anything holding you in Vegas."

Deion put his hand to his heart. "I'd love to call Madison Square Garden my home."

Home? My eyes grew three sizes bigger. When they started to talk about real estate and penthouse views, I tuned out. I thought the whole reason for this ruse was so Deion could keep his job … in Vegas, not so he could flip it into some opportunity of a lifetime. And Deborah knew exactly what she was doing when she said… "There's nothing tying you down in Vegas." I wanted to yell "I'm the one tying your son down, literally, and teasing him with my tongue."

"You know your cousin Aileen is a real estate agent. She could help you sell your place in Vegas."

"I don't think I'm ready for all that but eventually maybe." The pad of Deion's thumb gently caressed the side of my neck.

"I'll email you her contact information so you have it." Deborah's eyes settled on me. "Do you and my son live near one another?"

"No Deborah, I could never afford to live in that neighborhood. I have a two-bedroom one bath off the strip."

His mother was messy. And the enthusiastic way in which she was encouraging him to move was irking my spirit. I didn't know what Deion and I were doing but I did know I wasn't ready for it to end. Normally, after a few months a suitor would do something to get on my bad side. But Deck was easy going and he knew how to handle me both in and outside of the bedroom. Most men found it hard to deal with my personality but it never seemed to faze him.

I don't even know why I was here. Deck didn't need me to meet his mother. The goal was to sell this relationship to the press and Ramblers' organization, not to his family. It would have been easier if he'd just left me and

Ace back at the hotel. But he insisted we come and made a point to include us in every conversation. Maybe he just liked spiking his mother's blood pressure. At the end of the night, it was clear Deborah and I wouldn't be booking a spa day together anytime soon, which was fine by me. She was too bougie for my liking. *Seriously Debbie you slip a silk scarf over your head at night just like me.*

After returning home and seeing Ace off to bed, I found Deion on the balcony with the most amazing views of the city skyline. My arm was sore from constantly pinching myself. The fact that this man and this view was my life now … for however temporary … was still unreal to me.

Pointing to the glass of red wine in Deck's hand I asked, "I thought Brenden said no drinking?"

"One serving of red wine is allowed. It keeps your heart healthy." He extended the glass in my direction.

I took a sip, the serving seemed more appropriate for two people than one.

"My mom liked you." His hand caressed my cheek and acted like a pilot light igniting my lusty desires.

"No she didn't."

"OK she didn't, but she doesn't like anybody the first time she meets them."

Frown lines grooved the corners of my mouth.

"Seriously, she didn't like Destiny for like a cool three months."

"What?"

"She said the baby didn't look like it was mine."

"That child in there?" I pointed toward the suite. "She has your entire face."

"Now she does but as a newborn she was looking like Gollum."

I gasped out a laugh. "Don't do her like that."

"Yes, she's beautiful now but it was a rough six months." His smile lit up his face, I think he was happy … at work, at home, with me. Maybe I did know how to bring a man peace. "Stop acting like Ace was always a handsome kid."

"He was. From birth he was a cute baby. No cone head, no wrinkled skin. Perfect in every way."

"I'm going to need to see some baby pictures." Deck collected the glass back from me taking a long swallow.

Leaning against the railings, I studied his face. "Was it weird being back home?"

"Yeah, I don't know how my mother does it. That place is like a shrine to my dad. The pictures, the awards, the trophies."

"They met in college, right?"

"Yes, and to hear them tell it Morris and Deb fell in love at first sight. In all actuality it was a bit more complicated than that. Typical ups and downs and compromises … mostly on my mother's part." He offered me the glass. "You know the fucked up thing about my father's death? When he got sick, I thought he'd be OK. It was like a cold. I stayed in Vegas because he was supposed to be released from the hospital the next day."

"But that never happened?"

"Nope, he died and my mom was alone. And I regret

it. Raphael and I should have been there for her. My dad always told us if anything ever happened to him we needed to take care of our mother. Shit he'd been telling me that since I was like five years old. And when she needed me the most I was miles away."

"That wasn't your fault."

"Kind of was. I heard her voice … she was scared. And it terrified me. And so I did nothing hoping that if I did nothing, nothing would happen."

"I think you're being too hard on yourself."

"Well, that would make two of us."

"What's that supposed to mean?"

"Nothing."

I squared my back bracing myself for an argument. "Nah, if you have something to say fucking spit it out."

"It's just really rich coming from you. Telling me shit's not my fault and not to blame myself when all you do is blame yourself for the shit your father does. Sure, your pops has issues, but those issues don't belong to you. Yet for some reason you are content to wrap his mistakes around your neck like a fucking anchor. You have convinced yourself that you are unworthy of love. No strike that … you've convinced yourself that you don't even want it."

"How much wine have you had?" I tried to lighten the mood to hide the fact that his arrows were connecting.

Deion downed the remaining wine. His energy felt off. Maybe it was from having dinner with his mom or being back in his childhood home with reminders of his father but he was visibly agitated. He surrendered his hands in the air. "I'm just scared. I'm scared that I care more than you do."

"About what?"

"About us, the only thing that matters." He spat the words at me.

"Us?" I released a scoffing laugh "How does *us* factor into your out of state move?"

"I need to go where the money is. So Houston, New Jersey, California. Everything is on the table."

"Just like that you'd walk away from m … the team." I shut my eyes hoping he didn't catch my slip of the tongue.

"Listen I love the Ramblers' organization but I need to think about my future. My family's future. And that means securing a contract. My window of opportunity is closing. I have two maybe three good years left."

"So just fuck the Ramblers?" Deion didn't realize it but my question was about so much more than the Ramblers. If he left Vegas, he wasn't just leaving an NBA team, he was leaving me. And from his tone it appeared he hadn't even factored losing me into the equation. Which made sense considering our business arrangement.

"If another team is willing to pay me more … yes."

The sinking corrosive feeling in the pit of my stomach is what happens when you get attached to your fake boyfriend.

"What?" he asked. In the last four months Deion had gotten good at reading my moods.

"Nothing." My throat was thick with emotion.

"I mean Vegas is great but have you ever been to

*New Jersey*?" He said the state name in a heavy East Coast accent. "We could find a place—"

"And what? Play make believe until your knees give out and they retire your jersey?" Maybe he had factored me into his plans but not in a practical way. I couldn't just move across the state.

When I was twelve I dislocated my shoulder. My dad nicknamed me Jawbreaker because I never cried, even when he popped it back into place because we didn't have health insurance. I think I was more shocked than anything else. He said I was made of steel with a tough outer shell. And right now it was taking everything I had in me to keep the tears at bay.

"I don't know we could figure it out."

"I have a son, Deck. Pretending to be madly in love with you isn't a viable career path."

"Right ... because ... that's what this is all about ... pretending and make believe."

"And the money." I reminded him.

"Of course, the money." His face turned cold.

"It's late and we're both tired. I don't know ..."

"Sloane listen to me—"

"I gotta wash this shit off my face." I didn't want to try to figure something out that we both knew would never work. Heading for the bathroom, I turned on the faucet to muffle the sounds of me falling apart.

# DEION

The morning of the All-Star game started with a bang. My tongue was submerged inside of Sloane's pussy. It was early with everyone in the suite still asleep. I awoke at 5:37 a.m. to a buoyant dick and a desire to hear Sloane moan my name. When she screamed for me, it was as if she was fighting to conceal just how good I made her body feel. Her voiced strained and stuttered compelled to speak against her better judgment. The only noises were the sounds of me indulging in her sweet spot and the whimpers of satisfaction it produced. Sloane's long fingernails clawing at the sheets as I slurped. Making her body levitate was my newest magic trick.

Her vocal encouragement made my dick throb. Sloan's deep voice still thick with sleep said, "You're so good at this."

Last night she'd abruptly ended our conversation and when I crawled into bed, she pretended to be asleep even after several well-placed kisses. Sloane was mad. I was confused. If I was traded or signed with another team, I accepted it would be tough before it got better.

Logistically we'd have a lot to figure out. But I was willing to roll with the punches to make this work. When I reached for her this morning and she welcomed my advances I was relieved.

Biting at her thigh, I pulled myself on top sucking a nipple into my mouth before slipping myself inside. Sloane gasped softly as her hips shifted to accommodate me. In the still of the morning, I drove deep keeping pace with her gentle moans. Her arms hugged me tight absentmindedly stroking my back after each thrust.

Kissing her cheek, I whispered in her ear, "You're especially beautiful first thing in the morning."

"Liar," she groaned as we picked up the tempo.

My mind went blank as a dizzying tornado swirled inside of me gaining pressure making it difficult for me to hold back. I forced myself to think of my grandmother in her modest house dress and slippers until Sloane shivered and cried out underneath me giving me the all clear to release. Bearing down on her shoulder with my teeth, my body jerked and my face contorted before collapsing next to her.

We lay in silence as both our bodies reset. Sloane's left leg still twitching unprovoked.

"Sloane …"

"Hmm."

"Me leaving Vegas isn't set in stone."

"OK." Her eyes slammed into me as she released a low huff.

"In a perfect world the Ramblers will ante up and offer me what I'm worth. I'm not itching to leave Vegas but I need to prepare myself for the very real possibility the organization will no longer need my services come the end of the season."

"Why are you telling me this?" Standing, she slipped on one of the fluffy white hotel robes.

"Because it's obvious you're bothered by the thought of me leaving."

Her laugh was loud and brittle. "It's your life do whatever the fuck you wanna do."

"I'm not looking to fight." I stepped back into my boxers.

"This isn't a fight. I don't care if you move to Jersey, or Boston, or Timbuktu."

"What if I wanted you to move with me?"

Sloane grabbed the accent pillows from the floor, throwing them one by one at me in rapid succession.

"Quit throwing stuff at me," I yelled, while trying to block incoming fire.

"You know what fucker I'm not gonna let you do this," she shouted.

"Do what?" I asked through raised arms to protect myself from the onslaught of feather pillows. The last pillow was heftier than the rest narrowly missing my head.

"Make these bullshit promises. God why do men always feel the need to start offering up the world after good sex."

"This is about more than just sex and you know it."

There was a knock on the door.

"What?" I barked.

Raphael opened the door wide-eyed. "You two OK in here?"

"Yeah, we're good," I said, not bothering to ask why he was in our suite this early in the morning wearing shiny parachute pants.

Raphael's eyes went from the rumpled-up bed sheets to the pillows scattered across the floor. "Is this some kind of role play shit?"

"What do you want?" Sloane's tone was just as harsh toward him as it was to me.

"I'm about to order room service if anyone wants something."

"Just order enough for everybody," I replied shooing him away.

"Will do," he said, before closing the door behind him.

Crossing the room, I stood in front of her. "It's entirely too early in the morning to be this mad." I rubbed her cheek with the pad of my thumb. "We don't have to figure this out right now. Can we just rewind back to right after you came and the way you looked at me."

"How'd I look at you?" Her shoulders retreated from her ears.

"Like you had no intention of hurling pillows at my head." I laughed. "Remember in anger management they encourage us to take a timeout. So let's put a pin in this and just enjoy the day."

She dropped her arms which had been snug across her chest. Heading toward the bathroom she stopped short. "Are we not gonna talk about the fact that Raphael is wearing MC Hammer inspired pants?"

"Oh my God ... where do you even purchase pants like that?"

"I mean he always dresses a little off with the Tommy Bahama shirts ... but those pants are ridiculous even for him."

"And why were they shiny?" I yelled.

We burst into uncontrollable laughter.

---

I texted Sloane from the locker room and asked her to meet me in the tunnel of the Toyota Center. As my team of assembled West Coast players made their way to the court, I stopped short. The roar of the enthusiastic crowd was so loud it vibrated my chest. When Sloane's silhouette of curves and tussled curls came into view my heart jerked against its reins. Her big brown eyes darted over my anxious expression as she approached.

"What's up?" she asked slightly out of breath.

"I just needed to see your face."

"You should take a picture it lasts longer," she teased.

"I have several pictures, but none of them are safe for viewing in mixed company."

Sloane ran her hand down my arm. "Deck, this is the All-Star game. You just have to go out there and have fun."

"Yeah, I know. You're right." I nodded.

"Then why do you look so distressed?"

I knew this was basically an exposition game. Players weren't going all out at the All-Star event, it was purely for entertainment. Despite that knowledge I couldn't help but feel the weight of the moment. I'd been in the NBA for fifteen seasons and this was the first time I'd been invited to play in an All-Star game.

Clearing my throat I asked, "Do you think I'm good enough?"

Sloane's heavy hand made contact with my face slapping me hard. "What, do we all need to get into a big circle jerk and regale you with tales of how great you are?"

"I should have called my mother." I rubbed my cheek.

"Deion you deserve this moment. Don't let your fear tarnish this day."

"By the time my father was my age he'd played in a dozen All-Star games."

Sloane seeped a long breath of air. "I'm going to say this as respectfully as possible. Fuck Morris McCabe."

Shocked unhinged my jaw.

"Fuck him and his record-breaking points, his triple spinning dunks, and his well recorded legacy. This is no longer about your dad, Deck. This is about you. You as a player and a man. You don't need to live in the shadow of your father because you're paving your own path. You are Deion D'Money McCabe and no one can move the ball like you can. And this weekend is proof that the entire league recognizes your talent.

"We are done doubting ourselves." Her hands tugged at my beard. "Do you understand me. You earned this. You showed up for your team and Vegas every fucking day. You deserve this, baby. You are not an imposter you are the real deal."

My forehead wrinkled as I rubbed the back of my neck. "Do you really believe that?"

"I knew it the third time I met you." She smirked.

This was why I texted Sloane. When she wasn't telling me I was a beautiful unicorn she was genuinely filling my cup. This woman didn't take life too seriously but when it came to me, she didn't play. She wouldn't stand for negative talk about my worthiness, especially from me. I truly believe she would kick my ass if she could listen to my thoughts and hear the shitty things I said to myself.

I wrapped my hand around her neck pulling her closer. "I'm about to say something and I don't want you to interrupt me or deflect. Just let the words sink in. Promise."

"I promise." She fluffed her hair intentionally attempting to cover her eyes.

"You make me a better man and the day I met you was the best day of my life."

Sloane's nose wrinkled and her mouth flattened into a frown.

"You promised." I warned her before continuing. "I love you, Sloane Kaplan." Stroking her throat with the pad of my thumb our eyes locked. I could see the fear swimming in her pupils but I could also make out a glint of hope.

Sloane swallowed hard. "How do I know this is real?" her voice was a whisper.

Reaching for her hand I placed it over my heart

before resting my hand against her chest. "This is real." The roar of the crowd dulled and all I could hear were Sloane's slow heartbeats syncing up with the frantic beats in my chest.

Sloane broke contact. "The game is gonna start any minute now. You need to go. Your team is waiting for you."

I nodded planting a quick kiss to her cheek before heading to the court.

"Make me proud," she yelled after me.

Doubling back, I scooped her into my arms. Her kisses were like power boosters and when I dipped my tongue in her mouth my energy level re-upped. Reluctantly pulling away I said "I live to serve," before running up the tunnel toward the hardtop.

# SLOANE

UPON RETURNING TO VEGAS, I DROPPED ACE AT HIS father's house before heading back to my place. When I reached the landing of my second-floor apartment my father was leaning against my door.

"What are you doing here?" I dropped my luggage rummaging through my purse for the keys.

"Hello. How are you? Nice to see you again, Sloane."

"Hello Stanley. What are you doing here?"

"Can't a father visit his daughter and make sure she's straight."

"Yes, some fathers do, but you only show up at my place when you want something." I shooed him aside, unlocking the door.

"That's hurtful," he said, reaching for my luggage and following me inside.

"How did you even know I was coming home today?" Pulling back the patio blinds, I opened the slider door to allow fresh air to circulate through the living room after being unattended for the past four days.

"Tammie told me you'd be back home on Monday."

I loved Tammie but she was a little too friendly with my dad, oftentimes offering up information I'd rather remain private.

"So what, you've been staked outside my door waiting for my return."

"No … Tammie provided a bit of entertainment while I waited."

I scrunched my face in disgust. I could only imagine the type of entertainment they got up to. "Dad I've had a busy weekend and I need to wash clothes and run some errands so if you want money just ask."

Stanley pulled a cigarette pack from his back pocket.

"Don't even think about lighting up in here." I pointed a warning finger.

He sucked his teeth but stuffed the cigarettes into his jacket. "I saw you on the TV with that basketball play-er." Examining a picture of Ace and I on the shelf he continued. "I thought you said you and Ace would be spending the weekend visiting national parks?"

"Plans changed."

"You've been holding out on me."

"And you've been running your mouth. You don't know the first thing about Deion and me. You met him one time and all of a sudden, you're an authority."

"Are you mad about the interview?"

"What happen to Kaplan business should stay among Kaplans? Hmm? Cause that's what you always told Lee, Chet, and me when you didn't want us telling our teachers you were a neglectful drunk."

"That was different."

"Yeah, because they offered you money. How much did you get for the lies you told?"

"A thousand dollars." His chest thrust forward and he flashed a huge smile that showed all his teeth.

A heaviness clung to my limbs. I knew my dad was manipulative, and deceitful and yes, I'd been burned by him more times than I cared to recall. But every time he hurt me, it stung. "You didn't come over here to talk about Deion McCabe."

"I did actually." He bounced on the balls of his feet. "Look, baby girl this could be an opportunity."

"An opportunity for what?"

"To come up."

I recoiled taking several steps back. "No, Deion isn't one of your marks."

"That ball player is the best mark yet. He's rich, from what I can make out he's gullible, and for some reason he likes you."

"You're wasting your breath."

"Think about this rationally. A man like that is gonna get tired of your hood antics eventually and go find himself a model or singer to lay up with. And what will you be left with? Nothing. Men like him are users; they use people mining all your resources until there is nothing left. Right now, he thinks you're the best thing since sliced bread but eventually the bread will get moldy and he'll toss it out."

My father lived by the creed of kill or be killed. He believed everyone was waiting to stab him in the back so he was prepared to initiate the first blow. I'm not saying his thinking wasn't sound. I'd experienced it firsthand. Friends who you thought had your back throwing you under the wheels of a bus or aggressively trying to sleep with your boyfriend. *Maybe I need to find a better crop of friends*, but eight times out of ten, people were just out for themselves.

"Thank you so much for your advice but Deion and I are fine."

"Of course, you are and that's why you need to strike now before things turn sour."

"Strike?" This isn't some military offensive."

Stanley grabbed my arm pulling me to the couch. "Just hear me out. What does Deion McCabe have an abundance of?"

I wanted to say good looks, talent, and quality dick but I don't think that was the correct answer.

"Money. And we … you could use some supplemental income."

"So you want me to ask him to give me money?"

"It could be money or expensive gifts that hold a resale value. Have you been to his place?"

"Yes."

"Maybe he has stuff he wouldn't miss … a watch, some jewelry, maybe an unopened iPad."

I coughed out a stunned laugh. "You want me to rob him?"

"I'm not asking you to do anything you haven't done before."

You remember those late-night parties my father would drag me and my brothers to? Well while he was gambling, we were in the bedroom, where all the coats and purses were piled on the bed, pocketing money and anything that looked like it could be pawned. So no, I wasn't above stealing, I'd just outgrown the practice.

"That's gonna be a hard no." I gave his knee a pat before standing up and heading to the front door.

"You're dating a famous basketball player, you should have something to show for it when it ends."

"Who says it's gonna end?" I blurted out.

He took lazy strides toward the door, an unlit cigarette dangling from his lips. "Sloane as much as you hate to admit it you're just like me. Loving you is like trying to hold lightning in your hand, it's impossible."

My eyes darted to the carpet, an uncontrollable heat flushing my face. Opening the door, I stepped aside so he could leave.

Stanley left me with these parting words. "Love can make you dumb but there's no need to be dumb and broke. Just think about it."

Closing the door behind him I pressed my back against it. There was nothing to think about. I wasn't going to cat burgle Deck. My dad didn't know about my arrangement with Deion, and if he ever found out, his hand would be extended looking for a cut until the funds were depleted.

I was a grown ass woman with problems of my own but I'd been taking care of my father and brothers for years, it was second nature. Stanley taught us family always came first, even when that family was dysfunctional and co-dependent. But this money was mine and mine alone. I'd already opened a savings account for Ace. I wasn't going to let my father piss it away on the promise of the next great thing.

Despite his absurdity some of Stanley's points were spot on. This thing between Deck and I was finite. No matter what I might be feeling … and I'm not admitting to anything, especially not a rash of goose pimples whenever he was near. One day the novelty of being with me would wear off and when it did Deck would change his locks, update his security system, and get a new number.

---

DEION WAS POSED COMPLETELY NAKED WITH A BASKETBALL strategically covering his junk. Raphael and I accompanied Deion to the *Sports Illustrated* photo shoot for the body issue. He'd landed the cover and next month millions of people would get to worship this statuesque man like I did every night. I'd dated some physically fit men in the past but none like Deion.

God must have been in a good mood on the day she created this man. Deion's skin was a smooth saddle brown. His physique was like a tool and every muscle served a purpose. His long legs with their strong calf muscles ensured optimal performance when he was on the court. He had eight pack abs that until meeting him I thought were a myth and then there was his ass. It was round and firm and supported by his massive thighs.

"OK let's try something different, drop the ball and turn your body to the side." The photographer directed.

Deion tossed the ball aside, not at all shy now that his penis was on full display. And who could blame him if I had a dick like that I'd probably want to show it off too. Next to me the intern's mouth became unhinged when she caught a peek.

After his MVP win at All-Star Weekend, Deion's star seemed stratospheric. The media loved a comeback story and his story had it all. Tragic loss, underdog elements with an epic, albeit fake, fairy-tale romance. People were interested in the baller and bottle girl. And the fact that I was from around the way gave hopeless romantics aspirational relationship goals. If ordinary Sloane Kaplan could land a professional athlete, why not them.

While Deck jumped in the air per the photographer's instruction, I headed to the craft table for a bottle of water.

"Sloane?" a voice called from behind.

Turning I found the makeup artist who'd applied shiny stuff to Deion's skin behind me. She was also a frequent guest at sporting events and parties.

"Hey Katt, I thought that was you earlier." We exchanged quick hugs.

"Deion sure is looking good up there. You're a lucky girl. If he was my boyfriend, we wouldn't make it out of the bedroom."

I forced a smile, not really sure of the appropriate response. What I did know was she was staring a little too hard for my liking.

"It seems like Deion is everywhere right now. And the Ramblers are greeted by packed arenas and frenzied crowds. We could actually make it to the playoffs this year," Katt asked.

"They're definitely playing like a winning team."

"I bet the after parties are going to be lit." She performed a quick two-step.

"You never know they could make it to the finals." That was me being optimistic.

The Ramblers were a long shot. They'd played well but there were still some missing pieces preventing them from being great. It was no surprise management was looking to make some movement. That meant cutting or trading players with the hopes of upgrading to better ones. Hopefully Deion had done enough this season to prove his worth to the team. I know I sounded like a sports fanatic but after spending all this time with Deion it was kind of hard not to retain the information.

"What about you? What are your plans when the season is over?" Katt asked.

"Plans for what?"

"Just like players are on pins and needles hoping they don't get cut, so are the girlfriends. The summer is when you see a ton of breakups. During the season players are focused on the game but once the season is over, they have some time for reflection. And most decide they'd rather upgrade for a newer sexier model."

"Well I'm with Deion … so—"

"You're probably the most in jeopardy of losing your spot. Deion's star is on the rise; he can be more selective on who he chooses to date." I blinked rapidly processing her callous words. My bulging eyes probably hinted at my surprise at her blunt tone. "I hope I'm not offending you but we as women need to stick together. I've been in this circle for a minute and you're still a newbie. I'm just trying to bring you up on game. If you want to maintain this five-star lifestyle you need to start putting your feelers out."

"My feelers?"

"Yeah girl. What one man won't do another man will." Katt's demeanor during our conversation was bubbly and light. Like she didn't just inform me Deion would most likely chuck me to the curb and I needed to flirt hard if I wanted someone to come along and rescue me from the trash heap of discarded girlfriends. Was this really a thing? I wasn't naïve, of course ball players had options regular men didn't. But I wasn't interested in relying on some random man to save me.

I'd been taking care of myself since adolescence and I be damned if my entire self-worth got tangled up in some vain, egotistical basketball player who needed validation every day to function. *What the fuck was I doing?* I'd lost focus of my reason for agreeing to this. It wasn't Deion it was the money, plain and simple and it would do me well to remember that.

Katt nudged my shoulder with hers. "Tell me is *it* as good as I imagine it is." Her eyes were fixated on Deion's naked body.

If this chick thought I was going to give her a five-star review about Deion's sexual prowess she'd lost her damn mind. I wasn't going to help her find her new sugar daddy by stealing mine. "Actually, it's not good. You'd think he has all the tools and equipment to accomplish any task but bigger doesn't always mean better." Leaning in closer, I laid it on thick. "It's like a jackhammer five thrust and its lights out."

Her face fell with disappointment.

"Don't tell anyone that." I pulled my face into a pleading expression.

"Oh no of course not," she said, before walking off.

"Ooh you messy." Raphael seemed to appear from nowhere.

"What are you talking about?"

"You're over here lying on the efficacy of Deion's dick."

"Efficacy?"

"Yeah, I fell into a YouTube spelling bee wormhole last night."

"How much of that conversation did you hear?"

"Enough to tell you old girl is full of shit. Deion doesn't operate that way."

"I don't care. I don't. I'm just here for—"

"The money, I know." Raphael did that thing where his obsidian eyes bore a hole into the center of my soul.

"Don't look at me like that."

"Like what?"

"Like you know. Because you don't know."

"You're right I don't know you're in love with Deion. But I suspect it."

I grabbed several bite sized pieces of fruit and stuffed them into my mouth. "Have you tried this? You should try this, so good," I said around the food wedged in my mouth.

Raphael hooked his arm around my shoulder. He pointed to Deion who was standing perfectly still as the photographer captured pictures of his broad back. "Last season he was doing commercials for Lieutenant Car Insurance. You know that budget insurance place."

"Yes, I know it well."

"And now this."

My eyes settled on Deion in all his glory. Now that he was receiving his flowers it was difficult picturing myself in his life. Sure when he was a down and out player we had commonalities. He saw himself as a victim and I could relate, seeing how life had handed me one rotten lemon after the other. But his fortunes were turning while I was essentially in the same place he'd found me in. He'd outgrown me. Even if he didn't realize it yet.

"Are you OK?" Raphael stared at me with concern.

"Yeah ..." I cleared my throat. "I'm fine. I think I might be coming down with a cold or something," I lied, hoping to explain away this mistiness in my eyes.

The photographer called for a fifteen-minute break and Deion came bounding over securing the sash of his robe. "Hey, we're almost done. How's it looking?" He nicked a piece of cheese from the craft table.

"It looks really good. I'm sure the pictures are gonna be great," I reassured him. Without warning Deion scooped me up in his arms, planting a kiss in the crook of my neck. My whole body tensed. "What are you doing? Who are we trying to convince?" I whispered, observing the room.

"No one. I've just been daydreaming about kissing you for the past twenty minutes."

His lips found mine, and kiss me he did. My heart skipped several beats as he cupped my face in his hand, his fingertips submerged in my hair. The buzz of activity all around us washed away as his lips languished over mine until my toes curled in their Jordans. I loved the fact that he didn't care who was around because I felt the same way. If Deion was down I would fuck him right here and now on this craft table next to the artisan cheese.

Pulling away, I was finally allowed to breathe, my head spinning and my eyes dreamy. When he was around kissing me like this it was hard to focus. His smile lulled me into a false sense of security that I had no right possessing. This was fake, bogus, phony, it didn't matter that butterflies were nesting in my stomach or that Deion took care to ensure I was centered and appreciated. Pretending to be Deion's girlfriend had severely clouded my judgment. Instead of waiting for his size fourteen shoe to drop, I needed to grab cement and some bricks and start creating some distance.

# DEION

Booked and busy, with interviews on late-night talk shows and endorsement deals with Wendy's, Gatorade, and Old Spice, that was my current status. My jersey was one of the top sellers this season. I was in discussions to be featured on the cover of next year's release for the video game NBA 2K. My ascension was being framed as a comeback story with comparisons to Pippen, Duncan, and Thompson, all shooting guards who were famous for supporting their star player. Outside of work my focus was on family which included Ace and Sloane.

Unfortunately, the situation with Sloane was getting complicated as we got closer to the end of the season. It almost felt like she was slowly distancing herself from me. I'd invited her to join us on the set of my newest commercial, but she'd declined claiming she had errands to run and her apartment needed to be cleaned. I was tempted to remind her I was paying her for her time but truthfully, I wanted her to be here because she wanted to, not out of some financial obligation.

"After a long day on the court I rely on Old Spice to

keep me fresh and dry all day long." My cheeks hurt from smiling for the last two hours.

"Cut," the director called. "That looks good Deion lets do an outfit change."

Handing the bottle of deodorant to an intern, I headed to the dressing room for a quick change.

"Hey next time you deliver the lines you might want to mix it up," Raphael suggested, his feet kicked up on the small table.

"Oh yeah like what?"

He cleared his throat and donned his pearly whites. "Old Spice, funk doesn't stand a chance."

"Umm, I think I'll pass."

"If Sloane was here she'd agree with me." He wagged his string cheese in my direction. If Sloane was here, she'd have enlisted Raphael to help her nick as much food items as possible from craft services.

"Well she's not here," I said, discarding my T-shirt in a pile of rejected clothes options.

"And why is that?"

"She had shit to do." I held up two button up shirts. "Blue or gray?"

"Blue. I thought you were paying her so the only thing she has to do is you."

"Shhh." I flashed him an irritated look before closing the dressing room door. "The agreement was for Rambler events. This is extracurricular."

"Is that the excuse she gave you?"

"She's free to do whatever she wants."

Sloane had her own life and responsibilities to attend to and I needed to respect that. But the lack of a "Break your leg," text was distressing. *Maybe she was bored of me?* Normally dating a ball player was glamorous with exclusive parties and trips around the world. Dating me entailed nights spent curled up on the couch, going to the Whole Foods an hour before it closed because it was less crowded, and maybe if I was feeling frisky a late-night snack of grilled cheese and tomato soup.

After All-Star game weekend, meeting my mother and the talk of me signing with a team other than the Ramblers, the energy between us was shifting. Now when we were together it felt like only parts of her showed up. Her sarcasm was still there but the tender look in her eyes was replaced with a vacant stare. Her laughs were hollow, and sometimes even the sex felt performative.

Reaching for my phone, I typed out a text. "Do you wanna hang out after my shoot?" Staring at the screen I deleted the words one by one typing instead "I want to see you." No, that sounded too demanding. "I miss you and when you're not around I feel empty inside." Nope, too desperate. I settled on keeping it cool and unaffected with a simple text.

Deion: Hi, I wanna finger bang you.

Sloane: Who is this?

Deion: It's Deion ... Deion McCabe number twenty-seven for the Las Vegas Ramblers. The other night you made me come using only your tits.

> Sloane: That name sounds vaguely familiar.

> Deion: I miss you.

> Sloane: ...

Fuck me, someone take away my phone. Come for the sex stay for the stage five clinginess.

Raphael snapped his fingers to get my attention. "Did you hear me?"

"No, what?"

"What are you gonna do about your Sloane problem?"

"I have a Sloane problem?" I unbuttoned the blue shirt, slipping it on.

"Yeah, you two are clearly on separate pages. Truthfully, I don't even think y'all are reading from the same damn book."

"We're fine."

"God you're just like Dad."

"What do you mean?"

"You only see things from your point of view. And anything that contradicts your narrative you dismiss out right. You love Sloane so she must love you too and be ready to drop everything and move God knows where with her son so you two can be together. You haven't even considered how weird that is. Expecting someone whose known you for a couple of months to disrupt her entire life."

"You don't think she loves me?"

"I don't think you listen just like Dad. It was always

his way or no way. Mom, you and I were just along for the ride and she resented him for it. You need to make your expectations abundantly clear. The two of you have been playing house for so long it's become difficult to determine what's real. Tell her what you want so she can tell you what she needs. Because I get the sense she sees her role in your life as disposable.

"Did she tell you that?"

"Not in so many words no. But I'm a good judge of people. Everything's coming up Deion right now and I can only imagine she's trying to understand how she fits in."

"She doesn't have to fit in she's already in."

Raphael shrugged. "Sometimes humans need reassurance. Maybe Sloane wants to know she's not in this alone."

"In what alone? Love? Did Sloane tell you she loved me?"

"No. She didn't have to say it." Raphael rolled his eyes. "God you're stupid."

I looked at my phone, Sloane hadn't responded to my "I miss you," text. Maybe Raphael was right. I needed her to know that my plans for the future had her in the starring role.

---

THERE WAS A WEEK LEFT IN THE REGULAR SEASON AND THE Ramblers still had a slim chance of making it to the playoffs; although I wasn't holding my breath. I was more concerned with my basketball future followed closely by my future with Sloane. If Raphael was right, she was preparing herself for the end.

We were at a farm to table restaurant that Pratt raved about. The ambience was laid back with a modern vibe, there was an open kitchen and large windows that provided stunning views of the strip. Sloane smoothed down her floral dress, offering a soft smile over the candle light that flickered on our table.

"Old Spice sent me a case of their products. You should sort through it, pick some stuff out for Ace."

"I can't wait to see the commercial." Sloane fluffed her thick curls.

"Don't forget the billboard." I smiled. "Your boy is going to be plastered all over the city."

I watched as Sloane took a bite of pasta, her full lips hugged the fork. What I wouldn't give to be an inanimate object right now.

"Charmise told me Smalls got traded to the Washington Wizards."

"Yeah, he's pretty excited he and his wife hated Vegas so I guess it's a good thing for them."

"Any word about any other potential trades?" Her gaze rested on me with a heft behind it.

What Sloane wanted to know was if there was any discussion about me and a trade. Even though she liked to pretend she didn't care, I knew she was just as concerned as I was. Until that bit was sorted out it felt like our future was kind of up in the air. Where I ended up didn't change my feelings for Sloane but it seemed to be a sticking point for her.

"Sometimes no news can be good news. Plus, if a

trade was in the works Justus would let me know. He's not gonna let me twist on the vine."

"What does Brenden think?"

My agent thought I needed to be ready for any possible outcome. But I didn't want to raise Sloane's antenna unnecessarily. I was praying I got to stay in Vegas too but if I was traded, I would work hard to convince Sloane to make the move with me.

"He currently has me at a fifty-fifty split."

Sloane didn't respond; she focused on twirling pasta around her fork.

I knew asking Sloane to leave everything and everyone she knew to come start a new life with me was a long shot. But I didn't think it was far-fetched. Pretending to be in love with Sloane turned out to be easier than I expected.

I leaned across the table, reaching for Sloane's hand. "Listen, I don't know what's going to happen. If my contract's extended, maybe we could do some traveling. If I get traded then I'll need to get my affairs in order. Put the house on the market. Find a new place to live."

Sloane nodded but her facial expression was difficult to read.

"What's your custody arrangement with your ex?" I asked.

"What?"

"If we had to move, would he fight to keep Ace in Vegas or do you think we could come to some amicable arrangement?"

"What are you talking about?" She pulled her hand from mine.

"I think you should just start talking to him now, planting the seed that you may be moving."

"Vegas is my home. I don't plan on moving."

"Well I'm hoping we don't have to but—"

Her head flinched back slightly. "Why do you keep saying we?"

Before I had the chance to respond, two women approached our table. "Sorry to interrupt but aren't you Deion McCabe?" One of the women asked, twirling her wavy red hair.

"Umm ... yes, but—"

"Oh my God, I knew it, can we get a picture?" The woman pulled out her phone and thrust it in Sloane's face without a word. She grabbed the phone, offering zero objection as the women gathered around me leaning in close. Sloane appeared to be overly zealous. Smiling and encouraging the ladies to say cheese. When the redhead leaned in kissing me on the lips, Sloane's smile faltered. Reaching across the table she held out the phone which accidentally slipped from her hands and landed into the pitcher of water on our table.

"Whoops," Sloane said, I could tell by her tone the butter fingers were not by accident.

The women's face stretched in dismay as she stuck her hand into the water to retrieve her damaged phone.

"You should get that into a bowl of rice. I've heard that helps," Sloane suggested.

The redhead stared in disbelief as water dripped from her phone. The look she flashed in Sloane's direction was lethal. The waiter escorted the ladies from our table, one of them complaining loudly.

"Was that necessary?" I asked.

"I don't know what you're talking about. It was an innocent accident." Sloane shrugged.

"Nothing about you is innocent."

The drive home was filled with sounds of hip-hop playing through the car speakers. Sloane enacted the silent treatment once we left the restaurant. It wasn't unusual for fans to approach me. Female fans sometimes got a little handsy, rubbing my chest or pinching my ass. Sloane was often ignored or treated like she didn't exist, being pushed aside or tossed a phone like she was my personal assistant.

I tried my best to limit these interactions and correct people who stepped out of line but oftentimes it was just easier to let them get the picture so they could leave us alone. It was clear tonight Sloane wasn't having any of that.

As we pulled into the garage I asked, "So are you going to tell me what the problem is or are you going to continue with the silent treatment?"

Opening her car door, she ignored my words.

Following her into the house I said, "I asked you a question. Don't walk away from me."

Sloane spun on her heels. "You're my problem. This … everything."

"OK, well if I'm gonna fix it I'm gonna need you to narrow it down a bit." I entered the four-digit code into the alarm panel silencing the beeping.

Sloane took a deep breath and word vomit came out. "I just think the season is coming to an end and maybe it's best we go our separate ways … now."

"What are you talking about?"

"I don't think we need to prolong the inevitable."

"Where is this coming from? Is this because of what happened back at the restaurant?"

"At the restaurant, at Ramblers' events, at your mother's house. Everyone is silently thinking you could do better than me. Let's not pretend like you don't have options now."

"I always had options but I chose you."

"No, you chose yourself. Hiring me benefited you."

"So what is this? You're having second thoughts about our arrangement at the eleventh hour?"

"I'm a realist and I went into this knowing exactly what this was and how it would end."

"Are you even listening to me? Have you listened to anything I've been saying these past few months? Sloane I don't want this to—"

"Deion do you really see yourself with me two years from now, five years, ten? I think if you're honest with yourself you'd agree this was fun but it's not a forever thing."

"Why are you so afraid to let me love you? To let anyone love you."

"Because you don't love me," she shouted. "You love that people's perception of you has shifted. You love the endorsements and speaking engagements. You love the perks and increased playing time. But at the end of the day, you could give two fucks about me."

"All of that shit is great but none of it would be possible without you."

"And that's really it. You see me as some golden

goose laying eggs of opportunity in your path. But sooner or later you're gonna realize it was never me, it was always you. You made these things happen, not me."

"Why are you fighting this so hard?"

"I didn't want to say this before but … I don't love you. I never have."

"Bullshit."

"I'm a liar. I'm great at spinning a story and sometimes I even forget it's not real. This was always about the money for me, nothing more. I pretended to be falling in love because I knew that's what you wanted. It was about securing the bag. You wanted to be back on top and I needed money. We both got what we wanted."

"If you don't want to be here, I'm not gonna beg you," I said calling her bluff.

Scooping up her purse she headed for the front door. "I'll call a RideX from the front lawn." I was close on her heels when she opened the door, my hand reached out closing it shut. "I will scream," she threatened me.

"I'm hoping you do," I said, while undoing the sash of her wrap dress.

"This is never going to work. You need to let me go." As she was saying the words her hands were fumbling with my belt buckle. Propelling forward we stumbled into the bedroom, which was difficult to do with Sloane stroking my dick. I removed my trousers and boxer briefs before slipping her panties over her thighs.

Dropping to the bed, I pulled Sloane's warm core to my mouth savoring some well-placed kisses. With my fingers I pried back her folds and delighted in the sounds she made as I teased and sucked her sensitive skin. This pussy was mine and by the time I was done with her she would give up on any thought of leaving. Unhooking her bra, I massaged her breast as she worked toward her orgasm. Her hips frantic and demanding pressing against my open mouth. I eased back, sticking out a rigid tongue I let her take control as she rode my face. It didn't take long for her legs to box in my ears while her body shivered on top of me.

I didn't give her a chance to recover before turning her onto her stomach. With an extra heavy hand, I smacked her tattooed ass, causing Sloane to seep in air as her torso melted into the mattress. Running my dick over her slit, she whimpered for me to make myself at home. My head rolled back as I slowly slid inside, the pressure of her wet center making space for me forced a shiver to trip up my spine. As I reached her depth, Sloane gasped.

With each thrust I tried to communicate how much I wanted her. I needed her to know I wasn't going anywhere. Clearly my words weren't conveying the message, hopefully my dick could. This was about expressing my urgent need for us to be together and the best way to do that was to fuck Sloane in the most loving but disrespectful way possible.

I needed to see her face and kiss her lips. Crudely flipping her on her back, I reentered her. Dropping low, I sucked her lower lip into mine. Inches from her face I searched her eyes for proof that this ... us wasn't all in my head. Her hand slid down my abs and she pulled my dick out indulging in several deep throated sucks. I screamed her name fisting her hair so she could take more of me.

Pulling myself from her mouth, I sunk onto the bed and slid back into place. "Tell me it's mine," I ordered.

"Yes, it's all yours. I'm all yours."

Her confirmation egged on the intense long strokes I was performing. I intended to take all of it.

"Sloane, just tell me you love me. Even if you don't mean it." This time my tone was a plea as I deepened my stroke in hopes of eliciting a response.

"Make me come, baby," she whispered over my mouth.

Not the words I wanted to hear but enough to send us spiraling into twin orgasms so intense it was almost painful. I shuddered over top of her, giving her every last drop. Brushing her hair from her forehead, I studied her face as her eyes lit up and her features contorted. Sloane stretched out bearing her neck and I dipped my face in the crook awash in the scent of her. As we came down, our bodies still rocked against each other not wanting the connection to end.

I reluctantly released her, stretching I shook my body before collapsing to the bed. Sloane always took longer to recover than me so I just laid beside her massaging her scalp while listening to her hitched breathing and occasional body tremors.

When she finally returned to the land of the living, she found her spot in my arms. "Not gonna lie, I'm gonna miss this view when this is all over in a few weeks."

I rubbed her arm. I loved the way her body melted

under my touch. "You know you don't have to miss any of this …right?"

"I don't wanna fight any more. Not tonight." Her voice sounded sluggish.

I nodded thoughtfully. "When I was in high school I was the star athlete. And Junior year there was this play. I wanted desperately to try out for the play because I secretly loved musical theater. *West Side Story, My Fair Lady, Chicago.*"

Sloane flashed me a disbelieving eye.

"I know. It was unexpected and my father was not supportive. Basketball should be my only focus. There was no time for hobbies, especially ones that involved dancing and singing on stage." I heedlessly brushed my palm over her soft skin.

"So what did you do?"

"I auditioned and I got a part … a lead part. I went home super pumped, told my dad and he flipped. 'Damnit Deion you don't have time for distractions. Basketball is your ticket out.' Mind you we were upper middle class so what I was trying to get out of I wasn't sure."

"Let me guess, you dropped out of the play to appease your dad."

"No, I did the play. Even though I was scared and no one else believed in it, I believed in it."

"Why do I get the feeling you're about to drop the moral of the story?" She teased tugging at my beard.

"Moral of the story … things that are most terrifying are typically the most rewarding." We studied each other's faces the light from the moon made her look ethereal but it still wasn't able to hide the storm brewing in her eyes. "We can figure this out. You just have to believe in us."

Sloane buried her face in my chest when she finally pulled back. Her eyes were misty. "Deion, I love you and I truly want you to be happy."

I pulled her in tight. Hearing her say the words after wanting nothing else for so long was anticlimactic. I can't really explain it but the words felt weighted and fragile. I shook the thought from my head. She loved me that was all that mattered. Right before we drifted off to sleep, I said, "I love you Sloane and I always will."

In the morning Sloane's side of the bed was empty. On her pillow was a crudely scribbled note.

*It's over. Do not try to contact me. This was never about love it was always the money. Sorry I can't be who you want me to be.*

*S.*

# SLOANE

I HAD A MASTER'S DEGREE IN FUCKING SHIT UP. THE LAST few months with Deion had been beyond anything I could ever imagine. But I wasn't a dreamer and I needed to remind myself people like me didn't win big. People like me had to fight for every good thing. Every ray of sunshine. Like so many others I almost believed the hype. When you run a long con you're not the one that's supposed to fall for it.

I knew what this was at the door. It was fake. It was a lie. It was all a show. At this point I didn't even care about the rest of the money. What was most important was leaving with my heart intact. If I didn't walk away now, I would work myself into a place in which I was so madly in love with him that the inevitable end would tear me apart. Maybe we'd make it past the summer before he tired of me and moved on. I was already too wrapped up in him and his world. And to make matters worse I'd dragged Ace into this shit, officially knocking myself out of the running for mother of the year.

It had been two weeks since I'd seen or spoken to

Deion, choosing to cut myself off cold turkey. A string of Ramblers away games also help. Deion had been on the road for much of that time making it impossible for him to insert himself back into my life. I blocked his number and when he called me from Raphael's phone, I blocked him too.

The last thing I wanted to hear was his deep, silky baritone voice saying all the right things and making me waver. When Deion claimed he loved me I believed him. I believed him when he said he wanted to make this work. But I knew good intentions often led to empty promises that could never actually come true.

I called Fabio and told him to put me back on the schedule at Enclave. Thanks to the deal Deion struck, I was now guaranteed weekend shifts which were the busiest nights. Deion had also gotten Fabio to agree that I couldn't be fired for at least a year with the exceptions of theft or a homicidal rage. I guess I could consider that as Deion's parting gift to me.

I was sitting on the floor of Tammie's apartment with leftover Chinese food watching the Ramblers' must-win finals game against New York. A game I was supposed to attend until I freaked out and burned my relationship to ashes. I yelled at the screen every time Deion gained possession of the ball. Just because he was no longer my fake boyfriend didn't mean I didn't want him to win.

I'd blocked Deion's number and started attending anger management sessions way across town, all because I knew my resolve was weak and if I looked into his eyes or heard his voice, I would be pulled back in. Now as I watched him run up and down the court there was a pang of regret. But heartbreak is easier when it's on your own terms.

Tammie plopped down on her couch, the ice cubes in her glass clinking. "I hate to say it, sweets but you fumbled the bag."

Yes, I told her Deion and I broke up, a move I was now regretting.

"Back in my hay day I had a shot at Billy Ocean in his prime. He was taking me to fancy restaurants and nightclubs. Treated me real nice and like you I got into my own head and ruined it. Well, that and I slept with Lionel Richie."

I had so many questions but decided to let her statement fly unchallenged. "It's better this way. Waiting for him to end things would have been torture."

"How do you know he would have ended things?"

"I mean come on." I pointed to myself, in a stained shirt and messy pineapple ponytail, as a reference.

"You have a nasty habit of selling yourself short. Sloane you are smart, funny, and beautiful as all get out. Any man would be lucky to have you, Deion included."

"That may be true but I'm also a host of other things that cancel the positive attributes out."

"I'm reading this book and one of the things it talks about is recognizing and accepting that we are worthy of love in this moment just as we are."

"I'm not so sure about that." I shoveled chow mien into my mouth.

Tammie stood disappearing into her bedroom. When

she returned, she dropped a book in my lap. "I think you need this more than I do."

I turned the book over in my hand to examine the cover. The title read *Finding the Love You Deserve*. The urge to puke was strong. I didn't need a self-help book, I needed a fresh start. Sometimes I'd imagine what it would have been like if my mother never left or if I was born into an entirely different family altogether. *Would things have worked out better for me?* Maybe I'd be a boss lady making deals and checking my stock options. Or a soccer mom who baked cupcakes from scratch for the fundraising event.

Of course, all this daydreaming was quickly dashed when my father would call asking for money, or one of my brothers asked me to be their alibi. Deion had gotten a taste of my father's antics but he didn't have a clue of how dysfunctional my family tree really was. And I doubted a man who grew up in a two-parent household behind the gates of a posh, suburban community could relate.

I was thirty-four with no direction. If the time with Deion had taught me anything it was that I needed to get my life in order. I'd been thinking about going back to school. Maybe I could become a court reporter. I was a fast typer and I had an insatiable interest in other people's business. Perhaps I could get assigned to high profile murder cases and get all the gruesome tea. I'd done some research online, I could get a degree in as little as two years. And once I was certified I could make sixty thousand to start. No more working nights and weekends off. Added bonus, immersing myself into school would help to keep my mind off Deion and the fruitless scroll of his social media pages.

* * *

WHEN I RETURNED HOME FROM WORK IN THE WEE HOURS of Saturday morning, all I wanted to do was take a shower and crawl into my bed but when I got to my apartment door, Deion was seated on my doormat like an Amazon package.

"What are you doing here?" I glanced back the way I came tempted to retreat.

"You haven't been returning my calls. I thought maybe something happened to you. But here you are, dressed in booty shorts and smelling like weed."

"I was working. And I distinctly remember telling you not to call me."

He flashed me an incredulous stare. "Working ... where?"

"At Enclave." I shooed him aside so I could open the door. He didn't give me much room the scent of him invaded my nostrils and for a brief second I was tempted to climb him like a tree and stick my tongue down his throat.

"When did that happen?"

"I just thought it was time to get back to my life." I pushed the door open.

"You were eager to return to your nine to five?

Dropping my purse, I released an aspirated huff. "Look it may not be as glamorous as jet setting and adoring fans screaming your name but it's my life. And

I realized for the past few months my wants and needs have come second place to what you wanted."

"What do you want, Sloane? Please enlighten me because I've been trying to figure that out for weeks now."

It was four in the morning and I was exhausted. All I wanted, at this moment, was for this conversation to end. "I thought you'd take the hint and leave me alone after I blocked your number."

"Admittedly I may be a little slow on the uptake because one minute we're cool and the next you leave a cryptic note and go all Casper the Ghost on me."

"The last time we spoke we were not cool," I said, with a distorted snort.

"We made love. I kissed you goodnight, told you not to worry and when I woke up you were gone."

I nudged a malcontented shrug.

"So you're dumping me?"

"No … because we were never a couple. I'm terminating our agreement."

"Fuck our agreement. I don't care about that."

"You can keep the remainder of the money. Obviously, I don't expect further financial compensation since I'm the one who breached the contract." I pulled out all the legalese I knew, this was all business, nothing personal. Or at least that's what I wanted Deion to think.

"Sloane?" Deion reached for me but I flinched, taking several steps back until my legs connected with the coffee table.

"I don't want to talk about how we can make this

work. Because we can't. I meant the things I said the last time we were together. I don't love you. I never did." My tone resembled that of a robot because I'd practiced this speech over and over at least a dozen times. I never took a breath, if I paused for even a second I would crack and crumble under the weight of his earnest gaze. My prepared remarks would have to steer the course.

"I just got caught up in the excitement and newness of it all. I know you may feel there's something here but I don't feel that way. And it would be cruel of me to pretend I did. I had fun. This was fun. But it was never love for me. If I led you on or made you believe we could be more I'm truly sorry. I never wanted to hurt you. I just wanted to help you out while also lining my pockets.

"But it's clear now that further contact would just make things harder. I wanted to tell you earlier but I didn't know how and then you started talking about us moving and uprooting my life. And that just confirmed we were not on the same page. I wanted to ride it out to the end of the season but it just became too difficult. It's not you. You're a great guy but I was never looking for a relationship. This was all just make believe."

His face was haggard like sleep had evaded him these past two weeks. I'm sure his loss of sleep was more about the game than anything having to do with me. The Ramblers made it to the finals but were quickly eliminated in the first round. He'd been working so hard, I knew the defeat was a disappointment and I felt guilty that I wasn't there to hold him and tell him how proud of him I was, and that everything would be alright.

Deion scrubbed his face. "If this is what you want I'm not gonna fight it."

I hitched a shoulder that was less committed than my words would lead him to believe. I'd imagined this conversation a million times and, in each scenario, Deion pleaded for me doing everything in his power to prove we belonged together. So his defeatist attitude caught me off guard.

He moved closer, examining my face. "I wish you could see what I see when I look at you." He rubbed the pad of his thumb across my cheek and soft ribbons of excitement twirled in my center. "Tell Ace I said goodbye."

As he headed toward the door, I welded my jaw shut for fear I'd break and recant my well-rehearsed words from moments ago. When the door closed behind him, my shoulders rounded into a heap. I never expected Deion to fight for us. I'd effectively given him an out so he could walk away clean. He didn't have to be the bad guy who dumped the poor waitress so he could go frolic in St. Barts with a swimsuit model.

No, I didn't expect Deion to cause a fuss, but I was hoping for a meager objection. *This is silly.* I'd gotten what I wanted. I was single and once again in full control of my life. My emotions were another matter. I don't know if it was exhaustion or allergies, but my eyes grew misty as I swallowed the self-inflicted pain welling in my throat.

Crying doesn't count when you're in the shower. Is it

tears or water droplets? It's hard to tell the difference. After a half-assed attempt at a nighttime skin routine using some of the products Charmise had put me on to, I climbed into bed. My phone dinged from the night-stand table. Scanning the screen, there was a notification from my bank. Deion McCabe just deposited twenty-five thousand dollars into my account with a memo note that read "Contract completed."

# DEION

"Where the hell have you been?" Raphael asked.

"Sloane dumped me." I took a shaky breath.

"Again?"

I shot him an evil eye. The last thing I needed was his off-color sense of humor.

"I'm sorry to hear that." He was in my kitchen at five in the morning making himself a sandwich with most of the fridge contents scattered across the counter. The thing about being the baby of the family was you almost always got to act like a child forever. "So that's it? You just gonna let her walk away?" Raphael cut a triple stacked sandwich in two. Placing one half on a napkin, he slid it my way.

"What do you mean let her? This isn't a gangster movie. What do you want me to do … break her legs?" I took a bite of the sandwich and for a brief moment my mood improved. "This is good. What's in here?"

"The secret ingredient is horseradish. I'm thinking about opening up a shop."

I did not have the appetite for another Raphael

inspired business startup. I took another bite deciding to hold my tongue.

"I've had a front row seat to you and Sloane for the past few months and if I may, can I offer some observations?"

"Sure." I pulled a pickle from the center of the sandwich, dropping it into my mouth.

"Sloane is super observant. She watches people like she's casing the joint as part of a well planned heist. So she probably noticed how people treated you when you started racking up the wins. She also noticed the basketball world can be hella superficial. Most players' wives are trophy chicks they all fall into a similar cookie cutter aesthetic. It's almost like … copy, paste, delete, upgrade, repeat."

My brother didn't take anything seriously except for his weed and maybe his sandwiches, but every now and then he would have a moment of clarity. Sloane did mention the wives club possessed an unhinged energy she couldn't quite put her finger on.

Raphael continued, "Sloane isn't cookie cutter. She's the type of cookie you put in the oven and it spreads and you can't really tell what shape it was supposed to be but when you eat it it's amazing." He raised his palms. "Not that I've had her cookies but from the way you two be screaming and carrying on in the bedroom I imagine it's pretty good."

"She doesn't love me and she is not interested in this life," I said matter of factly, even though I didn't completely believe it.

Raphael rolled his eyes. "The last part may be true

but her love for you is not the problem. Like that woman would go to jail or hell for you. She's on that … Usher and Alicia type love … my boo." Raphael's voice cracked as he attempted to sing the last part.

"Well, the lifestyle part seems to be a real sticking point for her."

"It's your job to help her get unstuck."

"I can't believe I'm seriously taking advice from the man who used to eat crayons."

"I was six. Are you ever going to let that go?"

"No you were eating them like they were candy." Rolling my shoulders, I stood. "I need to get some sleep."

How did I manage to fuck up my life worse than it already was? I could never have two things going right for me at the same time. My career was reinvigorated but my girlfriend was totally tripping. OK technically she was never my girlfriend. But in my book she was, it was just a matter of semantics. Like that one uncle who's been dating the same woman for years, they have kids together and they're committed it just wasn't official. That was Sloane … she was my old lady. I was totally devoted.

When she said she didn't love me and gave two fucks about our relationship that shit hurt. Was she in full blown love like I was? Maybe not, but she cared more than she was willing to admit. Love was more about actions than words. And Sloane's silent actions spoke volumes. After a game she would bring me a heat pad for my sore muscles or massage the stress from my shoulders. At night when I was restless, she'd tell me stories of the bizarro capers of the Kaplan clan. My favorite was the plot to rob a credit union.

Sure, I could have tried to convince her to stay but her mind seemed pretty well made up. She wanted off the ride, who was I to force her to keep spinning in circles with me? Sloane was right about one thing, asking her to uproot her whole life for a man whose career was influx was selfish. Looking back, I can't believe I'd presented that to her as a viable option. No one likes uncertainty and I seriously expected Sloane to add not only herself but her son into my chaotic bullshit.

If I had any hope of winning her back, I needed to prove I was serious. High on my list was my meeting with my agent on Monday morning. Team offers had come in and that would determine my next course of action. If I had to move maybe Sloane and I could make the long-distance thing work for a few seasons. I just didn't want to lose the best person and petty thief I'd ever met.

"Deck, my man. How is it going?" Brenden Scott, my agent asked.

"I'm doing good."

"You're looking like money." Brenden slapped my back directing me to the couch in the corner of his office. Brenden was your typical agent, high energy, overly ingratiating, all smiles, alpha-male personality. "The season is over. Playoffs or not you played your ass off.

You can tell me … it's because of that hypnotherapist I referred you to. Am I right?"

"No hypnotherapist just finally felt the fog lifting."

"Clarity of mind. I love that." Flipping through his notes Brenden continued. "Checking out your stats you were in the zone this season averaging twenty points, five assists, and eight rebounds per game."

I nodded in agreement. When you come off the bench like I did you wanted to inject energy on the court that fuels your team. Consistently posting up those types of numbers each game, gave the starters some room for error. Because even if they were having an off night, they knew I would swoop in and help turn the tide.

"I know you didn't come down here to listen to me tell you how great you are. So let's get down to business. Your athleticism and hustle caught the attention of several teams. By far the most attractive offer was from the New York Knicks, with a three-year contract for twelve million." Brenden performed a little dance with his shoulders. "I'm not saying I'm the best agent in Northern America but I am one of the fucking best.

"New York is my hometown. I can show you around. And then getting to lace up and play in Madison Square Garden. Are you fucking kidding me. Big lights, big city, big opportunities. I am going to be making all those backroom deals for you. When you leave Manhattan in three years' time you'll be set for life."

All I could do was stare at Brenden with a blank expression. Brenden was always a lot to deal with but trying to process this information with his personality dialed up to a ten, was a bit much.

"I just told you The New York Knickerbockers want to hand you a blue and orange jersey and you look like I spat in your food."

"It's great. I mean twelve million is more than I could have hoped for at this stage in my career."

"But?"

"Was that the only offer?"

"Was that the only offer? Hell, no that wasn't the only offer. It was the best offer, ergo the only offer."

"Did the Ramblers come back with anything?" I leaned forward hopeful.

Brenden pinched the brim of his nose releasing a tight breath. "Yes, but it's not competitive."

"What is it?"

"Three years for ten million." He raised an apologetic shoulder. "Houston is also offering two years for six, but that deal is a nonstarter." Brenden slapped me on the knee. "Deck, my man, talk me through this. What are you thinking?"

"I'm thinking I've got some thinking to do."

---

THE HOSTESS ESCORTED ME TO MY TABLE, RESTAURANT goers pointed and whispered as I passed. For the first time in a long time, I felt confident the hushed tones and stares were positive and not because of some new scandal I'd stumbled into. Reaching the table, I tagged

Coach Justus on the back before sliding into the booth opposite him.

"How are you late when you invited me for drinks?" he joked.

"My bad, you know I can never be on time. What are you drinking?"

"A boilermaker." Justus pointed to his whiskey and beer.

"Shit, I don't know nothing about that," I joked before ordering a dark lager.

"So what's up?" Justus asked.

"I talked to my agent."

"Listen, you fought hard this season. And that hard work reminded people why they signed you in the first place. Gordon himself said you exemplify the Ramblers' way. You worked hard for every basket; you never stop hustling for the win. When others give up there's Deck draining a three, grabbing a rebound and assisting for another two to pull us back into the game. After what you did this season, extending your contract was a no brainer."

My jaw circled as I listened to Coach's words. Being wanted was a good feeling. "The Knicks offered me twelve."

"What did we offer you?"

"Ten."

Justus pulled his face into a frown. "Shit, so you're headed to New York?"

"That's the thing. I'm not so sure New York is the place for me." I scrubbed my face with my hand. "I get it this will probably be my last three years in the NBA. And if that's the case I should go where the money's at."

"But?"

"But … for all of my bitching I do consider Rambler Nation my home. The relationships I've built within the team. Going to New York would be like starting over and that oftentimes comes with its own bullshit. I just wanna play and hopefully be appreciated for it."

"What does Sloane think?"

I screwed my face into a frown. "Umm …"

"What?"

"We kinda broke up a few weeks ago."

"No, I like Sloane, she's a straight shooter."

"Yeah well she shot me straight in the heart."

"She dumped you?" Justus's brows shot up in surprise.

"I don't really wanna talk about Sloane to be honest."

Justus displayed the palm side of his hands conceding to my wish. "Vegas loves you Deck. You're like a wild card. You're a game changer. The Ramblers' organization was excited at the prospect of signing you for three more years. If you're looking for a support system, we got you. Now I've been in your shoes and I understand this is a hard choice. Whatever you decide I'ma have your back."

"Thanks, I appreciate that."

Maybe I should take the money and run. New York would provide a fresh start. Sloane was clearly moving on. She'd been MIA from the last several anger management sessions. After a lot of sweet talking and the promise of front row tickets to an upcoming game, Shelly the sessions leader, told me Sloane transferred to an anger management group in North Las Vegas. If Sloane was anything like me she had to miss me a little. That woman was all I could think about and I wasn't able to walk away from things I wanted. And loving Sloane and her loving me was something I was invested in.

# SLOANE

"Mom, did you know ants can carry twenty times their weight?" Ace asked.

"No, I didn't know that." We were zooming down the freeway headed to drop Ace off at his father's house.

"Yes, if a human could do that it would be like being able to lift four thousand pounds."

"Sounds like superhero powers to me."

"Yeah, like Spiderman or Black Panther."

"Yep."

Ace fell silent offering me a rare moment to get a word in. "So I was thinking when school lets out maybe we could go on a vacation somewhere fun. Maybe Disneyworld or—"

"You always said Disneyworld was an overpriced rip-off."

"I did. And I still think that. But I also hear its super fun and we deserve a bit of fun don't you think?"

"Can we invite Deck and Destiny?"

My stomach dropped hearing his name. I'd counted him and our time together as a fever dream, so to hear

Ace say his name just reminded me I had not in fact dreamt him up. What we shared was very real, however brief.

"I don't think so kiddo."

"I'm sure if you talked to him he'd want to work things out. He loves you, Mom."

"Ace, what did I tell you about staying out of grown folks business?"

"But Mom Deck is the greatest—"

"Ace, that's enough." I focused my attention on the road.

It took a minute to fall back into my usual routine. The past few months had been filled with fancy dinners, star-studded events, and sex that left my core gushy and hot like molten lava. Now returning to the normally scheduled program that was my life, meant spilled drinks, mind-numbing headaches, and achy legs from being on my feet all night. I knew Ace missed Deion just as much as I did, but eventually, with time he would get over it. Kids were resilient in that way.

Ace's arms were pinned against his chest, his bottom lip poking out. "Listen Ace I know this is hard but Deion and I decided to go our separate ways. No one's the bad guy. Sometimes romantic relationships don't work out for a host of reasons. Your dad and I didn't work out. But we still love you very much and we're both happy."

"You haven't been happy since Deck left."

"First, I left him and I miss him a bit but ultimately the decision I made was best for everyone involved. You can't see that now because you're young but maybe in time."

This is exactly why I never introduced Ace to the men I was dating, because I didn't want him getting attached. I'd let myself get caught up in the lights and excitement of it all and dragged Ace into this relationship with me. I never expected for Deion to be so kind and forge a friendship with my son. Ace's well-being was paramount to me and I'd been careless not protecting him these past few months. I would never make that mistake again.

Much of what I knew about being a good parent I'd learned from television. I'd come home from school and watch shows where the parents were present and asked questions like how was your day. Parents who knew who their kid's friends were and took an interest in their hobbies. I vowed if I ever had a child of my own I would be like those parents taking a genuine interest in my son or daughter's life and development.

I was now coming to grips with the fact that good intentions weren't enough. If I didn't fix the shit from my past, I could still unintentionally pass it on to Ace. I decided to reach out to my former therapist, and to my great relief she agreed to take me back on as a patient. It had only been a few sessions so far but this go round I was more open. And for the first time I discussed how being abandoned by my mother affected me and impacted the choices I made as a mom.

I wasn't perfect but I was doing the best I could. And with the money from Deion I could provide Ace with whatever he needed. A proposed vacation was just the beginning. I'd scheduled a meeting with a money management guy at my bank. I planned to open a college fund for Ace so he had a chance to be or do whatever he wanted when he got older.

The rest of the money would sit in savings until I determined my next move. I was seriously looking into the possibility of purchasing a home. Something I would never have been able to do before meeting Deion. All things supposedly happened for a reason, maybe the reason Deck and I connected was to get me to a better place financially.

IN MY WEEKLY ANGER MANAGEMENT MEETING I LISTENED AS a wiry haired woman cried while retelling how her anger destroyed many of her relationships.

"I just didn't know when to let things go. Even after my sister apologized although I was the one who was in the wrong I still held on to the hurt. Eventually she stopped coming around because she claimed I was always flying off the handle. The relationship with my daughter isn't much better. She's twenty-six now and barely talks to me. We bumped heads once she hit her preteens and it doesn't help she has my temper ..."

This anger management group was way larger than the prior one. There were probably fifty people in attendance in the medium-sized auditorium style classroom of the local community college.

After the woman sat down the class coordinator addressed the crowd. "Who would like to share next?"

The space was silent except for the occasional cough and rustling in squeaky wooden chairs.

"I'll go next," a voice called out.

My head remained low. I was just here to meet my probation requirement. This larger classroom setting was doing nothing to keep my interest. Unlike the group I'd left, it was easier to get lost in the crowd and skate through the sessions without really contributing anything of value. Also, the North Vegas snack selection left much to be desired. The donuts were stale, the coffee bitter, and there were no little packs of fruit snacks.

"Hello my name is Deion …"

My head snapped as I turned to look in the direction of the man standing. What the hell was Deion doing here? I'd chosen North Las Vegas for a reason, this location was in the hood and I knew it was a place Deion didn't frequent.

"I've struggled with my temper recently and I'm learning how to listen before reacting. In the past I would lash out with harsh words or my fist. But my time in anger management has taught me to be more considerate. Thinking through a problem instead of letting the fear or anguish lead me. A few weeks ago, someone I care about dumped me. And I didn't put up a fight because I didn't want to continue to hurt her or say things driven by my pain.

Deion's eyes searched through the crowd finding mine. I slumped in my chair trying to evade detection. But his words were like high beams making me the focal point. The space seemed to close in as my heart pulsed loudly in my chest.

"My walking away wasn't because I didn't care or because I was giving up. I just thought we both needed time maybe a little space. The old Deion would have let things stand, acted like I was fine without you. But I'm not too cool or tough to admit I want you in my life."

All eyes in the auditorium swung my way as people slowly made the connection Deion was addressing me specifically and not the group. I hated being the center of attention and my face grew hot from the scrutiny. Deion moved toward the aisle maneuvering down the steps until he was a few feet away from me.

"Sloane, all I'm asking is for you to give me a chance to love you. The thought of loving you is terrifying but not because I'm afraid you'll hurt me or me you. It's because I gave up on feeling this way a long time ago."

My throat was painfully dry and I swallowed hard making a way for my words. "Deion, just because you feel something doesn't mean it translates into a happily ever after," I said meekly.

"I know you don't think you deserve to be happy. I know you think life can only be what it's been for years … a struggle."

My eyes darted across the room to the group that was leaning forward with rapt attention waiting to see how this played out. "I ended things because it would never work. You're getting traded to another state and I can't separate Ace from his father. I can't do that to either of them so I'm stuck in Vegas. Relationships are difficult enough when both people are in the same city. The distance would make it damn near impossible to maintain and I don't want to get wrapped up in something that's careening toward a cliff."

"Do you love me, Sloane?" He raised his eyebrows offering a questioning gaze.

"Deion this isn't the time or place."

"As far as I'm concerned there's no better time or place because nothing else matters but this."

"Love is the least of our worries. We have too many other obstacles stacked up against us to win."

"Listen, maybe we try and it doesn't work but if we never try all we'll be left with is regret. I already have so many things I wished turned out differently. I don't want to add you to that list."

Every heartbreak I'd experience was never a surprise. I knew they were too good to be true or feeding me a pack of lies. Deion on the other hand actually wanted to adore me. Even when we were pretending his love felt real and tangible. It was something I could hold on to at night when the intrusive thoughts emerged from the recesses of my mind. He'd never wavered from the script saying the words and then backing them up with concrete actions. Was I really gonna let my fears hold me back from a chance at love? Real love with no strings attached, the only requirement remaining my authentic self.

The crowd started to grumble. "Girl who hurt you?" one of the women in the front row shouted.

"Everyone," I lashed out. "Everyone I've ever loved has hurt me." I turned back to Deion. "You agreed no promises."

"I'm not making promises, I'm stating facts. I love you. And I want to create a life with you and Ace."

"Who's Ace?" someone called out.

"You can't know that after a few months," I said.

"I can and I do. I want you to be mine, for real this time."

"Say yes sweetie," a salt and peppered-haired woman with a deeply lined face said.

Many around her were nodding in agreement.

Everyone eagerly taking his side left a bad taste in my mouth. "I don't believe in fairy tales," I shouted, before collecting my things and heading for the side exit. The sun blinded me and I had to take several steadying breaths to regain my composure.

Behind me the doors opened and Deion emerged. "I'm not trying to sell you some fairy tale. I'm not Prince Charming and my love for you isn't some magical potion. What I'm offering is real." He grabbed my hand pressing it to his chest the frantic pounding of his heart thrummed against my palm. "Me with all my flaws and insecurities. My nosy ass brother who'll insert himself in our relationship offering advice neither of us asked for. My bougie mother who thinks no one is ever good enough for me. And my nagging fear I won't be interesting or exciting enough for you."

Despite my best efforts tears were now streaming down my cheeks. My throat was tight and dry and it was a struggle to find the words.

Deion brought my hand to his lips kissing my palm. "No fairy tales, just reality."

I shook my head violently ripping my hand from his

grasp. "My reality includes a family with a long rap sheet. A father who is financially dependent on me. And who would rather see me steal from you than settle down with you. Brothers who will beg for favors because of who you are and what that means for them." I scrubbed at my face in an attempt to quill the tears. I love you, Deion … I do but you do not deserve this shit-hole of an existence I've grown up in."

Deion took tentative steps forward. "I want it all. Do you hear me? The messy, the chaotic, the joy, and the pain. I'd walk through fire for you, Sloane Kaplan."

My eyes reloaded with fresh tears. "I want to believe this. But in a few months, you'll just leave. It'll become too much, my family, my son, me. I am not the woman who gets her hopes up. I don't have expectations because I'm always being disappointed. Without fail.

"You want this now but you'll move to New York or Minnesota and the calls will become less frequent, the distance making it too tough to maintain. We'll start to grow apart but still try to salvage a relationship we both know we should've let go of a long time ago. Deion these past few months with you have been a bright spot and a pleasant surprise but the sun always sets. This relationship has more days behind it than in front of it. And that's OK because what we shared was beautiful. You made me feel special and I will never forget the love you poured into me."

I didn't cry often but when I did it was muddled and raw, wrecking me to the core. If a sink hole opened beneath my feet, I would welcome it. I'd even accept a heavy awning falling and trapping me underneath. The physical pain could distract me from the emotional torture of walking away from Deion when I loved him so much.

"The Ramblers offered me a three-year contract and I signed it yesterday morning," Deion said.

"What?" His words broke my fog of self-pity.

"I'm gonna be in Vegas for the next three years."

"Wait you're not leaving?"

"No."

Before I could stop myself, my arms were flailing pushing into Deion's body. My halfhearted shoves didn't faze him. I don't think he moved an inch. "Deion Fucking McCabe you should have led with that."

A dazed expression settled in his wide eyes. "I'm sorry I didn't know I ..."

Tossing my purse to the ground, I jumped into his arms claiming his lips. Deion supported my weight with his arm under my ass. With my legs clasped tightly against his waist; I plastered relieved kisses across his face.

Pulling away for a breath I said, "When I said I didn't love you I lied."

"Yeah, I already know that." He laughed full and free.

I smiled over his mouth before we resumed our passionate kisses, making up for the time we wasted apart. Don't confuse my unbridled enthusiasm for fool-hardy optimism. There were still several issues we'd have to work out. Primarily of which was setting boundaries with my father and brothers. But I was willing to commit to us, I was open to giving and being loved without reservations.

The secret to happiness wasn't being a perfect person, it was making a choice to set aside your fears and trust in a feeling greater than yourself. I was no longer settling for the love I thought I deserved. Instead of going for the easy layup I was attempting a three pointer at the buzzer and it was nothing but net.

# DEION

# EPILOGUE

THE OFF SEASON WASN'T LONG ENOUGH FOR MY LIKING. After several vacations with and without the kids, I was back in the training facility in preparation for the new NBA year. As always, Coach Justus was tough on the team as he worked to break some of the lackadaisical habits we'd picked up during our down time. There were also changes to the roster with a few new players, and me being moved to a starting position. Luckily the one thing that hadn't changed was my relationship with Sloane.

To my great surprise, it took very little convincing for Sloane to agree to move in with me. We decorated one of the bedrooms with all of Ace's favorite things so he'd feel right at home. I thought I was all done raising kids but now here was Ace who looked up to me and talked my ear off. He was smart and curious like his mother and I loved him immediately. Not gonna lie, I'd always wanted a son and now because of Sloane, I had one.

You know that saying life is full of surprises. Well, those words rang true with me. In mere months my life had been flipped upside down in the best possible way. I'd gone from a zero to a hero with my team, and was rewarded with a three-year contract that would most likely see me retiring as a Rambler. My weekends now included going to soccer games and visits to the Natural History Museum so Ace could bring me up to speed on the sharks and their eating habits.

Destiny was entering her senior year of college. Which was causing me to go into an existential crisis. While challenging, I had to accept she was an adult, and as her father I couldn't be prouder. Destiny made mistakes but that was part of growing up, and I honestly had no room to judge with a list of wrong choices spanning a mile. But I was confident Destiny had the tools to navigate this world, and as a parent that's all you can really ask for.

Raphael was still living in the guest house but he wasn't there to watch over me so much as take advantage of a rent-free living situation. Can't say I blamed him, and Sloane and I liked having him around. We were also set to open up a second dispensary. One night Sloane, Raphael, and I were talking about The Kush Consultant and Sloane asked why we were neglecting a very successful business. Raphael and I just stared at her, dumbstruck.

So we brought Sloane on as a partner and she and Raphael are overseeing the launch of the new location. Believe it or not we'd agreed to hire Sloane's brother, Chet, as the store manager for the new site. Chet and I hit it off right away, he was a hustler like his sister and had an easy-going spirit. I think Sloane was relieved we got along so well. It was obvious she really loved her brother.

Both Sloane and I successfully completed anger management. Sloane still had a year left on her probation but she was staying out of trouble. Like Sloane predicted, Stanley occasionally showed up begging for money or attempted to guilt Sloane for living in a fancy house while he was in a trailer park. Dealing with Stanley took its toll, but I reminded her she was not responsible for her father's failure to thrive. I was willing to help him when we could, but I was not going to fund his addiction.

I'd been in love before but I'd all but given up on experiencing it again, Sloane changed all that. When we were apart, I missed her. She occupied a large chunk of real estate in my brain. *What should we do this weekend? I wonder if Sloane would like this? How can I make her smile?* This was the narrative that played out in my head. When she was happy, I was at peace because I lived to serve her.

I pulled into the garage next to Sloane's hooptie Honda which she refused to get rid of because it was her baby. When I offered to buy her a new car, she said it was wasteful and she could just borrow one of the several I already owned. I wanted to spoil her but she always made it difficult, saying I should save my money. Sloane grew up having to pinch pennies and she just wanted us to be good financially. But I needed her to understand there were no limits, nothing was too outrageous or audacious. If she wanted it, it was hers because she deserved it.

Entering our house, I took a deep breath. The air smelled like her and it practically made me salivate. I loved that this place was ours. Before Sloane, this house never really felt like it belonged to me, but now it was a welcoming space because she was in it. We could live in a tent in Yosemite and it would feel inviting. OK maybe I was exaggerating a bit about camping in the forest, I was a city boy after all. But I was happiest when I was with her because we accepted one another just as we were. I didn't have to change for her to love me, she loved me in spite of my flaws. Neither of us had the answers, and that was OK because we were figuring it out together.

Sloane's bare feet slapped against the hardwood as she approached from the long hall. "You're home," she said, jumping into my arms and wrapping herself around me.

"Yeah, I am." I smiled against her lips before going in for a kiss.

# EXCERPT
# CHAPTER ONE

# JUMP BALL

## LAS VEGAS RAMBLERS

## BOOK TWO

# SARIAH

"Yes, just like that." I seeped in a breath of air, my hips rotating as I rode the face of the man I'd met at the hotel bar just hours before. Ho-ish? Yes. But what this man was doing to me was much needed after a stressful week in a foreign country. Plus, who doesn't travel to France and fuck a Frenchmen. It's essentially a rite of passage. Granted this Frenchmen's name was Roger, which was a huge disappointment. I was hoping I'd be screaming out the name Franz or Pierre, but Roger would have to do.

Right now, Roger had his hands planted on my waist and with an impressively long tongue, was satisfying my urgent need to bust a nut. My phone rang from its perch on the hotel night stand. Leaning forward, I fumbled for it, pressing the button declining the call, all the while never losing the connection between my lower lips and Frenchie's. Work had brought me to Nice and I'd spent the week enjoying the food, shopping, and finally the men.

Roger lifted me from his face and asked, "I want to feel your pretty mouth around my dick. Will you?"

"Listen, if you make me come I'm liable to do just about anything you ask," I said, with an enthusiastic nod.

He claimed hold of my clit, working hard to hit my spot and I showed him how much I appreciated the effort by stroking his dick through his briefs. It wasn't big but it had potential. My phone dinged several times notifying me of incoming text messages. The dinging was followed by another call.

I grumbled under my breath, "Ugh, let me be great," before shutting my phone off all together.

It took a whole lot of concentration for me to get my head back into the game but when I did, I quickly zoned out, writhing on top of Roger as the orgasm washed over me. I pressed my full weight on his head. Hopefully, he had good lung capacity because I didn't plan on releasing him until he'd sucked every last drop. With shaky legs, I collapsed onto the bed still rubbing my nipples in a euphoric state.

Roger stood, pulling off his underwear. "I want you to choke on it," he said.

I looked at Roger, then at his dick and back again. I can assure you no one was choking on it.

"How do you say fuck me in French?" I asked. It was late and I didn't want to spend fifteen minutes with his pale peen in my mouth. I needed Roger to hit my spot and then bounce.

"Baise moi."

"Baise moi. I don't think I can wait any longer," I moaned, opening my legs wide in an attempt to really sell it. Roger took the bait and opted for a soft, warm place to land. Donning a condom, he sunk on top of me.

---

After getting rid of Roger, I headed to the bathroom to take a shower. We had two more days in Nice and then we would close out our trip in Paris. I was traveling with my best friend and business partner Tracie Kirk. We'd launched our makeup line, Genuine Beauty, ten years ago and were finally branching out to skincare. She and I were in France to show off our products to retailers for pre order.

Genuine Beauty was my baby. Since I was a young girl I loved fashion and dressing up. When I turned sixteen, my mother finally allowed me to wear makeup. A little lip gloss or a dab of eyeshadow. It was then I started to recognize the lack of products that complimented the deeper tones like my mahogany-hued skin. Genuine Beauty revolutionized the beauty industry by introducing a range of foundation shades, and over a dozen nude-lip options that worked for more than just the lightest complexions. And we were about to shake the industry once again with our skincare line.

Piling my hair atop my head, I secured it under a shower cap. Before entering the shower, I turned my phone back on. I wanted to text Tracie so she could remind me what time we had to be out the door tomorrow morning. The information was written on my itinerary which was somewhere under the mass of papers on the coffee table. Tracie was far better organized than me, and I knew she would be able to provide the answer with little effort.

When my phone settled on the home screen after rebooting, I was inundated with text messages and missed calls from both my mother and Aunt Dina.

> Mom: Baby call me when you get this message.

> Mom: Sariah it's me again. Can you please call me back ASAP. It's urgent.

> Aunt Dina: Girl where are you at? Your mother is trying to reach you. Call us back.

> Mom: 911

There were several other text messages imploring me to contact them. I checked the last missed call. It was from my Aunt Dina. "Damnit Sariah, your father's had a heart attack and you can't even bother to answer your fucking phone. He's at Kaiser Hospital in Henderson. It doesn't look good. You need to get your ass back to Vegas."

I stared at my phone screen frozen with shock. Did Aunt Dina say it didn't look good? What the hell did that mean? She didn't mean … she couldn't. My father was the strongest man I knew. Yes, he was seventy-two but he was the picture of health. He worked out every day and he'd gone vegan after marrying Harper who, despite being with my father for ten years, was barely in her thirties.

I called Tracie. When she answered, I quickly blurted out, "My dad had a heart attack."

As if on cue, Tracie's mama bear instincts kicked in. "I'm on my way over."

In less than a minute, there was a knock on my hotel door. When I opened it, Tracie was standing there with wine and her laptop. Tracie's room was a few doors down from mine, and it appeared she'd wasted no time grabbing the essentials and heading my way. "We need to book you a flight back home. I can help you pack your bags. Where is your luggage?"

I pointed toward the bedroom, sinking to the couch as she buzzed in and out of the suite's living quarters. She finally climbed into an armchair, crossing her legs. Opening her laptop, she pulled up available flights.

"Tracie," I whispered. "He's gonna pull through, right?"

"What did your mom say?"

"I don't know, I just opened my phone to a shit ton of messages and my Aunt Dina's voicemail saying it didn't look good."

"Let's just get you a flight. There's one leaving at six in the morning. It has a couple of layovers—"

"We have a ton of meetings tomorrow. I can't miss those."

"I can handle them." She stood, retrieving a glass from the bar and poured out some wine, handing it to me.

I slurped down the white wine, holding out my glass for more. "The last time we talked it ended in a fight."

"Don't do that. Don't you dare." She pointed a warning finger in my direction.

I felt numb inside, disconnected from myself and what was happening around me. Crying would be helpful right about now, at least I would have a place to direct my energy, but I couldn't make the tears fall. I think my body went into self-preservation mode, cutting off my access to emotions so I didn't spiral. All I felt was confusion because nothing made sense. I knew I needed to call my mother but if I did, I would be able to hear the emotion in her voice and it would confirm my aunt's words, "It doesn't look good."

Tracie managed to book a first-class flight back home. It would make two stops, Munich and then Denver. I'd land at McCarran Airport in a little over seventeen hours. My father's driver, Mr. Charles, would pick me up from the airport. I was useless while I watched Tracie collect the items scattered across the living room and place them into my suitcase.

"How'd things go with the guy from the bar?"

She was trying to distract me to stop my brain from making an unproductive stop in the pits of despair.

"We had sex." My tone was dull and listless.

"Congratulations. At least one of us is getting some ass on this trip."

"What should I do?" I was in desperate need of direction.

"Get your passport and jewelry from the safe."

I stood going through the motions as I tried to open the hotel safe in my bedroom closet. "I can't remember the code," I called.

"It's Benji's birthday."

That's right, I always used Benji's birthday when I needed a numeric password. It probably wasn't the most secure password, but it was a date I knew by heart. Back in the living room, I handed Tracie the items I'd pulled from the safe and she stowed them away in my carry-on. Normally I was more helpful, but my brain was in a fog.

I touched my head and felt the plastic shower cap. "I need to shower."

"Good idea. A nice hot shower will do you good. While you do that, I'll finish packing the last few items."

I don't know how Tracie managed it, but she packed my things, booked my flight, and made sure I got to the airport on time. In my seat I shut the partition door, closing myself off from the other passengers. Lowering my window shade, I pulled a sleep mask over my eyes. I just wanted the seventeen hours to pass as quickly as possible.

I think I was six or seven when I realized my dad wasn't like other dads. My father was flanked by security and was dressed in impeccably tailored suits. He was always coming from an important meeting or heading to one. I remember the way people would treat him, especially other men. They would hang on his every word and laugh at his jokes even when they weren't particularly funny. When my father entered a room, people moved out of his way.

I asked my mother once, "Is Daddy the president?" Because the president of the United States was the only person my young mind could conjure up that wielded that type of power. My mother reassured me that while we weren't a part of a political dynasty, my father was very powerful. Grover Thornton was the majority owner of a basketball team, the Las Vegas Ramblers.

My brother Benjamin and I were his children, but I think the Ramblers were his pride and joy. In the hierarchy of my father's attention, it was the Ramblers, Benji, my mother, then me. My father had no use for a daughter. He didn't know how to connect with a little girl, a teenager, or an adult woman he couldn't sleep with. At least with Benji they could bond over sports, or he could show him how to shave the scruffy whiskers on his chin.

With me, all I got were questions about school. And when I started dating it was all about the importance of remaining a virgin. Then I went off to college and I think he was relieved he would no longer have to engage in those awkward conversations with me.

When the plane finally touched down in Las Vegas, I was exhausted. My attempts at sleep were frequently interrupted by intrusive thoughts. I just needed to lay eyes on my father. If I was able to see him I'd know everything would be OK. When it was safe to do so, I took my phone off airplane mode. There were no new text messages from my mother or aunt so I took that as a good sign. I texted Tracie letting her know I'd landed safely and thanked her for booking the flight and finishing up our trip alone.

Collecting my bag from baggage claim, I headed outside and easily spotted Charles, a tall and bulbous man in his fifties leaning against a Mercedes-Benz Maybach, one of my father's many cars.

"Hello Charles, good to see you again."

"You too, Ms. Sariah. I hate that it has to be because of this." He opened the door and I slid inside. I waited as he placed my luggage in the trunk. Charles had been employed by my father since I was in high school. He was like an uncle to me, even though my father didn't like us getting too familiar with the staff.

Charles climbed behind the driver's seat and we were off. Normally he was a chatterbox, wanting to give me updates on his kids or listen to me chat about my travels. But today he was silent. The soft sounds of jazz could be heard through the speakers. I leaned back into my seat watching the lights from the Vegas strip as we cruised down the freeway. My eyelids felt like they had weights attached to them and before long, I drifted to sleep.

I was awakened by the sound of the driver door opening and closing. Rubbing the sleep from my eyes, I peered out the window. Charles removed my bags from the trunk before opening my door.

"What are we doing at my mother's house? I thought you were taking me straight to the hospital?"

"Ms. Thornton asked that I bring you to her home." Was the only explanation Mr. Charles offered. I followed him into the house and could distinctly hear a hum of conversation in the family room. "I'll take your bags upstairs." Charles ascended the steps, bags in hand leaving me alone in the foyer. I walked toward the sound of voices. In the family room were my mother, my aunt and a handful of other relatives.

"Sariah, you're home," my Aunt Dina said when she caught sight of me.

My mother crossed the room walking toward me. She looked like I felt ... frazzled and depleted. I guess we were all operating under little sleep. When she pulled me into a hug her familiar scent provided temporary comfort. "I'm so sorry, Sariah," she said. "Your father is dead."

# THANK YOU. LET'S CONNECT.

Thank you so much for reading Defensive Stance. If you enjoyed Sloane & Deion's story, please help a sister out and leave a review or tell a friend. Your feedback is important to me and will help other readers decide whether to read my book too.

Feel free to connect with me virtually. I would love to engage with you.

- : @authorkashathompson
- : @authorkashathompson
- : @authorkthompson

HAPPY READING,

*Kasha*

# ABOUT THE AUTHOR

**Kasha Thompson** is a contemporary romance author. She writes authentic love stories that examine the complexity of falling and staying in love. Her books center black love with relatable characters, humor, and spice.

# ALSO BY KASHA THOMPSON

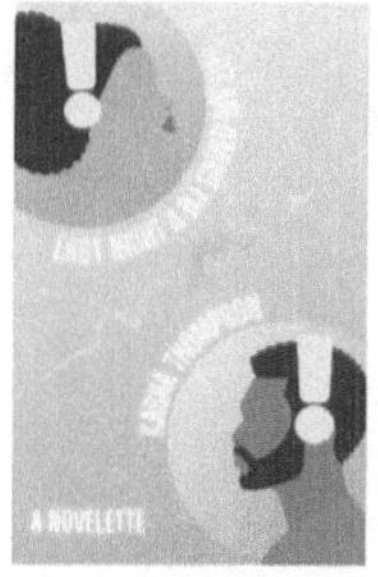